RIVERBEND FRIENDS™

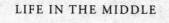

LIFE IN THE MIDDLE

Life in the Middle

RIVERBEND FRIENDS™

Stephanie Coleman

CREATED BY

Lissa Halls Johnson

A Focus on the Family Resource
Published by Tyndale House Publishers

Life in the Middle
© 2023 Focus on the Family. All rights reserved.

A Focus on the Family book published by Tyndale House Publishers, Carol Stream, Illinois 60188

Focus on the Family and the accompanying logo and design are federally registered trademarks and *Riverbend Friends* is a trademark of Focus on the Family, 8605 Explorer Drive, Colorado Springs, CO 80920.

Tyndale and Tyndale's quill logo are registered trademarks of Tyndale House Ministries.

Scripture quotations are taken from the Holy Bible, *New International Version,*® *NIV.*® Copyright © 1973, 1978, 1984, 2011 by Biblica, Inc.® Used by permission. All rights reserved worldwide.

The characters and events in this story are fictional. Any resemblance to actual persons or events is coincidental.

Cover design by Mike Harrigan

For manufacturing information regarding this product, please call 1-855-277-9400.

For information about special discounts for bulk purchases, please contact Tyndale House Publishers at csresponse@tyndale.com, or call 1-855-277-9400.

ISBN 978-1-64607-088-6

Printed in the United States of America

29	28	27	26	25	24	23
7	6	5	4	3	2	1

For McKenna,
my real-life inspiration for Tessa

Chapter
1

MOM'S TEXT CAME AS IZZY AND I rounded the corner out of the sophomore hallway.

It's final. Can I come pick you up from school? Now?

There was no question about what "it" was. She meant the divorce.

Mom and Dad told me last August that this would happen, and my dad had been living with his girlfriend since then. They even had a baby together a couple months ago. I knew Mom and Dad had signed the papers, and yet I still felt a touch of shock.

I read the text again. I also shouldn't have been surprised that Mom wanted to come pick me up from school. This was exactly the kind of situation I'd been telling Kendra, my therapist, about. Talking to Kendra before I responded to Mom would be a good idea.

"Tessa?" Izzy said from alongside me. "Something wrong?"

"One second," I said as I typed, Mom texted the divorce is final. Can we talk?

I tapped *send*. Not that long ago, I would've told Izzy nothing was wrong. I would've claimed I was fine. But after an entire school year of Izzy and our two other friends, Amelia and Shay, standing by me through my parents' split/separation/divorce, I was getting better at being honest with myself and others and not pretending everything was fine. I hesitated a second before turning my phone screen to her.

"Mom wants to pick me up," I said with a sigh. "Because it probably hasn't occurred to her that it's the last week before finals and I *need* to be at school this week."

Izzy bent closer to read Mom's text. "What does she mean 'it's final'?"

"The divorce. They'd already signed papers, but the court had to put some kind of stamp of approval on it."

Izzy winced. "Stars, Tessa, I'm sorry."

"It's not like I didn't know this was going to happen." I jammed my phone into the side pocket of my leggings as we turned toward the multipurpose room. "But I'm going to talk to Kendra before I respond. This is exactly the kind of situation I was telling her about."

"I wish I had a therapist," Izzy said, pushing her wild, dark brown hair over her shoulder. "Well, I do sometimes meet with Zoe outside of small group to talk about, you know, everything that's happened. But it'd be cool to have a professional counselor give me advice."

I bit my lower lip for a moment as I considered how to respond. I'd resisted therapy for a long time, but I liked Kendra a lot, and it *had* been helpful to talk to someone whose sole focus was on helping me and who wasn't biased toward either of my parents. I'd even felt a little disappointed when Kendra said she thought I was doing great and only needed to come once a month.

My phone vibrated in my pocket with Kendra's response.

Can you call now? I'm available until noon or so.

"It is kind of nice sometimes," I said. In my head, I added, *Though I'd prefer to have parents who adore each other and not need to be in therapy.* "I wonder if Ms. Larkin will let me make a phone call."

"I don't know," Izzy said. "Ms. Larkin is anti-phones. Maybe use one of your bathroom passes?"

Going to the bathroom at Northside High had become increasingly complicated since spring break and now involved a multitude of rules, thanks to several TikTok trends that led to weird vandalism. Like stealing soap dispensers or emptying the tampon dispensers into the sinks. Mom didn't allow me to have TikTok on my phone, so I never saw any of these dumb challenge videos firsthand, but I had to suffer the consequences all the same. Now we were allowed two no-longer-than-five-minute trips to the bathroom each day, and we had to sign in and out with our teacher. And we were forbidden from going during passing periods. Teachers stood outside each bathroom and guarded the doorways, like the toilets were crown jewels in a museum. It was ridiculous.

"I think I'll be honest with her," I said as I pushed open the door into the multipurpose room where our Drama 1 class met.

How weird that I'd started sophomore year hating this class, feeling like it'd never be over, and now I had only one more week of it. I would miss it a little next year. Not enough that I wanted to sign up for Drama 2, but I would miss Ms. Larkin and the guaranteed time with Izzy, Amelia, and Shay.

The room was in its usual state of pre-bell chaos. Marcus and Chad were doing rock, paper, scissors to see who got to sit in the hot pink stiletto chair. K-pop blared from Jaiden's phone and she, Amber, and Gage were doing a dance routine on stage. Amelia was reciting her audition piece for a summer production to Shay with such gusto that I could hear it from the door, even above the K-pop.

Ms. Larkin sat at her desk in the back of the classroom, tapping away on her MacBook, seemingly unperturbed by the noise. She'd been gone for a lot of the semester taking care of her sick mother, and it was nice having her calming, supportive presence back in the drama room.

While Izzy secured her phone with the others in the shoe organizer by the door, I kept mine in my side pocket and strutted across the multipurpose room directly toward Ms. Larkin.

She looked up and smiled. "Hello, Tessa. What can I do for you?"

Ms. Larkin was effortlessly lovely, with dark hair to her shoulders and dark eyes. If she wore makeup, it was the enhancing-what-God-already-gave-me variety, and nothing that was super obvious. I hoped I had the same confident aura when I was in my thirties.

I took in a deep breath. "Um, my mom sent me a text about her divorce, and I need to talk to my therapist about how to handle it. Can I make a phone call?"

Ms. Larkin blinked rapidly—the only sign that what I'd said surprised her—and her smile turned to sympathy. "Of course. What about the prop closet backstage? If you can get a signal in there, that should be quiet."

"Okay, thank you."

"Sure."

I considered dropping my backpack off at the black-and-white striped loveseat where I always sat with the girls, but Izzy was looking at me as she talked low and rapidly to Amelia and Shay. I assumed she was filling them in, and if I went over there, I'd have to talk about it. I kept my backpack with me and headed toward the closet backstage.

Kendra answered right away with her characteristic warm voice. "Hello, Tessa. Nice to hear from you."

"Thanks for being available so quickly." I settled onto a step-ladder beside a shelf full of wigs.

"Of course, what's going on?"

"Well, like I said in my message, Mom texted that the divorce is final." To my surprise, my throat cinched shut like a drawstring had been pulled. My eyes glazed with tears, and when I laughed it sounded more like a half sob. "I'm sorry, I didn't know I was going to cry."

"That's a fine thing to cry about." Kendra said, her voice as gentle and comforting as a fuzzy blanket.

I propped my elbow on my knee and cupped my forehead with my hand. My dark hair fell in sheets around either side of my face. "I've known for nearly a year, though. Shouldn't I be so adjusted to the idea that this feels anticlimactic?"

"You know how I feel about the word *should*." I could hear Kendra's smile.

I swallowed hard. "Yes, I know. I was calling because in the same text, Mom said she wants to pick me up from school. Like, right now."

"Ah. Have you responded yet?"

We'd talked about this more than anything else in the last few sessions—that I needed to separate my feelings from Mom's feelings. That being supportive of Mom was different than taking responsibility for her.

"No. I texted you right away."

"I'm glad we're able to talk about this together. Do you mind walking me through what you're feeling?"

I blew out a breath. "Lots of things."

"That's fine. Tell me about them."

"Well, upset, obviously. And like my mom needs me and that I should say 'yes, come pick me up.' Who better to understand and sit with her than me, right?"

"What else?" Kendra said instead of confirming or denying.

"Well, I also feel like I'm the absolute worst person for her to talk to. And since I have school and finals next week, I need to be here for the review sessions. And maybe I'm also annoyed that she texted me in the first place. Didn't she think this would upset me? Couldn't it have waited until after school?" I pulled my phone back from my ear. Eleven fifty-eight. "And I know you have to go at noon."

"So, in this situation, what belongs to you? What has God given you to control?" Kendra said without any hint of hurry in her voice.

We'd done this enough that I knew how to break it down. I took a deep breath. "I get to control if I respond or not. I get to control what I say." I paused and thought a moment. "I get to control the decision of whether I'll leave school or not." I considered a few seconds longer. "I think that's it."

"Okay. Do you want to respond to her?"

"Yes." I said. "Absolutely."

"Great. You've already made one decision. Are you going to leave school or stay?"

I bit my lower lip for a moment. "I want to stay. I need to prepare for finals."

"Okay. What do you think is the best way to tell your mom that?"

I closed my eyes, imagining the words in my head. "That I'm sorry, but I can't. I need to be in class. But we could talk after school, like before her art class and before swimming."

"I think that sounds good, Tessa. You're drawing a boundary around your school and swim time, but still communicating that you care about your mom, which I know is important to you." After a beat, Kendra asked, "Do you know when you come in next? I don't have my calendar in front of me."

"I think Wednesday the eighteenth."

"Okay, does a week from now feel soon enough considering everything going on? If not, I can have Jake call you to set up an appointment for sooner."

"I think I'm okay." I was about 50 percent sure that I was telling the truth. "Thank you."

"Okay. Let me know if you change your mind."

"I will."

"See you then, Tessa."

After Kendra hung up, I sat there in the prop closet for a few minutes, my eyes pressed closed. Oddly, it felt like prayer, even though I wasn't saying anything. I was sitting. Being silent.

This time last year, my life was basically perfect. Sure, Alex—the boy I had liked for years—was hung up on a different girl, but other than that, life had been pretty sweet. Good friends, good parents, good grades. I had a nice house, a sport I loved and enjoyed, and I thought I'd be celebrating sweet sixteen with a dream trip to Iceland with my dad, who was my hero.

And now . . .

A wry laugh slipped out as I looked at my surroundings. Now I was sitting in the prop closet on the phone with my therapist because my dad had decided to have an affair that had resulted in my half brother, Logan. My best friend for years, Mackenzie, had moved away and tried to commit suicide. Our other friends, who I thought I'd have through high school, were obsessed with partying and now felt like strangers to me.

I'd ended up with the boy after all—Alex and I would celebrate eight months together next week—and I still loved swimming. But those were pretty much the only things still intact from my old, perfect life. That and the house, which was more like a museum for a life I no longer had.

You'll get me through, God, I whispered as I turned off the lights in the prop closet. *You always have.*

Chapter 2

AMELIA SCRUTINIZED MY LUNCH TRAY, her green eyes narrowing. "Tessa, today of all days, you should let yourself eat something besides a salad for lunch."

I laughed and speared a cucumber wedge with my fork. "But I like salad." I showed her my Coke can wrapped in a napkin and lowered my voice. "And Alex bought me a Cherry Coke."

Amelia gave an exaggerated roll of her eyes as she opened her bottled vitamin water. "Contraband? You? My apologies. Clearly, you're handling this situation fine."

"Tessa's more likely to clean her room or go for a run when stressed," Alex said around a mouthful of grilled chicken strips.

I gave him a look. "That's not—"

He raised his eyebrows, and I reconsidered my denial.

"That's not *entirely* true. I've wallowed through my share of ice cream, thank you very much." I peeled back the napkin from my Cherry Coke and took a long swig as if to illustrate my point.

Alex smiled and beneath the table his knee settled against mine.

"Does the divorce being final change anything for you?" Amelia asked as Izzy and Shay arrived. Shay settled to my left with a brown bag lunch that I already knew was going to be a peanut butter sandwich, an apple, and carrot sticks. Izzy had a slice of pizza and a salad that was mostly bacon bits and shredded cheese.

"Yeah, it does. Legally, I'm required to spend every other weekend with my dad." I wrinkled my nose. "Which means Rebecca, too, obviously."

A moment of silence fell.

"And Logan . . ." Izzy glanced about the table, seeming unsure that this was the right response.

"Yep, Logan, too." I felt myself smile. Last time I held him, he fell asleep on my shoulder and laid there nearly an hour, his fuzzy head nestled against my neck. "That's not so bad."

"I'm afraid of babies," Shay said as she selected a carrot from her bag. "I only held one once, and I was sure I was going to hurt it. And then it threw up."

"Yeah. Babies do that a lot. I'm sure you wouldn't have hurt the baby, Shay," I said with a smile.

She shuddered. "I'm fine with baby animals. Just not baby humans."

"I like babies okay," Amelia said as she dipped her burrito in salsa. "I think I like them better than kids. I'll have to deal with a lot of children during our production of *Annie*. I've never been in a show with diverse ages. That'll be fun."

With Amelia, all conversational roads led back to the stage.

"I thought the summer show was *High School Musical*?" I asked.

She shook her head. "I thought so, too, but that's the show they're doing with their two-week theater camps. Those are more for kids who are only kind of interested in performance. *Annie* is for the serious actors."

Izzy poked at her pile of grated cheddar. "When do you audition?"

"Two weeks from now. I can't wait to be done with finals so I can focus on the show instead of my dumb classes."

Amelia's grin broadened as she continued talking. This would be her first time auditioning with Aspire, a Christian theater group, and she oozed enthusiasm. I hoped it went better than her previous auditions. Every time I'd seen Amelia on stage, she was brilliant . . . unless she was auditioning. Then she really struggled. But with all the confidence she gained after running our spring production of *Peter Pan*, hopefully auditioning would feel easier to her this time around. The terrible pixie haircut she'd gotten for herself—a bold attempt to help the casting team visualize her as Peter—had grown out a bit and was looking . . . well, not *good*, but better.

Alex's knee bumped against mine, and I looked at him. "You're coming Saturday afternoon, right?" he asked quiet enough to not interrupt the musical theater conversation the other girls were having. Amelia was trying to convince Izzy and Shay to audition. She had zero chance with Shay—she hated theater even more than I did—but Izzy looked interested.

My confusion must have shown on my face because Alex said, "My brother's graduation party? Not *this* Saturday, but the Saturday after. Do you have a meet?"

"No, thankfully. Mom and I will be there."

"Okay, good." When he smiled, his caramel-colored eyes crinkled a bit. I loved that. "Otherwise, I'll be totally bored. It's going to be mostly Clark's friends there."

I took a sip of my Cherry Coke. "How's your mom doing?"

Alex shrugged. "Same, I guess."

"Still crying most days?"

He nodded, causing his sandy hair to flop forward. "And Clark is pretty impatient about it. Which I kind of get, because she's been doing this for weeks, but . . ."

"Yeah, it's hard."

My thoughts drifted to my own mom. She'd responded with a simple, "Okay, see you after school," to the text I'd crafted with Kendra, but it wouldn't surprise me if I found her bingeing home-improvement shows when I got home.

"Tessa, what are you doing?"

I blinked back at the conversation to find the girls looking at me expectantly. "Uh, eating lunch?"

Shay grinned as she rewound her scrunchy in her low ponytail. "No, this summer. We're talking about our plans. I'll be at Green Tree Farm as much as possible. Or stuck helping at the store."

Shay's Aunt Laura owned Booked Up, the sole independent bookstore in town. It was a super cute store and Laura was cool with us hanging out there and doing homework so long as we were reasonably quiet and stayed out of the way of customers. If I were Shay, I'd want to work at Booked Up all the time, but her true love was horses, so it didn't surprise me that she'd soak up all the horse time she could at Green Tree.

"I thought you liked working at the store," Izzy said, a crouton falling off her fork and bouncing onto the floor.

"Lately it seems all I do is look for books that customers have put back on the shelves in the wrong place. Ugh. So incredibly boring."

Amelia cleared her throat. "Hopefully I'll be spending my summer as Miss Hannigan." Maybe her sudden accent was to indicate she was from New York City?

I didn't know anything about theater so being Miss Hannigan meant nothing to me, but Izzy bounced in her seat and clapped her hands. "Yes, you'd be perfect! And, stars, I don't know what I'll be doing this summer. A little bit of everything, I think! I'll still need to help with Sebastian, but not as much as I used to. I started learning Japanese on Duolingo. And Mrs. Kirby asked me to watch her chickens and cat while she's gone on a cruise. And I might do some art lessons with your mom, Tessa. And of course I have some baking to do! So many things I want to explore!"

Since Alex was sitting beside Izzy and conversation had naturally worked around the circle, all eyes shifted to him.

"I'll be a counselor at Outdoors with Christ. It's a—"

"No. Way." Amelia groaned. "My brother and sister were obsessed with OWC as kids, so my parents made me go. Worst week of my life *ever*."

Alex's smile was the patient one that he'd probably use all summer long with kids. He never came right out and said anything, but I was pretty sure that Amelia was the most challenging of my friends for him to get along with.

"Yeah, not every kid loves it, that's for sure."

"This is a camp?" Shay asked without quite meeting Alex's eyes. He didn't eat with us every day, and she could still be somewhat shy around him.

Alex nodded. "It's an outdoor Christian camp about thirty minutes outside of town. I went every summer as a kid and so did Tessa. There's fishing, swimming, archery, hiking, all kinds of stuff."

"You're outside all day every day." Amelia gave a theatrical shudder. "It's the absolute worst."

Shay smiled. "Doesn't sound so bad to me."

"I'm the fifth-grade boys' counselor, so I'll be in charge of eight to ten fifth-grade boys for a week at a time, basically."

Shay flinched. "*That* doesn't sound so great."

"I think my neighbor mentioned she'll be working there this summer too. She was so excited," Amelia said as she balled up her trash. "Lots of people like it. Tessa, what about you?"

"Swim lessons. So, I'll have my own swim practice starting every morning at seven, and then I'll teach lessons from nine to noon."

Amelia's face flickered with a frown. "That stinks. I think

practice at Aspire starts at one, and then I'm busy all day. When are we going to see each other this summer, girls?"

Nobody spoke.

"We'll figure it out," Izzy said after a few moments of silence. "We need to."

—⁓—

Instead of finding Mom on the couch in front of HGTV, she was sitting at the kitchen counter, peering through her reading glasses at her laptop. My mom was forty-four, but her hair was almost completely steel gray and had been for as long as I could remember. She kept it cut in a bob that hit barely below her chin. Even though I knew she'd stayed around the house today, Mom still had her full face of makeup on, complete with her signature lipstick and black liquid eyeliner. Her bright red mouth frowned at the computer screen.

"Did it do that update thing again?" I asked.

Mom's head snapped up, as if she hadn't heard me come in the garage. "Oh, hi. No, it didn't. I'm trying to understand money stuff and my brain hurts."

I'd been better at math than my mom since third grade. I leaned my backpack against the wall. "Like work money stuff?"

"No. General life money stuff." She sighed and pushed her glasses up into her hair. "Your dad has to pay a certain amount of money every month, and I'm trying to figure out how much it will be when you factor in the mortgage and utilities and my car payment and pool fees . . ." Mom made a fluttering motion with her hand to indicate that the list went on. "I don't think it'll go as far as I originally thought."

A tightness formed in my chest. "Oh."

Mom must've heard the concern in my voice because she looked up right away. "We're going to be totally fine, Tessa. I'm sure of it. I guess I've never paid close attention to what things cost or how much money I make until I had to fill out all the divorce paperwork and—" she shrugged "—now I will. But it'll be fine. We'll be fine." She closed her laptop and pasted on a smile. "How was your day? Feeling ready for finals next week?"

I swallowed. A fake smile and closed laptop didn't fill me with confidence that our financial situation was going to be fine. "Yeah, I have ELA and drama finals on Monday. I feel pretty good about those. Mom, do you want me to look at the money stuff and—"

"Absolutely not," Mom said with the same forced smile. She leaped up from the barstool and headed for the pantry where we stored our traditional after-school snack of sugary cereal. "I'm not worried, and you shouldn't be either. Actually, you know what I was thinking about this afternoon? Iceland."

That seemed random. I wouldn't have been more surprised if she told me she'd been ruminating about cheetahs or refrigerators. "Iceland? Why were you thinking about that?"

"I was thinking we should go." Mom grinned at me as she pulled out the box of Cookie Crisp. "I know I'm not your dad, and it was supposed to be a special trip for the two of you. But I think we could still have fun, don't you?"

"Mom . . ." I glanced at the closed laptop. "A trip to Iceland isn't exactly cheap."

"We're two smart girls. We can earn money, right? You have your job at the pool this summer, and my summer art camps are filling up faster than ever." Mom pushed her grin even higher. "Let's figure out how much it would cost to go and start saving. What do you say?"

My heart raced with a mix of excitement—I'd longed to go to Iceland for years—and anxiety. If Mom was still figuring out how much our mortgage cost every month, should we be planning a trip like that?

"Would it be so bad to go with me instead of Dad?" Mom asked, her smile slipping a bit.

"No, that's not it at all," I said in a rush. "I'd love to go with you. I . . . I want to make sure we have enough money to keep the lights on first, you know?"

"I'll take care of that," Mom said above the sound of Cookie Crisp filling our cereal bowls. "And you can take care of planning an awesome trip for us. Deal?"

I hesitated, but what else could I say? "Deal."

Mom beamed and threw her arms around me. "Yay! I'm so excited, Tessa. It's been eating away at me that you lost out on that trip, so you've made me very happy by agreeing to this. Now, start planning!"

I squeezed her back and tried to ignore all the obstacles that could pop up and were out of my control. Hoping and planning were dangerous.

Chapter

3

AFTER FIFTEEN MINUTES OF SITTING IN the Hastings' basement, scrolling Instagram while Alex played *Super Smash Bros.* with his brothers and cousins, I decided I was ready to be done with Clark's graduation party.

"I'm going to take off," I told Alex in a low voice once they'd finished a battle.

He looked surprised. "Oh, okay. Want me to quit?"

"No, that's fine. I need to get home anyway. Mom said she wanted to talk to me about something this afternoon."

Alex made a face. "That sounds ominous."

"Yeah," I said with a sigh. "I assume it's about custody stuff. I think she and Dad were waiting until school was out to talk with me about scheduling the every-other-weekend visits."

Alex's fingers threaded through mine. "I'm sorry."

"Me too."

Clark launched the next battle, so I gave Alex a swift kiss on the cheek. "Bye."

"Call me later?" he asked, his eyes locked on the screen where Donkey Kong was pounding his fists, and other *Mario* characters I didn't recognize were jumping around making weird sounds.

"Call me later?" mimicked Finn, Alex's younger brother. Then he burst out laughing. "Dude, I totally just pushed you off the cliff."

I rolled my eyes—not that anyone noticed—and left the Hastings boys to their game.

As I cut through the kitchen on my way to the garage, I found Mrs. Hastings leaning over the sink, weeping. I froze, then instinctively took several steps back, hoping to silently rewind before Mrs. Hastings realized I'd intruded on her private moment. I could go quietly out the front door and get my bag from the mudroom later—

Alex's mom looked up, surprise registering on her tear-streaked face. "Oh, Tessa." She attempted a smile. "Sorry, dear, come on in."

"I was getting my bag . . ."

"Of course." Mrs. Hastings wiped under her eyes with her fingertips, dragging flakes of mascara into her blond hair. "Sorry, I was having kind of a . . .," Mrs. Hastings chuckled self-consciously. "I don't know. An emotional breakdown is the most honest description, I guess."

Through the picture windows, I could see Mr. Hastings stacking folding chairs, cleaning up the yard from the afternoon's festivities. I swallowed and looked back to Mrs. Hastings. There was no one else here to help me through this.

"Because of Clark?" I asked.

"Yeah. I mean, this is it. The last event of high school. It's over." Mrs. Hastings clenched her jaw, but her mouth trembled anyway. "I imagine it sounds silly to you, but I can't believe it's here. I feel like he just started kindergarten."

I never understood when my mom said stuff like that. Moms

appeared to have their own fantasy timeline running in their heads that was completely disconnected from reality.

Instead, I said, "It doesn't sound silly. My mom says the same kind of thing."

"Summers always go by so fast. We basically have only a few weeks left of being a family." Mrs. Hastings teared up again as her voice climbed higher. "And then Clark will be off at school. And Alex will be a junior, and Finn only has one more year in middle school. Everything is going so fast, I can't—"

I jumped when the back door opened and Mr. Hastings called in, "Honey, can you— Oh, no, what's wrong?"

Mrs. Hastings laughed an I'm-completely-freaking-out-but-trying-to-cover-it-up laugh. "I'm scaring Tessa away, that's all."

I tried smiling and looking comfortable, as if I dealt with my boyfriend's mom imploding emotionally on a regular basis. "That's not true at all."

"I think Tessa's impossible to scare," Mr. Hastings said as he closed the door. He walked around the counter and fit his arm around his wife. "Remember that time she babysat Finn, and he threw up on her?"

"That was disgusting," I said, smiling at him. Looking at Mr. Hastings felt like I was getting a sneak peek of Alex in his forties. "And that was the last time I ever babysat, so it maybe doesn't prove your point."

Mrs. Hastings smiled at my joke and rested her head on Alex's dad's shoulder. Something in my gut clenched. When Mom cleaned up from my graduation party in a couple years, who would comfort her? Whose shoulder would she lean on?

"I think I'm tired," Mrs. Hastings said as she closed her eyes. "Tessa, your mom always hosts parties so effortlessly. I don't know how she does it."

"She used to," I said. "She hasn't in a long time, though."

"Well." Mrs. Hastings looked hesitant. Uncomfortable. "That's understandable."

I swallowed and looked at my bare feet. So, not only had I offered zero comfort when she was crying, but now I'd made the situation even more awkward by dragging in my parents' divorce. *Well done, Tessa.*

"You'll still be a family, you know," I said to my painted toenails. "You said there's just a few more weeks of being a family. It'll look different with Clark at Purdue, but you'll still *be* a family."

Silence stretched between us. I wiggled my toes.

"Thank you, Tessa." Mrs. Hastings's voice was low and husky. "Yes, you're right. I tend to get a little theatrical when I'm tired."

I looked up and smiled. "One of my best friends is theatrical twenty-four seven, so I'm used to it."

Alex's parents smiled back.

"I'll go out through the garage," I said.

Mrs. Hastings crossed the kitchen and folded me in a hug. "Thanks so much for coming. And tell your mom thank you too. I was barely able to talk with her when she was here, but it wouldn't have been a party without the two of you."

I doubted this. Mom had been abnormally quiet while she was here. Usually she loved a good gathering, but she was still getting used to navigating parties as a divorced woman.

"I'll tell her, thanks."

I waved goodbye to Alex's parents, grabbed my Kavu bag from where Alex had stashed it in the mudroom, and exited through the open garage. I'd been coming to the Hastings' house since second grade and could probably count on one hand the number of times I'd gone through the front door.

The afternoon was unseasonably chilly for May twenty-first, with a thin layer of gray clouds that made everything feel gloomy and damp despite there being no rain. My mind rewound and replayed my conversation with Mrs. Hastings as I walked up the

LIFE IN THE MIDDLE || 21

sidewalk toward my house. I should've offered her a Kleenex or hugged her or something. Izzy was way better at emotional conversations than I was. She would've known what to say and do, and then she would've shown up with a plate of baked goods an hour later. Mrs. Hastings would probably tell Alex, "Your girlfriend found me crying and then stood there awkwardly." Not that Alex would be surprised. Even though I'd worked through a lot of it in counseling, when dealing with my own emotional turmoil my tendency was still to deny it, shove it way down, and grieve privately beneath a shell of "I'm fine."

I pulled my phone from my hoodie pocket to text Alex a preemptive apology for being awkward with his mom, but before I could, my gaze caught on a familiar and yet unsettling sight. Dad's Jeep was parked in our driveway. My whole body tensed, as if I was a knot in a rope and someone had pulled both ends tight. Why was he here? Were we going to have the custody conversation with all three of us?

Maybe he and Rebecca had ended things? There was an awkward flutter in my chest, like a butterfly with a broken wing attempting flight. Because if Dad and Rebecca ended things, what would that mean for my half brother, Logan? Would I wish the same painful experience on him—Dad walking away—that happened to me?

Yes, I realized. Yes. If it meant having my family back, I really would.

The realization made me feel a little nauseated, especially as a part of my brain that I couldn't seem to shut up rattled off rationalizations. Logan wasn't even two months old. He wouldn't remember being part of a family of three. Rebecca could find and marry someone else. Someone who was *not* my father. She could have more kids with that man, and Logan wouldn't know the difference. *Maybe he'd even be happier*, some sneaky voice whispered.

I tucked my phone back into my pocket, my message unsent,

and closed my eyes briefly. *That was awfully ugly, God, wasn't it?* I opened my eyes, took a deep breath as if I were getting ready to swim a 400 and trudged the rest of the way up my driveway. I turned the doorknob and nudged open the door. My presence was announced with a succinct beep-beep, courtesy of the new alarm system Mom had installed after reading a news story about single women being targeted by burglars.

"Tessa?" Mom called. It sounded like she was in the kitchen. Maybe the dining room.

"Yep."

"Your dad and I are in the kitchen. Can you come here, please?"

"Mmhmm."

My heart pounded so loudly, I couldn't hear if they were talking to each other or not as I wound through the living room and found them sitting at the kitchen counter several feet away from each other. Any hopes that this was a "We've decided to reconcile" conversation died a swift but painful death. Their smiles were far too stiff.

My gaze flitted between the two of them. The last time I saw them alone in a room together was the morning they told me about their divorce.

"Hi, Tessa." Dad looked like himself—same bald head, same glasses, and same neutral-toned button-down shirt—but more tired than usual. Probably because he had a two-month-old baby at home.

"Hi."

"How was the rest of the party?" Mom asked with an empty smile on her face.

The image that came to mind was Mrs. Hastings—tear-streaked and grieving—leaning on the shoulder of her husband. Thinking about that hurt.

"Fine."

"How's Alex doing?" Dad asked.

"Fine."

"He was our waiter a couple nights ago at Taqueria El Rancho," Dad said. *Our* referring to him, Rebecca, and Logan.

"Yeah, he told me."

Alex had said Rebecca wore Logan in a sling the entire dinner, and she'd told Alex the sling had been given to her in exchange for promoting it on her Instagram account. As if he cared about baby slings. I knew which one he was talking about, because I'd seen her touting it when I'd spied on her. Well, it wasn't spying if she posted it on Instagram.

If Izzy, Shay, and Amelia knew I had clicked "follow" on Rebecca's Instagram, they would groan and tell me to unfollow immediately. That no good could come from that. They weren't wrong. Stalking Rebecca's Instagram was a habit I knew I should break but also didn't really want to. She has twenty-seven thousand followers, because apparently you can be an Instafamous kindergarten teacher, so it's not like she'd ever notice that I followed her.

I leaned against the kitchen island. "So, why are you here?"

Mom and Dad exchanged a look. Dad gestured to Mom, indicating that she should speak, which made me scowl. Why was he in charge?

"Your dad and I have something we want to discuss with you." Mom folded her hands on top of the counter and leveled her gaze on me. "Please be honest with us."

This didn't sound good. "Okay."

"We've been talking about the house and what to do with it. We're considering a couple options, but we don't want to discount how it affects you."

"What to do with it?" I echoed. I cut a glare at my father. "You said I wouldn't have to move. You said you were committed to making this as easy on me as possible. Or is that yet another lie of yours?"

Dad cleared his throat, but before he could speak, Mom

jumped in. "Hold on, Tessa. We *are* committed to that. And if staying here at the house is important to you after you listen to the options, then that's what we'll do."

I gave Dad another suspicious look. "What are the other options?"

Mom answered, not Dad. "There are two we're considering. One is keeping the house until you've graduated. After that, I would look for something more suitable. The other option is selling the house now, and you and I pick out a place together."

It sounded like my mother would prefer the latter. There was something warmer in her tone. I bit my lower lip. "What about your business?"

Mom shrugged. "It would come with us. I can teach art classes elsewhere just as easily. We would look for a house that accommodated that. A place where I don't also have to clean five bathrooms." Her smile looked forced. Weary.

"I clean my own bathroom," I said quietly.

"Four, then. I think you know what I mean. This house . . .," Mom sighed and gave an exaggerated look around her. "It doesn't fit who we are anymore."

Because a family of two didn't merit a spacious house and five bathrooms, but a family of three did?

Dad cleared his throat again. "We understand this has been your home for your whole life. We know Alex is a few houses down. If keeping the house is important to you, then it's important to us."

Mom nodded. "Absolutely."

"I'd like to think about it," I said slowly. "Is that okay?"

"Of course," Dad said as Mom said, "Sure."

I looked at both of them, sitting at a counter that I'd sat at countless times eating my breakfast or doing homework. Behind them, through the row of windows, were the trees that lined the walking trail I took to the pool for practice. There was a literal lifetime of memories in this house. The idea of packing up and leaving the place where we'd been a family caused an ache behind my ribs.

"Okay." I turned and walked out of the kitchen, feeling aware that they'd talk about me after I left. Instead of taking the stairs in twos, I stepped one at a time, running my hand along the cherry-wood banister that I used to slide stuffed animals down as a little girl. I couldn't leave here. There was no way.

I paused at the top of the staircase, but if Mom and Dad were still talking, I couldn't hear them. Not that long ago, I'd stood at the top of this staircase and listened to them shouting at each other in the living room minutes before Dad loaded up his suitcases and left for good. That had been over nine months ago, but the memory still made my stomach ache.

I ran my hand along the banister and imagined living in a place where I hadn't learned my father wasn't who I believed him to be, where I hadn't watched my mother become a shell of herself for almost a month, and where I hadn't lost what mattered most to me in the whole world.

Yes, we'd been a family here. But here, I realized, was also where we'd fallen apart.

Chapter
4

"Maybe moving wouldn't be so bad," Shay said in that careful way of hers, like she was thinking through every word before she said it. She glanced at Izzy and Amelia, as if waiting to be corrected.

The four of us were at Booked Up. During the school year, we frequently did homework in this corner of the store, but with finals over and school out, we instead sipped at our drinks from the coffee shop around the corner and chatted.

Amelia rolled her lips over her teeth, as if she needed to do something physical to keep herself from responding. That probably meant she disagreed with Shay.

"Yeah," Izzy said in a bright voice as she braided a strand of hair. "I mean, your house *is* kind of big for you and your mom. It's a lot for her to take care of. Maybe a new place where you could create new memories would be nice?"

"Yeah." Shay bobbed her head as she absently stroked the

bookstore cat, Matilda, who was curled up on her lap. "Fresh starts can be good."

I took a drag of my iced coffee and glanced at Amelia. She flipped through an issue of *People*, pointedly not saying anything. "Amelia, you look like you have a different opinion."

Amelia sighed heavily. "Didn't your dad make all kinds of promises about you not needing to move? I'm angry that they're even asking you this. Like, why should *you* have to change something because of a decision *they* made?"

"Yeah—"

"And, yes, it's a big house. But it was a big house when your parents bought it too. If your mom didn't want to take care of a big house, she should've spoken up then."

The flash of fury in Amelia's eyes was heartwarming. The raw version of Amelia could be a little terrifying—unless she was in your corner and fighting for you.

"But she wasn't a single parent then either," I pointed out. Izzy stayed laser focused on her braid and Shay kept petting Matilda, as if trying to stay out of the conversation. "She and my dad always split the cleaning. Or during busy seasons, they'd hire it out. She can't afford that anymore."

"Then why doesn't your dad pay for it?" Amelia flopped back in the armchair. "Why shouldn't he still contribute? He's the one who wanted the divorce. He's the one who cheated. Why are you trying to make his life easier by moving?"

No one said anything for a moment. Shay's aunt poked her head around the corner. "Hey, girls." Laura glanced around the group of us. "Can we keep it down a bit back here?"

"Sorry, that's me." Amelia held up a hand. "No surprise, right? I'll rein it in."

"Thanks, Amelia." Laura flashed her a smile, and then disappeared from view.

"When I'm a grown-up, I want to look as cool and put together as your aunt," I said to Shay. "She puts off some serious Lorelai Gilmore vibes."

"I don't know who that is," Shay said with a smile. "But yeah. Laura's cool."

Izzy groaned and swiped open her phone. "I'll add *Gilmore Girls* to the list. Hashtag Izzy fail. We're just watching the original seasons, though. Not the reboot. Don't get me started on that."

Izzy and Shay got together regularly to "catch Shay up to this century," as Izzy put it. That appeared to be code for watching a lot of Izzy's favorites on Netflix. They both had more time on their hands than Amelia or I did, although Izzy was still often busy keeping an eye on Sebastian, her brother, who was high on the spectrum. Even that responsibility had been significantly reduced. I wasn't sure that Shay cared about understanding pop culture references, but she appeared to enjoy the time with Izzy.

"Back to your dad." Amelia's volume registered lower than normal, which probably took considerable effort for her. "If I were you, my answer would be no. Not just no, but, *No. Way.*"

"Yeah," I said into my iced coffee.

"Plus, Alex lives three houses down from you," Amelia added. "That's pretty perfect."

"Yeah."

"And don't you walk to and from swim practice?"

"Yeah."

Amelia cocked her head at me. "All these 'yeahs' have 'buts.'"

Izzy giggled as she sipped her hot chocolate, and then coughed when she sucked the liquid in weird. "Sorry. I have a little brother. I can't not laugh at that."

Amelia rolled her eyes and refocused on me. "What's the argument *for* moving, Tessa?"

I thought about yesterday, when I'd stood at the top of the stairs, and how the brutal memory of overhearing Mom and Dad's marriage end had engulfed me. "I hear what you're saying, and that's where I started too. When they asked me, I thought, *No way am I doing that.* But then . . ." Tears welled up, and I tried to cover by taking a long drink of my coffee. If the girls noticed, they were nice enough to not call attention to it.

"But staying at that house isn't going to fix my parents. Mom didn't come out and say it, but I think she wants to move. I think she wants that fresh start you talked about, Shay. If we do it now, I can help her. But if I ask her to wait until I go away to college, that's basically asking her to do it alone. Hasn't she suffered enough?"

"What about what *you* want, Tessa?" Izzy asked in a gentle voice. "That matters too."

"I'm only home for another two years. It seems like Mom's preference should get more weight, you know?"

The girls were silent, and then Amelia exhaled slowly. "You are a much nicer person than me."

I exhaled a sharp laugh. "That's not true. Everything you said about my dad and the promises he made me was stuff I said on the phone with Alex last night. I've had more time to come around to the idea. Because, yeah, I *don't* want to make my dad's life easier. I *want* to keep him on the hook for what he did to us. But this time, if I keep him on the hook, my mom stays on the hook too. I don't think that part's okay with me."

Amelia sagged her shoulders as if she'd read "act dejected" in a script. "I think I get that," she said. "But I still hate it for you."

"Thank you."

Izzy picked a piece of fuzz off her rainbow striped leggings. "What did Alex say about you moving?"

"Well . . ." I pursed my lips. "When we talked last night, I was still really angry and adamant about saying no. I haven't exactly told him about my change of heart."

Izzy winced. "Do you think he'll be mad?"

I hesitated. "Maybe not *mad*. But it's not what he would pick, of course."

The girls didn't seem to know how to respond to that. In the lull of our conversation, a customer's voice reached us. "Thank you! He's nine weeks old and *not* a fan of sleeping!"

Rebecca. I felt myself go stiff in my chair. I glanced at my friends, but none of them appeared to be tuned in to Rebecca's loud voice like I was. They maybe hadn't even noticed.

"Well, that's tough, Tessa," Izzy said. "I'm praying for you."

Shay brushed cat hair off her jeans now that Matilda had leapt off her lap. "Yeah, me too."

Hearing Rebecca had disoriented me so much that it took a few seconds to remember what we'd been talking about. "Thanks," I murmured.

Izzy kept talking, but I was half listening. More like one-quarter listening. The other three-quarters of my brain was dialed in to Rebecca's interaction with Laura. I couldn't make out Laura's words, only Rebecca's loud, showy voice. It was like she thought we were all her Instagram audience, eager to know what she thought.

"Too blessed to be stressed, though," she carried on. "He's our little miracle baby."

My jaw ached, and I realized that my teeth were clenched. *That's not true,* I wanted to yell. *All that talk about blessings and miracle babies isn't true!*

Because how could Rebecca—the woman who'd willingly had an affair with my married father—be blessed by God with a *miracle* baby? That didn't align with what I knew of God, who valued marriage and kept His promises. Why did Rebecca get to feel blessed while I felt bitter?

Amelia waved a hand in front of my face. "You in there, Tessa?"

I blinked back into the present. "Yes. Sorry."

All three of them offered me sympathetic looks, and I felt an unexpected flush of joy as I considered their faces. The last year had been a dumpster fire in so many ways, but not when it came to friends. God had provided some good companions to come alongside me during my walk through the valley.

Chapter
5

When I told Mom that moving would be fine with me, it was obvious that she had hoped this would be my answer. She squealed, hugged me, and basically hopped on the phone right away to get "pre-qualified." I didn't even know what that meant.

Still, I hadn't expected to be riding around two days later in the back seat of a realtor's SUV to look at houses. Mom knew Shelley through teaching art classes and the two chatted warmly in the front seats. Shelley's SUV smelled new, and the seats were like comfortable recliners. With the warm sun slanting through the window, it wouldn't have been too hard for me to be lulled to sleep as we drove through town. Especially as the houses blurred together in a chain of generic three-bedroom, two-bathroom ranch homes painted in neutral tones.

The only house we'd looked at so far that had stuck out to me was the one that backed up to my grandma and grandpa's place.

Mom and I had looked out the back window right into Grandma's raised flower beds. "Well, that's a 'no' right there," Mom said with a wry laugh. She didn't exactly have a bad relationship with my grandparents but living behind her former in-laws had some obvious downsides.

As Shelley navigated through an older part of Riverbend, she and Mom chatted about selling our house. "Liz and John are motivated buyers," Shelley said above the soothing voice of her GPS system offering guidance on where to turn. "I can't tell you how many houses I've shown them in the last month, but they keep coming back to wanting to be in your neighborhood so they can be close to the trail system. And I know they would pay top dollar for a house that's as beautiful as yours *and* backs up to the trail. I know you'll need to talk it over with David, of course, but if I'm right, you wouldn't even have to go through the hassle of listing your place."

"That would be really nice," Mom said.

Of course someone wanted to snatch up my house. My house was beautiful, like my life had been beautiful. Listening to Shelley talk about dumb Liz and John made me feel like a toddler who'd been guilted into sharing a prized toy, and then was forced to sit there and watch while the other child played with delight.

"They'd love to come take a look whenever you're okay with it," Shelley said as she pulled alongside the curb.

Never, I wanted to say. *We're never going to be okay with it.*

"I'll look at my calendar. The sooner the better because of art classes starting up." Mom let out a small gasp. "Oh, how darling is *this?*"

I looked out the window. The exterior of this house was the most unique we'd seen, a mix of red brick, forest green stucco, and limestone accents. It had large gables and a bright red door that made me think of a gingerbread house—along with the fact that it was small.

"It definitely has curb appeal," Shelley said as she shut off the ignition. "Older, maybe, than what you want."

"I don't know," Mom said, unbuckling. "An older home could be fun."

Really? Wasn't the point of this move to limit how much housework was on her plate?

The walk up the driveway was peppered with comments like "I love this shade of green," "Look at those cute bushes," and "What a great garage door."

"There's only enough space for one car," I pointed out on that last one.

"True." Mom's tone was dismissive. "One of us could park in the driveway."

"One of us" meant me. I tried to send Shelley a message with my eyes—*help me talk sense into her!*—but she was focused on inputting the code to access the key.

The front door opened into a tiny living room that I could already tell my mom was going to love. The walls were painted a rich red, the doorways were all arches, and a whitewashed fireplace took up most of one wall. Other than the bright white trim, there wasn't a neutral color in sight.

"Oh, I *love* this," Mom said as she ran her hand along an arched doorway. "So much character."

Shelley meandered through the living room and dining room in about twelve steps. "It's quite charming."

"What do you think, Tessa?" Mom asked without looking at me. "This has much more personality than any of those other houses we looked at this morning."

It *was* cute. "It seems like a place we shouldn't get too excited about until we've seen more than the living room. And read that document thingy owners have to fill out."

"Seller disclosure," Shelley supplied. "Extra important in an older home. If I remember right, this place was built in the 1930s."

"Wow, I think this is walnut." Mom admired the banister running up the narrow staircase. "We don't build houses like this anymore, you know?"

"With sparse electrical outlets and creepy basements, you mean?" I said.

Mom shot me a look that meant "not helpful" but didn't respond otherwise. I followed her and Shelley through the dining room to a tiny kitchen. I raised my eyebrows. Mom loved cooking and our current kitchen was the size of the whole downstairs of this gingerbread house.

"Well," Mom said slowly. "I won't need as much space if I'm only cooking for two. And there won't even be two of us to cook for in a couple years."

I felt a weird prickle in my chest at the reminder that this was short-term for me. Whatever house we picked out, Mom's opinion was the only one that really mattered.

Shelley opened a few cabinets. "Cabinetry is in good shape. And I bet this door goes to the basement." She crossed swiftly to a narrow door, causing several floorboards to creak their protest.

Mom grinned at me. "Now you can't sneak out of the house and go to parties."

I rolled my eyes.

Shelley opened the door into a narrow stairwell that descended into blackness.

"Uh, nope," I said. "I'll stay up here."

Mom and Shelley went down the groaning stairs while I lingered awkwardly in the small kitchen. Nobody lived here currently, which was obvious after my morning of looking at houses. Some were full of stuff, complete with irritated dogs closed in the laundry room. Others, like this house, had been staged with a few pieces of furniture. The staged ones always looked nicer, and it made me itch with suspicion. What did a small place like this look like when somebody lived there?

Mom's voice floated up to me. "Really, we don't need that much storage. This could be a good opportunity to thin out some of the clutter."

"Is three-quarters of our house clutter, Mom?" I muttered.

Because, no, we didn't need the big house we lived in, but she was downplaying how huge of a change a house this size would be.

There was no obvious master bedroom because none of the three bedrooms had attached bathrooms. Mom declared she'd never liked master suites anyway.

"Would your bedroom furniture even fit in here?" I asked as I eyeballed the bed that currently took up most of the main floor's bedroom. Mom slept in a king-size sleigh bed.

Mom pursed her lips as she considered this. "I could sell that bedroom set. The one in the guest bedroom would suit this house much better anyway."

The second floor had two small bedrooms, a bathroom, and a short staircase leading to a quirky loft. The desk staged in the middle implied this was intended for an office space, but it was warm and stuffy. The big skylights probably meant you roasted in the middle of the day.

"I'm not sure I could ask for a better space for work," Mom said. Unsurprisingly. "This has great natural light."

"All these stairs could be a deterrent for some of your older students," Shelley said. "Or students with disabilities."

"Mmm, true." But Mom continued to look around the space with an indulgent eye. Then she surprised me by adding. "It *is* a little warm up here."

I bit back a snarky comment—*wait, it's not absolutely perfect?*—and strolled to the window. I could see the clocktower in downtown Riverbend, which wasn't a downtown like Indy, but rather a single street with hundred-year-old buildings. If we lived here, I'd be close to Shay and Booked Up. It was probably a five-minute walk to her or Grounds and Rounds or Taqueria. That'd be nice when Alex was working.

Swimming would probably be a ten-minute drive from here. Dad had given me a car last Christmas, a secondhand sedan a guy at his work was selling for a good price. When he gave it to me, I think he hoped I would drive to his place more. But his place was Rebecca's place. I'd been there a handful of times, and . . .

I frowned mid-thought. Didn't they live a few blocks away from downtown? I pulled up Google Maps on my phone. Sure enough, the pulsing icon showing my current location was several streets away from the waypoint labeled "Dad."

"For an older home, there are lots of updates that would make life easier," Shelley said as I tuned back into the conversation. She had the seller's disclosure in one hand and looked at it through her reading glasses. "Looks like this has been rented out with Airbnb for the last year. The previous owners took care of the copper pipes, and the roof was replaced several years ago. Probably after that hailstorm with the ping-pong size hail. I think that's when half the roofs in Riverbend were replaced. The windows aren't original, but they were replaced in the '70s, so . . ."

To my relief, Mom was looking a little less like the heart-eye emoji. Although that probably meant she was seriously considering this. The house crush was over, and now she was deciding if it was worth putting a ring on it.

"So, the windows would need to be replaced soon." Mom ran a hand along her beloved walnut handrail. "Or I'll take the hit in utilities."

This could be my new home.

The thought stirred a weird slush of anxiety and excitement in my chest. It was one thing to think abstractly about a fresh start and new house. It was another to potentially be standing within its walls.

Mom turned and looked at me. "Tessa? Thoughts?"

Shelley kept her eyes on the disclosure document, but I could feel her listening.

"Well." I swallowed. "I've never lived in an old house like this."

"I haven't for a long time," Mom said when it became apparent that I wasn't going to continue right away. "But I love house projects. That part could be fun for me."

"We won't know until an inspection," Shelley added, "but it seems to have great bones. I haven't seen any concerning cracks inside, but we should check the foundation when we're outside."

"Let's do that now," Mom said. "I'm not going to overlook a foundation problem."

As we walked back down the stairs, I tried imagining myself here in this house day after day. Sleeping in that yellow bedroom with the slanted ceiling and built-in shelves. Getting ready for school in the small bathroom with the pedestal sink. Picturing myself living here was hard . . . but that would probably be true of anywhere, right? I'd only lived in one house before. And it wasn't hard to picture Mom being happy here.

Outside, the backyard was small, but big trees shaded a stone patio.

Shelley gazed up at the leafy branches. "Those will keep you busy in the fall."

Mom gave a good-natured groan. "Surely there's a nice neighbor boy who'll want to earn a few bucks."

Shelley grinned, then glanced at a notification on her watch. "Carrie, I'm sorry, my son is trying to heat up lunch and has a question. Do you mind if I give him a quick call?"

Mom waved Shelley away. "Of course not. Take your time."

As Shelley walked off, her glittery iPhone pressed against her ear, Mom turned to me with a cautious smile. "You don't love it."

She looked sad, and my heart softened. "It's not that."

"Then what is it? I can tell you're hesitant."

I looked away from her. "It's hard to think about moving. That's all."

"I know, honey. It's hard for me, too."

"You know it's pretty close to Dad's, right?"

Mom frowned. "They're on the other side of downtown."

I pulled up the map on my phone and handed it to her. "Just by a couple streets. I don't think they're even a mile away from here."

"Well, I don't love that." Mom's frown deepened. "But I also don't love the idea of *not* buying this place just because they live within a mile."

I thought of Sunday afternoon at Booked Up when I'd overheard Rebecca. *Too blessed to be stressed!* "You'd potentially run into them more."

"Yeah," Mom said on a slow sigh, as if she were a leaking balloon, only she was leaking enthusiasm instead. She returned my phone and gazed up at the house in contemplative silence.

After a few seconds, she said, "The first few years of our marriage, when we lived in Bloomington, we had an old house and I loved it. When we moved to Riverbend, I tried to talk your father into restoring a house around here, but he had no interest. Which probably made sense." Mom shrugged. "I was pregnant with you, and he had a new job with more money and more demands on his time. He said that wouldn't leave much time for house projects, which was true. Buying a newer home was a practical thing to do. Unsurprising." She chuckled humorlessly. "That's your dad, right?"

I swallowed hard. Dad had a way of acting as though his practicality was a positive trait and Mom's whimsy was a negative. Something to be pruned away at the least and eradicated if possible. But I didn't see it that way. Yes, sometimes practical was the smart decision, but what if it came at the cost of joy? If a home like this brought Mom more pleasure, then that was the right answer even if it might not be as practical.

"This is the house you want?" I asked.

Mom bit her lower lip. "If the inspection comes back good, then I think I would love to live here. I know it would be a big adjustment for you but moving will be months away. We have to get our place ready to sell, so you'll have all summer at home."

That would be good. "If this is the house you want, it's fine with me."

Mom's eyes were a mix of excitement and hesitation. She needed more than my mere acceptance, apparently.

"It's a cute house," I added. "It reminds me of a gingerbread house."

Mom's eyes sparked. "Yes. Like something from a fairy tale, right?" She put an arm around me and squeezed as we looked up at the gabled roofline. "I think God will write some amazing chapters in our story here, Tessa Rae."

Chapter
6

Can you call me when you get a chance?

I stared at the text from my dad. Not too long ago, I would've angrily swiped it away and felt almost no guilt for ignoring his request. Now, I stared at the words and thought through the possible responses. I could delay the call . . . but I wasn't doing anything except sitting in my car outside Taqueria El Rancho, waiting for Alex to get off work. Now was a convenient time to make a phone call.

But responding to Dad right away made me feel icky. Like if I did what he asked right away, I would make his life too easy. I'd seen Kendra yesterday, so it wasn't hard to picture her kind smile as she said, "Tessa, it sounds like you're still trying to punish your father for what he did to you." We'd talked a lot about that since this coming weekend would be my first to stay with him and Rebecca. Kendra had suggested that during this transition we could resume having appointments once a week, and I'd taken her up on it.

I stared at Dad's text again. I couldn't remember when he'd last asked me to call. If I delayed calling him back, I'd be stressed about what he might have to say. Once again, keeping Dad on the hook would keep me on the hook too. Now that I knew to look for all the ways that punishing him meant punishing me, too, I saw it all the time.

"Stop being a baby and call him, Tessa," I muttered to myself and tapped the telephone icon.

Dad answered, chuckling. "Well, that was fast."

I squashed the irritation that flared in me. "You caught me at a good time. I'm waiting for Alex to get off work."

"Do you two have plans today?"

"Just hanging out."

"Well, I'll make this quick so you can get on with your afternoon." In the background, I could hear a printer churning out pages. He must be at work. "You know how teachers have continuing education they have to do?"

"Uh, no. I don't know about that."

"They do. And they can earn certificates so they're qualified for . . . honestly I don't really know. Other teacher stuff. The reason I mention it is that this summer, Rebecca has an in-person class she needs to take for her continuing ed, but of course there's Logan to consider."

There was a sour taste in my stomach, like I'd swallowed expired milk. "Okay . . ."

"The class is four weeks long, starting June thirteenth. It's every afternoon from noon to five. I'm calling to find out if you're open to the idea of babysitting Logan for those four weeks."

I didn't know what to say. Babysitting wasn't my favorite—even before Finn Hastings threw up on me—but I actually kind of adored Logan. Getting some time with him and not having to put up with Rebecca sounded nice. But wouldn't Mom feel hurt if every day I left the house to go babysit for the woman Dad left her for? Left *us* for?

"It's fine if you want to think about it," Dad responded to my silence. "I know you're teaching swim lessons most mornings. I don't need an answer *right* now, though it'd be helpful to have one soon. We'd pay you fifteen hundred dollars for the month—"

"Fifteen hundred?" I couldn't help echoing. "Like, one thousand five hundred?"

Dad chuckled. "We're paying you fifteen an hour. Believe it or not, that's a bargain for us, considering daycare costs around here."

That hourly wage was more than what I made teaching swim lessons. Taking the job with Logan would mean that in four weeks I would be well on my way to paying for two roundtrip tickets to Iceland. Or a week of staying in a hotel or Airbnb. But . . . it would also mean having to interact with Rebecca *every* day . . .

The back door of Taqueria El Rancho opened and out came Alex in his bright red uniform shirt carrying a plastic bag full of to-go boxes. He squinted in the sunlight and grinned at me.

"I'd like to think about it," I said.

"Sure." Dad said. "Maybe you could have an answer by the time you come over tomorrow night?"

My grip on my phone tightened. "Okay. Alex is here. I got to go."

"Sounds good, sweetie. I love you."

I hung up as Alex popped open the passenger door and folded himself into my car. I had been taller than him until eighth grade, and his six-foot-one body still threw me off sometimes.

He leaned across the console for a hello kiss. "Were you waiting long?"

"No."

Alex cocked his head and studied me for a second. "Was it a bad phone call? You have that line between your eyes."

"It was my dad." I scrunched up my nose.

Alex made a crinkled nose face back at me that was really cute. "About this weekend?"

"No, actually, Rebecca has to take some kind of class this summer and they wanted to know if I'll watch Logan. Like a nanny, I guess."

Alex arranged the bag with our lunch at his feet. "That sounds awkward."

"Right?" I turned the ignition and the air conditioner kicked on, blasting my face with warm air. "But they also want to pay me fifteen hundred dollars for the four weeks."

Alex let out a low whistle. "I could deal with a lot of awkward for that amount of cash."

"Seriously." I pulled at my ponytail, tightening it. "What would I tell my mom, though?"

"Sounds like a conversation for after queso. We could eat at Founder's Park?"

"Sounds good." I put my car in reverse. "You want to see the house we're buying?"

Alex gave an exaggerated sigh. "Yeah, I suppose I'd better know where to find you."

Telling Alex that we were moving hadn't been as awful as I expected. Probably because I was bawling the whole time, and he didn't want to pile onto my misery. He also said he hadn't been too surprised by the news. "Your house is pretty big for two," he had said, same as basically everyone else.

I turned on Cherry Street to cut into the neighborhood. "We're on Walnut," I said. "It's this first street, the one that runs parallel to Main."

I turned and slowed my car to a crawl as we passed the new house, which sported a "Contract Pending" banner across the original real estate sign. That happened fast.

"It looks nice," Alex said after a moment. "Interesting. Small, but nice."

"Yeah. The Realtor said the previous owners bought it to rent out on Airbnb but they weren't making enough."

"So, the contract is pending, but you won't move until August?"

"That's what Mom said." I pressed the gas pedal now that we'd passed the house. *My* house. "We have to get our place ready to sell. Though, while I was with Kendra yesterday, this couple came and looked at it. Liz and John. I guess they're both doctors."

"Liz and John," Alex repeated with false disdain. "I hate them already."

I smiled and knew without looking that he was smiling too. "Mom met them and said they're nice. No kids, but they're about to adopt."

"So, no cute teenage daughter?"

I cut him a look.

"Just joking," Alex said. "Got to laugh so I don't cry."

Founder's Park was only a few streets over. When I was little, Founder's was shabby with old metal equipment and cracked swings, but sometime in the last few years it had been renovated. I parked under a tree in front of a playground shaped like a pirate ship that was loaded with kids of all ages. There were lots of moms pushing strollers along a paved trail that circled the playground and dog park. One woman had long, brown hair and aggressively pushed a sleek stroller. I studied her for a moment to be sure it wasn't Rebecca. Relief filled me as I determined it wasn't. Could I handle interacting with her five days a week for an entire month?

"How about over there?" Alex gestured with the bag to a shaded bench alongside the walking trail.

"Sure."

He took my hand as we walked over. It was the kind of summer day you dream about, with cotton ball clouds and a warm breeze that kept the humidity from feeling too oppressive. Even so, as I sat, I felt tired. Heavy.

Alex must've sensed this. He popped the plastic lid off a round Styrofoam container and offered it to me. "Queso fixes many things."

My mouth smiled, but I didn't mean it. "Being forced to move?"

"Well, no." Alex dug inside the to-go bag and produced a bag of tortilla chips. "Think smaller."

For a few minutes, we ate in silence and watched kids shriek and laugh and climb.

"Do you have OWC orientation tomorrow or Saturday?" I asked.

"Tomorrow." Alex grimaced. "And Monday morning I have to be there at seven."

"That's early for you."

"Tell me about it. And I found out that every Friday is 'bonfire Friday' so campers don't get picked up until nine."

I made a face. "And you probably can't be on your phone at all during the day, can you?"

"Nope. We check them in when we arrive, and we get them back when we leave."

"Like being in drama class," I said with a wry smile. "Well, guess I'll talk to you again in August when school starts."

He offered a sad smile and draped his arm around the back of the bench. "I suppose queso doesn't fix this either, does it?"

Something about him sounding as blue as I felt made my insides turn warm and fuzzy. We'd known each other long enough that when I wanted to, I could look at him and see the little boy he'd been when we met. The dusting of freckles over his nose that had faded by middle school, the soft jawline that was now defined. I rested against him.

"It won't be so bad." I kept my tone light, like maybe I could fake myself into feeling better. "Everything will wrap up by the end of July, and we'll still have a few weeks before I move."

"Right." Alex gave my shoulder a squeeze. "You're right."

My phone, which was in the side pocket of my leggings and wedged between Alex and me, vibrated.

"Someone wants you," Alex said, moving his leg away from mine so I could get my phone more easily.

"It's my mom."

When will you be home? Something's come up. We need to talk.

Alex read the message alongside me and made a noise in his throat. "*That* doesn't sound good."

"Nope." My thumb hovered above the keyboard as I considered how to respond. "It definitely doesn't."

When I got home several hours later, I found Mom in one of the guest bedrooms, where it looked like the closet had thrown up everywhere. The bed was covered in brightly colored dresses obscured by dry cleaner bags, hat boxes—had I ever seen my mom wear a hat?—and shoeboxes. Mom sat cross-legged in the middle of it all, a stack of binders on either side of her. One was flipped open on her lap.

"Hi, honey!" Mom chirped as I loitered in the doorway. Her eyes were wide and a bit frantic—Crazy Project Eyes, Dad used to call them.

"Hi."

She closed the binder, stacked it with a short pile of others, and grabbed another. "How's Alex? What'd you guys do?"

"Uh, he's fine. We ate food. Walked around downtown."

"Mmhmm." Mom flipped open the new binder. "Baseball cards," she murmured to herself as she closed it and set it in a different stack.

"Doing some late spring cleaning?" I asked. I stayed close to the door. The energy in the room was freaking me out.

"You know what sounds good? Chinese food. We haven't had Fortune Wok in a long time." Mom opened the next binder on the pile. "*More* baseball cards." She jerked her head to look up at me. "Does that sound good to you?"

"Baseball cards? Not exactly."

Mom shot me a look.

"Yeah, sure." I thought about a couple weeks ago, when I'd come home from school and found her worrying about money. "I'm happy to eat at home."

"I've been craving that crispy beef dish. With the snap peas? What do you want?"

I glanced around the chaotic room. A lot of this was my Nana's stuff that my mom had shoved in the closet after Nana died a few years ago saying she'd go through it "later." Why was today the time to do it? My chest suddenly felt like a block of ice.

"What's going on?" I asked.

Mom had been reaching for the next binder but paused. She folded her hands together and put them in her lap. I leaned against the wall, feeling too antsy to sit.

"So, I told you yesterday that there was a couple coming to look at the house? They're clients of Shelley's—"

"Yes, Liz and John. The nice doctors. I remember." My words all came out clipped. They were buying the house. Of course they were. It was an amazing house.

"Yes, that's them."

"They want to buy it."

Mom blinked at me a couple times. "They do."

Despair clenched my chest, like my heart was trapped in a block of ice. I took a deep breath. No need to be upset about this. Someone was going to buy it. It might as well be them. At least they didn't have a cute teenage daughter.

"Okay," I said slowly. "I guess it'll be good that we don't have to go through showing the house."

Mom stiffened. "There's a little more to it, Tessa."

And not a good thing, that much was clear from her tone. Maybe they *did* have a cute teenage daughter.

"They'd like to move in Friday the tenth."

I blinked rapidly as I processed this. "Friday the tenth," I echoed.

Mom nodded, tears welling up in her eyes. "*June* tenth. Like, two weeks from tomorrow."

"What?" The syllable came out fast and high. "That's impossible. Tell them no. No way."

"The thing is, Tessa, they're flying to China on Monday the thirteenth to adopt their baby—"

"That's not my problem." I had no idea my voice could get that shrieky. "Why should that be my problem? They should've planned better! Tell them no!"

"We can do that," Mom said quietly.

"And we will, right? You promised me one more summer. You *promised*."

"I did." Her voice had a strained quality of unshed tears. "But Tessa—"

"No. No 'but Tessa.' We are *not* moving on June tenth."

"If we do, they'll pay our moving costs. They'll hire movers who come pack everything up for us, load it up in the truck, drive it to our new house, and unpack it all. Do you know how expensive that is?"

"If we move in August, *I'll* pay for it," I said, pacing along the wall. "Dad and Rebecca want to pay me fifteen hundred dollars to babysit Logan. You can have all of it."

"Wait, what?"

"Dad called this afternoon. Rebecca has to take some kind of class for her work, and they want to hire me to watch Logan. I thought the money could help pay for Iceland, but it can go to this instead."

Mom's eyes looked extra wide thanks to the ring of smeared eye makeup around them. She took in a deep breath, opened her mouth, and then closed it. She shook her head and opened her mouth again. "We'll circle back to that, but even if you did babysit for them this summer, what Liz and John are offering us costs *thousands* of dollars. Not only that, but they're also nice people and they want to bring their baby home to their actual house—"

"And that's more important than keeping your promise to me?"

Mom tucked her hair behind her ears and said to her lap. "I understand you're upset, but it seems like the right thing to do."

"How come nobody ever feels like keeping a promise to me is the right thing to do?" I snapped.

Mom looked at me. "Tessa . . .," she began.

But she trailed off, and I didn't care to stick around. I marched down the hall and slammed my bedroom door behind me.

Chapter 7

GIRLS, I CAN'T BELIEVE THIS. We're moving June 10. JUNE 10. Even though my mom promised me we'd stay in our house this summer.

Izzy: 😣 😣 😣 😣 😣 😣 😣 😣 😣 😣

Shay: But that's only two weeks away.

Tessa: I KNOW IT'S ONLY TWO WEEKS AWAY. The buyers bribed her by paying all our moving expenses.

Amelia: Why? They want to move in quickly?

Amelia: BTW, the callback list will be emailed out on Saturday. I feel like I'm dying.

Tessa: They're adopting a baby so they want the weekend to get settled before they fly to China to get her.

Izzy: At least it's for a good reason. And you won't have to go through showing your house. Been there, done that. Do not recommend.

Amelia: I mean, I think I did pretty well. There were a

couple higher notes that I didn't hit during my song, but for Miss Hannigan that should be fine.

Shay: Tessa, I'm sorry. That has to feel disappointing. Amelia, I'm sure you did great.

Izzy: It'll be so fun to see you on stage! Tessa, want to come over? I'm hanging out with Bash.

Tessa: Thanks, but no. I'm leaving for Dad and Rebecca's now. First weekend over there. 😣

Amelia: I feel pretty good about my chances of getting Miss Hannigan. I bet at least one of the parents saw Peter Pan the night I filled in for Theresa. Don't you think?

Shay: Praying for you, Tessa!

Izzy: Yes, all the prayers! 🙏🙏

Amelia: Break a leg, Tessa!

Amelia: It's possible they'd cast me as Grace or maybe Molly.

Amelia: But probably not since I'm older. I'm perfect for Miss Hannigan.

———〰———

When I pulled alongside the curb at Dad and Rebecca's house, Amelia was still monologuing via text about how even if she didn't get a callback, it was probably because she so perfectly fit the role of Miss Hannigan. I knew she was feeling anxious about the audition and I understood . . . even still, I wanted to text back, "DID YOU EVEN READ MY TEXTS?" I didn't *really* care right now about who she thought the orphan parts might go to. I had enough problems of my own, thank you very much.

My stomach did an uncomfortable flip as I looked at Rebecca's small ranch house and imagined myself spending two nights trapped inside. I'd been doing mental gymnastics to make this weekend not feel like a big deal, telling myself things like "It's just

Friday night through Sunday dinner, which is a little longer than a swim meet. I can survive that."

But sitting there in the driveway, a duffel bag in the passenger seat, it felt harder to deny the weird weight the weekend carried. My first weekend living the divorce-kid life of shared custody. Of leaving my mom, who had a definite I'm-depressed-but-don't-want-you-to-feel-bad-especially-because-I-just-broke-a-promise-to-you vibe all afternoon. Driving to my dad's girl-friend's place.

Dad had been texting all through the day and his excitement was crystal clear:

We thought it would be easiest for you if we had some basics on hand. What kind of toothpaste do you like? Are there any other toiletries I can pick up for you? So excited to see you tonight!

If you have clothes that you'd like to leave here, feel free to do that.

Maybe tomorrow we could go pick out some things for your room here? Not sure what plans you have already. Think about it.

I've put a phone charger in your room so don't worry about bringing yours.

His enthusiasm along with my reluctance made my stress climb higher. Kendra and I had talked about this at length on Wednesday. I closed my eyes and repeated the words we'd worked on together. "It's okay to feel what I feel," I murmured in my increasingly stuffy car. "This is new, and it's normal for new things to be uncomfortable."

We'd also scheduled an appointment for me Monday morning. "Just in case," Kendra had said. "If you feel fine waiting till Wednesday, we'll cancel it."

If I hadn't been sweating from the heat, I would've been tempted to linger in my car longer. I popped open my door as

Dad came down the front walkway, a huge grin on his face that made my stomach curdle with guilt.

"Hi, honey! I'm so glad you're here."

I made myself smile but didn't make myself agree. "Thanks."

"Can I help with your bags?"

"I just have one in the passenger seat—"

"Great! I'll get that." Dad opened the door. "How's the car working out for you?"

"I like it a lot." I swallowed hard and tightened my ponytail. Why did *talking* to my dad have to feel so stressful?

"My first car was a Camry," Dad told me for at least the third time since he'd given it to me. "Bought it used and it got me all the way through college. Great car."

I pressed the remote lock once he'd closed the door, and then we looked at each other for a moment.

"I've made pancakes for dinner," Dad said, his smile never wavering. "I hope that's okay."

"I'm always up for pancakes."

"Just like me."

A year ago, being like him was a point of pride. Now . . . not so much.

"Let's head inside." Dad gestured to the door, like which direction I should go had been some great mystery to me. "Rebecca is bathing Logan. He's pretty cute in the bath, if you want to take a peek."

There was a strange tightness in my chest at hearing Dad's affection for Logan. *Lord, help me*, I prayed swiftly as I crossed the threshold into Rebecca's house.

The first time I visited was last October, before Logan, and the house looked as if the whole place had been staged for an Instagram shoot. And maybe it had. Every wall was painted a shade that Sherwin-Williams probably called something like "Neutral

Background." There had been a lot of decor proclaiming a love for fall or encouraging me to choose joy.

My second visit came right after Logan was born, and it looked more like they were hosting a baby shower—maybe because they were. There were lots of balloons and gift bags with an abundance of sky-blue tissue paper.

But this was different. Even from the entryway, I could tell a baby *lived* here now. An infant swing took up most of the floor space in the living room, and its bright greens and oranges did *not* match the decor. A variety of pacifiers littered the coffee table and another two were perched on the TV cabinet. And the white couch had an old bedsheet draped over it.

"Logan has reflux," Dad said.

I didn't know what that meant, but apparently you didn't want it on your couch.

"Your room is this way." Dad headed down the hallway to the first bedroom. It was an overly decorated room, mostly occupied by a queen-size bed covered in a white duvet and loaded with seven throw pillows (seven!) in various reds and blues. The artwork over the bed was a pallet painted like an American flag. A gallery wall was crowded with photographs of soldiers, presumably relatives, from the 1940s and maybe '70s, too, with a few shadow boxes of uniforms or medals that looked like a big deal.

"This has been the guest bedroom, and it's kind of a shrine to the Simmons family."

I couldn't imagine a room feeling *less* welcoming.

Maybe Dad could sense this. "But we can change things in here so that it's more your style."

"No." My voice was sharper than I intended. "This is fine. I'll hardly be here."

Dad set my duffel bag on the crowded bed. "I know, but we want you to feel at home when you're with us, so we're happy to change . . . this." He made a sweeping gesture with his hand. "Rebecca's family has a long-standing tradition of military service. This is her twin sister, Rachel. She served in the Air Force."

I glanced at the photo of a woman who looked strikingly similar to Rebecca. I should say *something*. "Mmm."

Down the hall, a door opened. "I think your sissy is here, Logan," Rebecca said in that high voice people tended to use with babies. "Should we go see if we can find her?" Several seconds later, Rebecca stepped into the doorway. "There she is! There's sissy."

As if we'd all been playing a game of peekaboo.

Most of the time when I saw Rebecca, it was the two-dimensional, glammed-up version on her Instagram account. Seeing the walking-and-talking variety of Rebecca was jarring. She had her long brown hair up in a messy bun and had obvious silver roots at her temples. She wore glasses and a T-shirt that read "Mama Bear" and was splattered with water.

My focus quickly shifted to Logan. He wore the blue-striped, zippered pajamas that Izzy helped me pick out when I went to visit him in the hospital. And he smelled divine. What about baby lotion made a baby smell *so* good?

I couldn't resist grinning at him.

"Hi, Logan."

His gray-blue eyes searched the room and landed on my face, melting me even further.

"Hi, sissy." Rebecca waved his hand for him. "I recognize my name now and like to look at people."

I groaned inwardly. Was the entire weekend going to be like this? Rebecca talking through Logan? If so, I was definitely *not* cancelling that Monday appointment with Kendra.

My phone buzzed and I peeked at it long enough to see that it was Amelia. It all depends on the interpretation of the director . . . I shoved my phone back in my pocket. That could absolutely wait.

"Dinner's ready," Dad said into the silence.

Rebecca looked up from Logan. "Did we have extra syrup?"

"No, I put it on the list. Which is getting long." Dad turned and started down the hall. "I'll stop after work on Monday."

"I might be able to go in the morning," Rebecca said, trailing after him.

"I don't want you having to go to the store on a Saturday."

I lingered in the Americana room with the photographs of Rebecca's ancestors for company. Their conversation chilled me. It was so *ordinary*, all this talk about extra syrup and who would do the grocery shopping. Like conversations I'd overheard my parents having for years . . . only now my dad was having them with someone else. I inhaled deeply—*it's okay to feel what I feel*—and exhaled. *This is new, and it's normal for new things to be uncomfortable.*

Beside the kitchen table, Rebecca settled Logan in some kind of reclining seat. There was an arch that went over it, and when she flipped a switch, lights turned on and music played. Logan's blue-gray eyes widened, and his arms and legs moved in an uncoordinated dance of excitement.

"Okay, Dad, we have ten minutes to shove down dinner," Rebecca joked as Dad carried a platter piled with pancakes in one hand and a plate of bacon in the other.

I lingered awkwardly between the living room and kitchen table as Dad set the food in the center of a round table set for three. I thought of Mom eating on the couch alone tonight. I waited to see which two seats Dad and Rebecca took before drawing closer.

Dad smiled warmly as I sat. "I'll pray. Heavenly Father, thank You for this weekend and that Tessa is able to be here with us. Thank You for the food You've blessed us with this evening. Help us to show Your love to those around us. In Jesus' name, amen."

"Amen," Rebecca echoed.

I'd grown up listening to my dad pray prayers like that before every meal, but never before had they grated on me like this one did. *Really?* I found myself thinking. *You're not going to listen to that, God, are You?*

It was one thing to sing on Sunday mornings that nothing could separate us from God's love, and another to be sitting at the table with my dad—alongside his live-in girlfriend and the child they'd created while he was still married to my mom—and hear him ask for help showing God's love to others. How about *not* cheating on my mom? How about *not* abandoning our family? That would've felt a lot more loving to me.

So, did I *really* believe that nothing could separate us from God's love?

"Guests first," Rebecca said brightly as she nudged the platter of pancakes my direction.

"Thank you," I murmured, not meeting her eye.

"When is your next swim meet, Tessa?" Dad asked as I selected several pancakes for myself.

"Two weeks from now in Fort Wayne." The timeline registered in my head. "I don't know if I'll compete or not since that's the same weekend Mom and I will be moving." And legally I was supposed to be *here* every other weekend, which would *also* be two weeks from now. "And it's also my weekend with you . . ."

Dad gave me a reassuring smile. "Don't worry, we'll figure that out. I can get you to your swim meet if you want to compete."

"I think Mom will need me." My last word trailed off. Talking about Mom felt weird with Rebecca sitting right there.

"She has the movers," Dad said dismissively, as if the physical act of moving had been my concern rather than the emotional. "That Saturday is the eleventh? Let me look at my calendar."

"You can't on the eleventh," Rebecca said. Her voice was calm enough, but there was an undercurrent of irritation. "We meet with Jillian that morning."

Dad didn't look at her but scrolled his calendar on his phone. "I need to be there for that?"

"I would like for you to be."

The Fort Wayne meet wasn't my favorite. The pool was small and always way too crowded—which meant the meet always ran long—and there were no good restaurants near the aquatic center. Skipping it wouldn't break my heart, especially because I absolutely wasn't going to abandon Mom the weekend we moved.

But it bugged me that Rebecca thought their meeting with Jillian—whoever she was—trumped Dad's parental obligations to me. Why should getting me to meets always fall on Mom's shoulders? Especially on a weekend that was "theirs"? That didn't seem fair.

"This meet is pretty important for qualifying for Hoosiers," I said oh-so-innocently as I sliced my pancake with a fork. I *had* missed Dad's pancakes. "I'd hate to miss it. Maybe you could drop me off."

Dad snorted. "I'm not driving three hours to Fort Wayne to 'drop you off.' Let me talk to your mom. We'll figure it out." He put his phone away. "What's Alex up to this summer?"

Conversation turned lighter for the next few minutes. Alex's responsibilities at OWC, how my school year wrapped up, what classes I'd enrolled in for junior year, and then Logan let out a shrill cry. It startled me, but Rebecca laughed.

"Now, come on, Logan. You're two minutes early." She used her foot to bounce his seat a couple times, and then shoved an enormous bite of bacon in her mouth before leaning to unbuckle him.

"I could hold him," I heard myself offer. "So you can finish eating."

Rebecca looked at me, and I realized it was the first time since my arrival that we'd looked each other in the eyes. I turned away.

"That'd be great, Tessa." Rebecca's voice was soft. "It's been months since I ate all my dinner without interruption."

I reached down to the bouncing seat, suddenly unsure about

how to lift Logan from it. He was over two months old; did I still need to support his head?

"Let me help," Rebecca said in the gentle voice that all elementary school teachers had. She lifted Logan from under the arms—apparently, no, I didn't need to support his head anymore—and offered him to me.

Her smile was so warm, it made me uncomfortable. "You won't break him. I promise. He likes being walked around, especially if you turn him out so he can see."

I stood with him, loving the cozy feel of his round, fuzzy head against my arm. As I walked the length of the kitchen, Logan stopped crying.

"We love our sissy, don't we?" Rebecca said. "You're so good with him, Tessa."

I didn't answer, but I liked the compliment more than I cared to admit.

———————

After Logan was in bed, it got real awkward real fast.

Dad and Rebecca sat next to each other on the couch, and I took an armchair, feeling like a chaperone on a date. I scrolled Instagram on my phone, hyperaware of the silence in the room and that my dad's hand was casually resting on Rebecca's leg.

"Do you have any plans tomorrow?" Dad asked. "You don't have to hang around here on the weekends you're with us, you know. I mean, you should always feel welcome. We want you here. But I don't want you to feel like you can't make plans with friends either."

I had made zero plans. Why hadn't I made plans?

"Yeah. Um, I'm getting together with my friend, Izzy, tomorrow afternoon."

"That's great," Dad said. "Have I met Izzy before?"

"Maybe. Izzy Valadez? Her family goes to Faith Community."

"Hmm. Doesn't sound familiar."

"You can have friends over here, too," Rebecca said, looking up from her phone. "We want you to feel at home here."

She bit her lip and looked back to her screen. This was new for Rebecca, too, it occurred to me. She'd never had a teenager quasi-living in her house before.

"Thank you," I said slowly. "That's kind of you."

Dad beamed at me, and I looked away.

"Tessa, did you get a chance to look at your calendar and make a decision about nannying?" Dad asked.

"Oh. Yeah, I would like to do that."

I glanced up and found them both smiling at me, which some-how made the whole situation feel even more like a betrayal of my mom. She'd brought it up with me today after we talked through what all needed to happen in the next two weeks to prepare the house for moving. I could tell Mom didn't like the idea of me watching Logan every day, and she hoped I would turn down the job, but also that she wouldn't come right out and *ask* me to say no. Especially since she was already asking me to move in two weeks when she'd promised me one more summer at home.

"That's great," Dad said with an enthusiastic nod. "Really great. Thank you, Tessa."

"Yes, thank you," Rebecca echoed. "Logan will love having you here every day."

I ducked my head so neither of them would see me smiling.

"If there are any days you aren't available, let me know," Dad said. "Grandma would probably fill in."

"Okay."

Seeing my grandma post pictures on Facebook of her and Logan had been kind of weird. Especially because sometimes people who weren't in the know left comments like "Did David and Carrie finally have another baby?" Awkward.

"There is something else we'd like you to put on your calendar."

Dad sat forward and clasped his hands together, sending a spark of panic through me. That was Dad's Important Conversation pose, whether he knew it or not. Were they moving? Were they pregnant again? Was that even possible?

My throat felt dry as I said, "Okay."

"Friday, July fifteenth, Rebecca and I are having a small wedding. It won't be anything big or fancy, but we'd like for you to be there."

Considering I was sitting in the house they lived in together and their baby was asleep down the hall, why did this announcement make my heart clench in my chest?

"Well, it'll be a *little* fancy," Rebecca said with a nervous laugh.

I needed to say *something*. But not "congratulations." Not "I'm happy for you." Not "that's great."

Swallowing felt hard. "Okay."

They both blinked at me. Rebecca bit her lip and looked back at her phone.

Dad cleared his throat. "I'd like it if you'd be the one who stood up with me, but of course I understand if you don't want to."

"What do you mean by 'stand up with you'?"

"Like, be my best man. Only, you know. You're my daughter." His smile hung brief and weak before disappearing. "You don't have to. Just think about it."

Um, no. I was *not* doing that. Shouldn't the best man be someone who supported the marriage?

"We're kind of going out of order." Rebecca's laugh was stiff and nervous. "Getting married *after* having a baby and all, but that's how it worked out . . ."

"Yeah," I said to my hands, silently adding, *sorry my mom and I got in the way of you getting married before your "miracle baby" came along.* My heart felt like it was pounding in my ears.

"You don't need to answer now," Dad repeated. "The wedding isn't until July fifteenth, so about two months away."

"Seven weeks from today," Rebecca corrected.

"Right. And I looked at the calendar to make sure it doesn't conflict with Hoosiers, assuming you qualify, and it doesn't."

"Okay," I said, still to my hands. Hoosiers was a state-wide meet for competitive swim, and I normally cared a lot about it this time of year, but right now I didn't *at all.*

Dad and Rebecca were getting married. *Married.* The divorce had been final for two weeks, and they were already getting married. Which I knew didn't change anything about the situation, but I still felt betrayed.

I took a shuddering breath. The only thing that would make this worse was crying in front of them and being comforted. "I think I'll go to my room now," I said in a small voice.

"Sure, honey." If Dad was trying to hide his disappointment in my reaction, he wasn't doing a good job. "Whatever you want."

I couldn't help huffing a disbelieving laugh as I stood. "Yeah, whatever *I* want," I said under my breath as I left the room.

Because absolutely nothing about any of this was what *I* wanted.

Chapter

8

MOVING WAS AN ENORMOUS PROJECT, even if someone was packing for you and moving your stuff.

As the calendar flipped to June, Mom and I were like the embodiment of one of those graphs you see in math class, where, as one quantity increases, the other decreases. Mom appeared to be energized by the move. Her delight with cleaning out closets, sorting, and selling unwanted items on Facebook Marketplace grew each day. She got up early to tackle her to-do list, worked a full day teaching art lessons, and then worked late into the night.

I, on the other hand, felt increasingly depleted as the days ticked by. After a morning of swim practice and teaching swim lessons, I would walk home at lunchtime and find a list of things Mom wanted me to tackle that afternoon. Every day, I felt more like taking a nap. Today was no exception. I grabbed string cheese and an apple from the kitchen and then read my list as I climbed the stairs to my room.

There was apparently a pile of Dad's old stuff that Mom wanted me to drive to his place. There was another pile of items that she needed pictures of to sell on Marketplace. There were boxes of things to be driven to Salvation Army. And there were other items on the list that my eyes skimmed over before I shoved it in my hoodie pocket.

All of it could wait until I'd eaten, showered, and maybe napped.

I flopped onto my bed and hoped my hair was dry enough that it wouldn't soak into my pillow and leave it smelling like chlorine for weeks. I looked up at the familiar ceiling, covered in glow-in-the-dark stars that I'd arranged in constellations when I was twelve. I should probably take those down. I couldn't imagine the movers climbing around on a step stool and scraping plastic stars from the ceiling.

When my phone buzzed on my chest, startling me, I realized I had dozed off.

The notification was a Marco Polo from Amelia. The angle was weird because she'd balanced the phone in the cupholder of her car. Her eyes were red and puffy.

"Girls, I can't even." Amelia's voice was a mix of anger and sorrow. Her eyes were on the road, and her eye makeup was everywhere except where it was supposed to be. "Mrs. Taylor asked me to be the stage manager for *Annie*. Stage manager! Can you believe that?" Amelia's lip crumpled and she appeared to be fighting hard to not cry. "I knew I messed up on a couple things in my audition, but I thought I did a good job, and yet again Amelia Bryan is asked to be off-stage. Oh, and understudy, which is basically a slap in the face. The show runs for two weekends. The main characters will have to be barfing their brains out to miss the show. Ugh, I missed my turn."

Amelia gave the steering wheel a harsh turn that made me flinch even from the safety of my bedroom.

"Well, Theresa did get sick before *Peter Pan* and I got to be on stage, so it's not like it never happens. But I don't want to be hoping and praying my cast members get sick so I can have my shot. And there's no way I'm going to convince my parents that theater is a viable career option if I'm never getting cast for anything, even at this level!"

Amelia's message went on for a solid ten minutes. So long that I eventually propped my phone up on my bookshelf and started prying stars off the ceiling. It broke my heart to hear her so upset, and there was only so much I could say or do to comfort her. Amelia was a talented actress, and I felt like once she figured out how to audition better, she'd start getting bigger roles.

Right as Amelia's message wrapped up, my phone buzzed with a new notification. I thought it would probably be Izzy responding to Amelia—Izzy was often the first to respond—but instead it was Alex. That was weird. This was week one of camp, and I knew he checked his phone in with his supervisor when he arrived and didn't get it back until the campers were picked up at seven.

Can't get together tonight. So sorry. Will call and explain more after camp.

Ugh.

I tapped a long row of crying emojis which was marked as "Delivered" but wasn't seen, even when I checked back thirty minutes later. Not really a big surprise. It had probably taken significant maneuvering on Alex's part to get *that* text sent to me.

I sighed, tucked away my disappointment, and recorded what I hoped was an encouraging response for Amelia. It felt hard, not because I didn't believe in her, but because I was feeling so drained myself. I ended the message, looked at the list from Mom, and laid back down instead.

—∿—

I stood at the Fortune Wok counter, waiting for our order. Only one table had people sitting there, which wasn't too surprising considering it was eight o'clock. I'd learned in the last few days that "moving time" was different than normal time. Eight o'clock was a totally normal dinner time—maybe even a little earlier than we'd been eating—when you were in a season of sorting out and relocating your entire life.

My phone vibrated as a waiter brought out a brown paper bag with "Carrie" written in black Sharpie on the side. I took the bag, thanked the waiter, and answered Alex's call as I pushed open the door, which jangled lightly. The evening air hung thick and heavy.

I pressed the phone against my ear. "Hey."

"Tessa, I'm so sorry about tonight." Alex's voice had that slight echoing sound that it got when he used his earbuds for phone calls. Clark was once rear-ended by a driver who was texting and the whole Hastings family took phone use in the car very seriously.

"It's okay. What happened?"

Alex huffed a frustrated exhale. "My mom got movie tickets for the five of us. When I told her I had plans with you, she said that was fine, but then started bawling about how long it's been since the five of us did something fun together, and how soon we won't be able to do that because Clark will be leaving."

Poor Mrs. Hastings. "She's struggling with him graduating."

"She is," Alex said on a sigh. "I don't know how much longer I can be patient."

"Well, I was looking forward to hanging out tonight, but I have plenty to do."

"Yeah?"

"Yeah. There are piles everywhere in our house. Mom keeps leaving me these lists of things she wants me to do, and then looks at me like I'm the most disappointing human ever for not completing them. Meanwhile, she's like a moving machine. It's like a superpower I didn't know existed. She forgets to eat, she's so into it. I'm walking to my car from Fortune Wok because she's currently sorting our kitchen."

"Fortune Wok sounds amazing right now. I'm already sick of campfire hot dogs and I have six weeks to go."

"You're welcome to come over." I dangled the take-out bag as if he could see me. "I ordered chicken in orange sauce."

Alex whimpered. "Now you're being mean. I'm pulling into the theater parking lot. Mom picked one halfway between OWC and Riverbend so that I could make it to the eight fifteen showing on time."

"Very thoughtful," I said as I nestled the take-out bag onto my passenger seat.

"Oh, yeah," Alex said sarcastically. "She's always thoughtful about forced family fun time. If you think you'll be awake, I might call again on my way home from the movie?"

"Yeah, sure. I'll turn my phone off if I go to bed."

We exchanged goodbyes, and I set my phone in my cupholder before push-starting my ignition. The streetlamps flickered on as I backed out onto Main Street. I'd driven this street countless times, coming to Shay's or Grounds and Rounds or Taqueria, but there was a different feel in the air tonight.

On impulse, I cut down Cherry to drive by the house that would be my new home in about a week. There were a few people out walking their dogs or shooting hoops in their driveways, but otherwise the neighborhood was quiet. I paused in front of the dark house. In a couple days, the windows of that house would glow at night. It would be full of our belongings, and of Mom's hopes for a brighter future.

But for now, we were still living in the uncomfortable in-between. Like we had one foot out the door of our old life but couldn't yet fully step into our new one. The murky middle, Kendra had called it, and that's how I felt inside. Murky.

My stomach growled. Murky *and* hungry, apparently.

My phone buzzed with a text from Mom. **Where are you?**

Coming home, I typed, and then punched the gas.

Coming home . . . while I still could.

A week and a half later found me alone in the new house for the first time, and it felt every bit as weird as I would've expected.

Mom was with Dad and Shelley, signing documents of some sort, so it was just me in a sea of neatly labeled and stacked boxes. No one had remembered to sign me up for the swim meet—including me—nor had anybody mentioned that it was my weekend with Dad. I'd decided not to ask about that. Instead, I wandered through the downstairs, trailing my hand along whatever I could touch. The back of the couch, the textured wall, the unfamiliar size and shape of the antique door handles. "It's okay to feel what I feel," I whispered into the emptiness of the house. "This is something new, and it's normal for new things to feel uncomfortable."

My breathing had become shallow. I closed my eyes and inhaled deeply through my nose. The house smelled like cardboard. I repeated the words from Kendra a few more times, and then mounted the narrow, creaky stairs to the bedroom I'd chosen. The walls were a warm, sunshine yellow that I already knew would clash horribly with my gray and aqua bedding. The ceiling had some funky angles to it, which my mom declared "charming" and there was a bookcase built in around the one small window. The view was nothing exciting, just the side of the neighbor's house.

The movers had set up my bed frame and even put my mattress on it. I needed to sit down. After two weeks of spending my time at swim practice, teaching swim lessons, and moving all my worldly possessions, my whole body ached in new ways. And on Monday, I would add "nannying" to that list.

Mom and I hadn't talked much about me watching Logan for the next four weeks. She'd confessed a few days before as we drove to Salvation Army that it was weird for her to think about me spending that much time with Logan. "I can't promise that I won't sometimes turn into an angry-Hulk mom, but I understand why you want to do it."

"I don't know that I *want* to do it," I had replied. "But I think it's worth it for the money."

I absolutely did not tell her that I was looking forward to the one-on-one time with Logan. Time when I could play with him without the watchful eyes of Dad and Rebecca on me. And without Rebecca doing that weird thing where she talked for Logan.

I'd opted to not mention the impending wedding. That could wait. As could unpacking my room. I stared up at the popcorn ceiling—why had that ever been a thing?—and wondered if my stars would even stick to a surface like that.

When the doorbell rang, it took me a few minutes to register what the sound was. It sounded more like a church bell chiming than a doorbell.

"What now?" I muttered as I dragged myself off my bed.

When I opened the door, Izzy stood on the other side, holding up a round plate of chocolate cupcakes with peanut butter icing. "Surprise!"

My mouth flopped open like I was a cartoon character. "You are my favorite person in the whole world right now."

Izzy shrugged away my theatrics. "Cupcakes have that effect on people. I thought you might need some cheering up today."

"Do I ever. Come on in. My mom is—" But my sentence died on my tongue as my eye caught on something at the brick house across the street. Or rather, some*one*.

A boy stepped out of his front door, holding a leash with a small black dog at the end. With his thick black hair and dusky skin, he was easy for me to recognize, even before he started across his lawn with that confident gait I would know anywhere.

"Abraham!" I called out.

He startled and searched for who had called out to him. I waved my hand and skirted around Izzy to head down my front steps.

"Tessa?" he said with a laugh. "*You're* the new family?"

"Yep."

Abraham's dog strained at the end of his or her leash, whimpering in a way that sounded like excitement.

"This is my friend, Izzy." I gestured as she walked down the grass with me. "Izzy, this is Abraham. He swims on Blazers with me."

Izzy waved. "Yeah, I recognize you."

"Yeah, I recognize you, too," Abraham said.

Izzy's whole body went rigid, and her carefree smile slipped away.

Abraham must've noticed because he added. "From T's Instagram. You're the cupcake girl."

"Oh." Izzy laughed self-consciously and held out the plate to him. "Guilty. Want one?"

"Thanks," Abraham said as he selected one from the edge. Abraham flashed her a grin that had broken half the hearts on our swim team and then flicked his focus back to me. "My mom was telling me that she'd met the woman who'd be living here and that she had a daughter my age. I had no idea you were moving."

I shrugged. "It happened fast."

"Guess you won't be walking to swim team anymore, huh? We could carpool."

"That'd be great."

Abraham grinned. "Cool. I better walk Maxine before she overheats. I'll see you around the hood."

"Guess so."

Abraham held up his cupcake. "Thanks for this," he said, and then took a huge bite.

"Sure," Izzy said. "Enjoy."

Abraham and Maxine walked away, and I turned to Izzy. "That was weird."

"Mmhmm." Izzy had an expression on her face that I couldn't quite read.

"What?"

"I don't think Alex is going to love that *he* is your neighbor." Izzy pointedly looked at Abraham's retreating figure. "That boy is clearly into you."

I rolled my eyes. "Abraham is into all girls. I don't take it personally."

She made a grunting noise that sounded like a growl. "I'm just saying, you might not want to carpool with him *every* morning. He could get the wrong idea."

"I can handle myself, Izzy." I couldn't keep the irritation out of my voice. I barely managed to resist saying, *I'm not you.*

I swallowed hard, as if to bury the almost-spoken words. Last winter, Izzy had her first boyfriend, and it went about as bad as a relationship could go. She ended up with fake nude pictures of herself—along with other girls from school—on Snapchat and then in a Dropbox account that the male population of Northside were paying to access. The whole situation was completely disgusting, and it still sometimes shocked me that sweet Izzy—who still named her stuffed animals and was currently wearing leggings with smiley faces printed on them—had gotten wrapped up in such a scandal.

"I know you can," Izzy said, blissfully unaware of how close I'd come to insulting her. "But staying out of temptation isn't the worst idea."

"Abraham isn't a temptation to me," I said. "Yes, he's cute. But he also flirts with everything female."

"Typical," Izzy muttered.

"Besides, I have zero interest."

"Does he know that?" Izzy picked up one of her own cupcakes and took a bite. "Because he didn't look like he knew that. He looked like Christmas had come early."

"He knows. And he's met Alex." I picked up a cupcake as well. "It won't be a problem."

"Oh-kay," Izzy said, dragging out the word in a way that made it clear she only kind of believed me.

I rolled my eyes. "Want to come in?"

"Absolutely." Izzy grinned at the house. "Stars, I think this is the cutest place I've ever seen. It's like something from a fairy tale."

Those words again. "Life sure doesn't *feel* like a fairy tale right now."

Izzy gave me a sympathetic look as she passed through the open door. "I'm pretty sure that's why God created cupcakes."

I laughed. "Or rather, why He gave me a friend who loves to make cupcakes."

Izzy's laugh filled the house, and as I closed the door, I realized having her there made the whole place feel a little warmer. A little safer. A little more like home.

Chapter
9

"This is where we keep the extra wipes." Rebecca opened the cabinet of the changing table. "And extra diapers. Currently he's wearing size one, but here's a package of size two in case you're changing him and it seems like he needs to go a size up."

Rebecca had asked me to come early so that she could help me get settled. That had seemed ridiculous when she first texted it, but now I wasn't sure we'd have enough time to get through what had turned into the most tedious bedroom tour ever.

Fifteen hundred dollars, I repeated to myself as Rebecca detailed the post-diaper cream options. *Fifteen hundred dollars.*

"You probably won't need to give him a bath, but let me show you how, just in case. Sometimes after his naps, he has blow-out diapers."

Blow-out diapers? I didn't know what that meant, and I didn't want to find out.

I trailed behind Rebecca to the hall bathroom I used when I

stayed here. This was the first time I'd been alone with Rebecca. Or alone-ish. She was holding Logan as he slept. Instagram Rebecca had a cheerful, confident vibe. Real Rebecca was also cheerful, but in a jittery kind of way. At least so far. Maybe the jitteriness was because of me. What had she thought about asking me to take care of Logan these next four weeks? Had that been her idea or Dad's? Did he have to talk her into it?

I hadn't been paying attention to Rebecca's instructions about how to give Logan a bath. Whoops.

". . . scream for a little bit, but that's okay," Rebecca said with a shrug.

"Okay," I said in the silence, hoping that was an appropriate response.

Rebecca pulled out all the washcloth and towel options, showed me which lotion to use, again reviewed the diaper cream options, and pointed out the five backup outfits she'd lined up on top of the dresser. Five. Next, she showed me how to properly heat the bags of breast milk that were stored in the refrigerator. I tried to not make a face—I knew it was immature to freak out about breast milk—but the sight of the bags stacked in the fridge grossed me out.

Fifteen hundred dollars, Tessa. What's a little breast milk when it's buying you a trip to Iceland?

"Oh, Logan loves walks! If he gets grumpy, the best way to calm him down is to take him outside." Rebecca strode through the kitchen into the front room and rested her hand on a black stroller frame parked near the door. "So, the infant seat snaps in here, and you push these red levers to lock it in. Down here, by the wheels, you push these red levers to lock the stroller. That's super important. And always, always, always buckle him. It can be easy to forget at this age, since he lays down in the stroller, and he isn't moving around, but it's still quite important."

I resisted rolling my eyes. She thought I needed reminders about basic safety like "buckle up"? But all I said was a pleasant, "Okay."

"Hmm, what else?" Rebecca's Apple watch began beeping at her, and she gave it a startled look. "Already? I haven't even shown you how to do tummy time. Or take his temperature. Or get him to take medicine if he has a fever."

"I'll be fine," I said. "If he starts running a fever, I'll call you or Dad."

"Don't call David. I mean, your dad. He has a big presentation this afternoon. If you need something, text me and I'll try to step out of my class."

Something about having Rebecca counsel me about how to interact with my dad made me feel cold inside. I reached for Logan. "We'll be fine." I wanted my voice to sound soothing, but it came out stiffer than I intended. "Promise."

Rebecca passed Logan to me, who didn't even open his eyes with the transfer. "Goodbye, love," she cooed to him. She kissed his cheek.

When Rebecca looked at me, her smile wavered. "I've never left him with anyone before. Other than David, of course."

"I'm his big sister. I'll take good care of him."

"Yes," she said in the tight voice of someone trying not to cry. "Okay. Thank you, Tessa. Try to keep him on the schedule that I posted on the fridge. I'll be home by five thirty."

She kissed Logan one more time, grabbed her bag—one I recognized from promotions on her Instagram—and walked out the garage door with one more wave.

In my arms, Logan stirred but didn't wake.

I carried him over to the window to watch Rebecca's tiny Volkswagen back out of the driveway. "Bye, Mommy," I said for Logan.

Then I realized I'd spoken for him in the exact same way

Rebecca did that drove me crazy. "I won't do that again," I promised my sleeping brother.

I sat on the sheet-covered couch and watched Logan sleep. I didn't have much experience with babies, but he really was the cutest one I'd ever seen, with his fuzzy blond head and his eyelashes fanned over his round, pink cheeks. I took a picture and sent it to Izzy.

"I'm glad you're here," I whispered to him, and then instantly felt a pang of guilt. How could I both adore Logan and hate what my dad did to my mom, considering Logan was the embodiment of his affair?

"But that wasn't your choice, was it?" I ran my finger over his plump, slack cheek. His skin felt like a flower petal. "You didn't pick your parents any more than I picked mine."

Still. I thought of my mom several blocks over, unpacking in our new house, scrambling to get ready for art camps while Rebecca had seemingly gotten everything she wanted. "Too blessed to be stressed!" she'd told Shay's aunt.

How was that fair?

My thoughts were such a tangle, that I felt relieved when Logan woke up crying.

—◊◊◊—

When I pulled in the driveway of the new house a little after 5:30, it was all I could do to muster the energy to turn off my ignition and trudge into the house. My arms and lower back ached in weird ways I'd never experienced, and my ears were still ringing from the sounds of Logan crying. I smelled like spit-up and sweat.

Apparently, mornings were Logan's happy time, but afternoons and early evenings he tended to be "fussy," as Rebecca put it. Also, I'd learned that "reflux" meant Logan spit up All. The. Time. And a blow-out diaper was when poop leaked out the sides and up the back of his outfit in some weird, seemingly gravity-defying phenomenon. I'd been too nervous to give him a real bath, but we'd gone through three of the five outfits Rebecca had laid out, and in the future, I'd bring a change of clothes for myself, too.

Mom was frying bacon and it was maybe the best thing I'd ever smelled in my life. When I dragged myself into the kitchen, she grinned at me over the frying pan. "Hey, you! Abraham's mom, Prisha, has a greenhouse and she already has tomatoes. She brought us some. Isn't that amazing? I love that you already have a friend in the neighborhood. That's so wonderful." Her gaze flicked over me. "Rough first day?"

"I'm not sure I've ever been so tired. Or smelled so bad."

Mom's smile turned empathetic. "Want to shower before dinner? Bacon should be ready in ten or so minutes but take as long as you want."

My stomach grumbled, reminding me that the last thing I'd eaten was a granola bar I snarfed on the drive between teaching swim lessons and watching Logan. I'd assumed that I would be able to eat while he was eating. I hadn't realized that I would be holding him constantly. I'd tried putting him in that bouncy chair thing Dad and Rebecca had used during dinner that one time, but Logan had made his dislike for that idea known immediately.

"Yes. I'll be right back down."

I trudged up the stairs. Instead of showering, I opted to run a bubble bath. I soaked mindlessly in the lavender-scented water for ten minutes before drying off, throwing on pajamas and padding back downstairs barefoot.

Mom had our small, round table set for two and was smearing mayonnaise on toasted bread as I entered. She smiled at me. "Better?"

"I at least smell better."

I hadn't known what kind of mood to expect from Mom when I got home from spending the afternoon with Logan. Would she be grouchy? Pouty? Nosy? But she seemed normal. Not just normal, but maybe even more cheerful than I'd seen her in a while.

Despite hosting two sessions of art camp today, she spent dinner talking about all the things she'd gotten done around the house. She'd put fresh shelf liner in the kitchen cabinets, visited with Prisha, and used a drill to hang curtains in the living room. Using the drill appeared to be a particular source of joy for her.

Mom seemed happier than she had in a long time. Freer. She was still her, but it was like before she'd been a pastel version of Carrie and now was colored with bold, vibrant colors.

"I'm glad you had such a great day," I said as she paused to take a bite of her BLT. I was nearly done with mine since I hadn't been talking.

Mom hastily chewed and swallowed. "I can't explain it, Tessa. I thought I'd be sad today with you over at your dad's, but I feel so happy here in this house. Like it's home in a way that our house no longer could be. For me, anyway." Mom smiled softly at me. "I know you said yes to moving because of me. I know it's not what you wanted. But I'm so happy here, and I love that I get to share that with you, even if it's only for a couple years."

Thinking of our old house made my throat feel thick. It was hard to imagine *this* house ever feeling like it was really my home.

I swallowed hard. "I'm happy you're happy."

Chapter
10

"The time with Logan is amazing," I said to the back of Izzy's head as she considered a variety of sprinkles options on the store shelves in front of her. "Well, mostly. Monday was pretty rough, but the rest of the week was great. It's everything besides Logan that makes the job awful."

Izzy and I were on our way to Taqueria to meet Shay and Amelia for lunch, but Izzy had wanted to stop at Paprika's first. She'd claimed she was going to "pop in" for red sprinkles, but I wasn't at all surprised that we were still there five minutes later as she gazed at a display of Fourth of July decorations.

"What do you mean by 'everything besides Logan'?" Izzy asked as she considered a jar of red, white, and blue stars. "These are cute."

"I mean the constant interactions with Rebecca. The regular texting. All the reminders about how to do things right. 'Don't fasten the diapers too tight.' 'Always buckle him into the stroller.'

'Be sure to keep him on schedule.' Like I don't know those things anyway. I'm relieved they had already planned to go out of town to visit Rebecca's dad or I'd have to stay with them this weekend. Did I tell you that she *hugged* me yesterday? It was so weird."

"You're not a hugger."

"I'm not *not* a hugger. I'm fine hugging people I like."

"I bet she didn't mean anything by it," Izzy said. "Sometimes I hug people without thinking. It's a reaction. I hugged Deputy Packard once."

He was our SRO at Northside. "Izzy," I said with a groaning laugh.

"I know, I couldn't believe I did that! He clearly felt weird about it. Oh, look at *these*." She bent to look at sugared American flags, her wild hair falling forward.

My phone buzzed with a text from Amelia to our group thread. Where are you two? Shay is starving.

"Izzy, we got to go," I said as I typed back, Order queso. Dragging Iz out of Paprika's now.

Izzy sighed. "I love this store. Maybe I should get a job here."

"You don't have a car, and it's too far from your house to walk."

She sighed again but headed toward the checkout counter. "I could ride my bike. But I'd probably spend my whole paycheck here. I need to work someplace where I wouldn't be tempted to buy anything. Like Jiffy Lube."

But knowing Izzy, she would probably get super into car maintenance and feel like she needed all the right kinds of oil and filters. Izzy could be a bit squirrel-brained and had a hard time focusing, but she also had a genuine interest and enthusiasm for a wide variety of things. I loved that about her.

"Hi, neighbor," Cody said as Izzy dumped three jars of sprinkles on the counter.

Cody Nichols was in our grade, and I'd hung out with him quite a bit in middle school. Once we got to high school, our core group—me, Mackenzie, Alex, Cody, Michael, and April—drifted apart for a whole host of reasons. But he and Alex were still good friends, and I'd always liked him.

Cody held up his bare wrist, miming checking the time. "You've only been here for ten minutes, Izzy. You're already done?"

She laughed and shrugged. "I blame Tessa."

Cody grinned at me. He had a squeaky clean, Captain America kind of charm to him. "You're bad for business." Before I could respond, he quickly turned back to Izzy. "What are you baking this time?"

"These are for my parents' big Fourth of July party. I found this recipe for strawberry cupcakes with cream cheese frosting. I was going to do red and blue sprinkles, but I like these stars better."

"Party, huh? Am I invited?" Cody asked as he tapped on the screen of the payment system.

"Oh, you wouldn't want to come," Izzy laughed. "It's a bunch of my family from out of town, and they're crazy."

"I don't know, crazy sounds pretty fun. Ten fifty-two is your total."

As Izzy tapped her debit card, I glanced at Cody. He was blushing. Did Cody have a crush on Izzy?

"Izzy's cupcakes are the best," I said. "Iz, you should take one to him on the Fourth."

Izzy looked up at me, her eyes wide. "Cody's had them before."

"They *are* the best," Cody said. "I wouldn't say no to one."

"Uh, okay." Izzy fidgeted with the tassel on her wallet. "But is Paprika's even open on the Fourth?"

Cody's smile hung crooked, and he was looking everywhere but at Izzy. He *definitely* had a crush on her. "No, but I'll be at home."

"Oh." Now Izzy looked flustered. "Well, okay. I'll bring you one then."

"See you then." Cody glanced at me. "Bye, Tessa."

We waved bye and headed into the sweaty outdoor air. I looked at Izzy, expecting to find a huge grin on her face after such a successful interaction with Cody, who she'd once described as "hunkadorbs." But instead, her jaw was clenched.

"Is something wrong?"

Izzy cut me a sharp look. "You made that really awkward."

"What? I didn't mean to make it awkward. But Cody was clearly flirting—"

"No, he wasn't," Izzy snapped. "He was being polite."

I swallowed hard. Had Izzy ever talked to me like that before? "Um, sorry, but I disagree. He really wanted you to invite him to the Fourth of July party—"

"We're not all looking for boyfriends, Tessa." Izzy picked up her pace on the sidewalk, causing her dark brown waves to bounce even more wildly.

I rushed to keep up with her. "I'm sorry, I thought you liked him—"

"I don't. We're just friends, okay?"

"Okay. Sorry," I apologized yet again.

Our two-minute-long walk to Taqueria was filled with stony silence. I relived the conversation at Paprika's, trying to pinpoint how I'd erred so grievously. But no matter how I looked at it, it seemed like Izzy was overreacting.

Taqueria El Rancho was crowded and noisy, the Saturday lunch hour in full swing. I didn't see Alex anywhere, but Amelia waved her arms with gusto and was easy to spot even before she called out in her big theater voice, "Izzy! Tessa!" I tried to not be embarrassed by how many people turned and looked.

I slid into the booth beside Shay, who had the bowl of queso and chips drawn so close to her they may as well have been in her lap. I laughed. "So. It really *was* Shay who was hungry. I figured it was you, Amelia."

Amelia barked a laugh and cut her gaze away. "Why, because I'm fat? No, Shay was the hungry one today."

My face burned as if she'd smacked me. "No, that's not at all what I meant." My tone pitched weirdly high. "I thought you were doing that thing where you said the other person is impatient or hungry or whatever, but it's actually you who is? Not *you* like you Amelia, but *you* in the general sense of the word. *That's* what I meant, not that you're . . ." I couldn't even bring myself to say the word *fat*.

Amelia looked at the menu in front of her and asked, "How was Paprika's?"

I shrunk back into the booth and felt both Izzy and Shay's gazes on me. While, yes, I was aware that Amelia was bigger, her size wasn't something I gave much thought to anymore. It was part of who she was, same as I didn't spend time dwelling on Shay being quiet or Izzy being Mexican American. I hated that I'd hurt Amelia. But I also hated that she'd assumed the worst about what I'd said.

I focused on the menu but wasn't really looking at it. Within the span of five minutes, I'd unintentionally offended two of my best friends.

Shay nudged the queso bowl my way and offered a sympathetic smile. I tried to smile back. With how the afternoon was going, I probably shouldn't even look at her.

Fresh bowls of queso and chips glided onto the table, and I looked up to find Alex standing there in his bright red Taqueria polo. He smiled at me, and even though it was the other-people-are-watching variety, being smiled at still felt nice.

"Hey there." He winked. "You look like this girl I used to know."

I couldn't think of anything clever to say so I just smiled back. Between his work schedules and Mrs. Hastings's Forced Family Fun, I hadn't seen him since the morning the movers arrived to pack up my life.

"We still on for tonight?" I asked.

He flinched. "Yes, absolutely. But with a slight schedule adjustment."

Anger sparked in my chest. "Ugh. Your mom?"

"Only kind of." Alex glanced at Izzy. "You want something to drink, Iz?"

Logically, I understood Mrs. Hastings was going through a hard season, but my life wasn't exactly a cakewalk right now. How come her inability to deal with her grief meant I never saw my boyfriend? I was so sick of how everybody else's choices—Dad's affair, Mom's desire to move, Mrs. Hastings's obsession with family time—negatively impacted me. I worked so hard to make good decisions, yet still had to suffer the after-effects of the bad choices of others.

Alex jotted down everybody's lunch order. When he got to me, he raised his eyebrows. "Usual?"

"Yeah."

"Don't be mad, Tessa," Alex said as he shoved his order pad in his back pocket. "We have to make a quick stop around six, and then we can go on our date."

I narrowed my eyes. "Where is this quick stop?"

"My cousin's birthday party, but it'll be superfast. In and out." He smiled harder—probably because I was giving him a disbelieving look. "Promise."

He gave me one last attempt at a convincing smile, then turned to take care of another table.

"Sorry, Tessa," Izzy said. Her expression had softened, so that was a perk of the dumb cousin birthday party.

"I wouldn't normally care, but it's been like this all week." I dipped a chip into the queso. "He cancelled on me twice because his mom keeps making plans. She's all emotional about his brother leaving for school and wants the five of them together all the time. Which I understand, but I'd like to see him too."

"He's the fifth-grade boys' counselor, right?" Amelia asked. She also didn't seem as mad at me. Another perk.

"Yep."

"Remember how I said my neighbor is also working there this summer?" Amelia pulled out her phone. "Turns out, Josie is the fifth-grade girls' counselor. I saw pictures of them on Instagram."

I blinked at her. "Her and Alex, you mean?"

"Yep."

"That's weird because they're not supposed to have their phones with them. It's in their contract."

Amelia shrugged and passed me her phone. "I think they sign stuff about not dating fellow counselors, too, but it happens all the time."

The first thing I noticed about Josie was that she had her arm looped around Alex's shoulders. The second thing I noticed was that she was 100 percent adorable with a natural, outdoorsy vibe. A high, dark ponytail, a bright smile, and cheekbones like a runway model.

My chest itched in a way that was familiar, but that I hadn't felt in a while. Not since the beginning of sophomore year when Lauren McConnell's eyes basically turned into throbbing hearts every time she looked at Alex.

The itching intensified as I read Josie's caption.

The best weeks of summer are at OWC! I have the privilege of hanging out with fifth-grade girls who love Jesus and want to serve Him better. And this is my partner in crime! Swipe right for OWC shenanigans.

"Shenanigans" included a selfie of Alex and Josie wearing crazy costumes that involved neon green shirts covered in feathers, another selfie of them side by side with marshmallows shoved in their mouths, and a short video of them racing each other to the top of a cliff. With the sound on, I could hear the cacophony of kids chanting both Alex and Josie's names. Josie got to the top first, but I was pretty sure Alex let her win.

Shay had been looking over my shoulder. "She probably isn't allowed to post pictures of the kids. That's the way it is at Green Tree Farm. So, if she wants to post pictures, she has to post them of herself with other counselors."

"She's not supposed to have her phone with her at all," I said stiffly as I handed Amelia's phone back to her. "Alex checks his in every day."

"You don't need to be worried, Tessa," Amelia said. "Josie's great. She's not the type who'd go after another girl's boyfriend."

So, Josie was beautiful, loved Jesus, and had a heart of gold? Yeah, she didn't sound like a girl I should be worried about at all . . .

Shay patted my shoulder in an awkward attempt to comfort me, and then pulled her hands back into her lap.

"Even if she *was* the kind of *chica* who went after another girl's guy," Izzy jumped in, "it wouldn't matter because Alex is crazy about you. You know that."

Really? whispered a mean version of my own voice. *How many times this week did he have a great time with Josie and then cancel his evening plans with you?*

"Yeah," I said with feigned confidence. I forced a smile and reached for the chip basket. "I'm sure it's not a big deal."

Chapter 11

"I'm so excited your friend Izzy signed up for art class next week," Mom said as we lugged stools from the creepy basement to the attic.

"She's really excited," I said. "She talked about it a lot at lunch today."

Once our food came, lunch had gone a lot smoother. I'd decided to attribute my conflicts with Amelia and Izzy to hangriness rather than any real problems that needed addressing.

"And you know who'll be in my afternoon session next week? Kayleigh Jones."

"Oh, nice." I huffed as I finally reached the attic.

Kayleigh swam on Blazers with me, but she was nine, so we didn't exactly swim together. Last summer, I'd helped her get back into swimming after she lost her mom to breast cancer. I was glad this summer seemed to be going so much better for her.

"I wonder how Phil is really doing," Mom said as she arranged the stools around the table. "He sounded good on the phone today, but I can't imagine what he's been through these last couple years with Sandy's battle. And now to be raising a daughter on his own . . ."

Mom and Sandy hadn't been close friends, even though our families go to the same church. But our church isn't very big, so everyone basically knew everyone. Especially in a sad situation like with the Jones family.

I followed Mom back down the three flights of narrow stairs to get the last of the stools.

"So, I saw on Instagram that your dad and Rebecca are getting married," Mom said as we started back up again.

I felt so surprised, I nearly tripped. "Do you *follow* Rebecca?"

Probably most moms are bad at social media, but my mom was abysmal. She never uploaded a profile picture and had set her account to private, even though it was supposed to be for her Carrie's Creations business. I suspected she mostly used Instagram to keep an eye on anything *I* posted.

"I don't. I'm already paying enough for therapy, thank you very much. But a couple of my friends do, and they sent me screenshots." Her voice had an oddly neutral quality considering the conversation topic. "I wasn't surprised. When we were taking care of paperwork at the old house, your dad mentioned that they were trying to set a date." Mom glanced at me as she rounded the corner to the next staircase. "You don't seem surprised. Did you already know?"

"Yeah," I said to the back of her head. "They mentioned it the first weekend I was there."

"Ah."

I felt a stab of guilt. "Sorry, I should've told you. I didn't know how."

"I get it." Mom sounded a bit breathless as we climbed the final steps. "It's a weird situation. I don't know how to feel about it, honestly. In one way, what does it matter to me if they're married or not married? They already live together. They already have a kid. But also, there's a strange finality to it. Like . . . we're genuinely over." Mom's voice wobbled and she turned away. "Sorry. I thought I could bring it up without getting emotional. Apparently not."

"You don't have to apologize for that." I plopped onto the stool I'd hauled up. "I get it."

When she turned her face to me, her eyes were glassy, but no actual tears had fallen. "How are you doing with it?"

I shrugged. "I don't know. Same as you, I think. Like in one sense it doesn't matter, and in another sense, I want to cry every time I think about it."

Mom nodded. "I'm sure they'll invite you to be there, so be thinking about if you want to say yes to that or not. If you don't want to go, I'll back you up."

"Thanks," I said softly. Should I tell her that not only had they invited me, but Dad wanted me *in* the wedding? And that despite me not yet giving an answer, yesterday Rebecca had asked for my opinion on bridesmaids' bouquets because as the "best daughter" I would have one too?

"Oh, baby." Mom crossed the few feet between us and wrapped her arms around me. "I'm so sorry for all this."

I hugged her back. "It's not your fault."

"I'm not blameless," Mom said into my hair. "If therapy has taught me anything, it's that."

The doorbell rang and she squeezed me tighter.

"That's Alex," I said, feeling relieved to escape the conversation.

"Oh, good." Mom released me and wiped under her eyes. "I feel like all you've done so far this summer is work and move. And you've been so busy, you've barely unpacked your room. I'm glad you get to go out tonight."

I'd been much more excited about the evening before learning that Alex committed us to stopping by his cousin's birthday party.

In his text this afternoon, he said Mrs. Hastings had grown teary when he told her we had plans. I'd been tempted to reply, "If I cry *because* we have to go, will you back out?" Why were guys so easily swayed by a few tears? I loved Mrs. Hastings, and I loved how much Alex cared about her, but all this crying was getting ridiculous.

It's a thirty-minute detour, I told myself. I could put up with thirty minutes if it meant having the rest of the night to ourselves. Right?

I opened the door to find Alex standing on the front porch wearing a Pacers T-shirt, athletic shorts, and sneakers. I'd spent thirty minutes curling my hair for our date, and he showed up looking like he was headed to cross-country practice.

His smile looked like he wanted to take a nap instead of go out. "Hey, you ready?"

"Yeah. Do you want to come in and see the house?"

Alex glanced at his watch. "If it's quick."

The annoyance that I hadn't quite been able to shake relit quickly. "Are you in a hurry?"

"No, but Jameson's party starts in ten minutes."

"If we're popping in, then it doesn't matter if we're a few minutes late, does it?"

Alex must have noticed the undercurrent of irritation in my voice because his eyes widened. "Not really, but the sooner we get there, the sooner we can leave. That's all."

"And we wouldn't have to go at all if you'd told your mom no and stuck with it."

"Well, I didn't," Alex said tersely as he pushed his hair off his forehead. "I've already said I'm sorry about a dozen times."

"Hi, Alex," Mom said as she jogged down the stairs. "How are you doing?"

Alex put on a friendly smile for my mom. "Fine, thanks. I like your new house."

"Come on in and take a look."

Alex didn't check his watch this time, just stepped across the threshold. He made a show of looking around. "It's nice."

"It's coming together," Mom said. "I'll let Tessa give you the official tour."

Alex looked to me expectantly, and it was all I could do to not roll my eyes at him. *Now* he was interested in seeing where we live? Now that my *mom* had invited him in?

"This is the downstairs." I pointed up. "That's the upstairs. There you go. There's your tour."

Mom laughed. "Oh, Tessa."

I snatched my Kavu bag from the hook near the door. "We have to go, or we'll be late for Alex's cousin's party."

Mom's face flickered with a frown. "You're going to a party?"

"Jameson's turning five," Alex said with a smile. "It won't exactly be a kegger."

Mom's laugh rang loose and loud, and I found myself feeling jealous. That was supposed to be me tonight, laughing and feeling joyful. Instead, I was a tangle of irritated and disappointed.

"I guess that'll be okay," Mom said with a grin. "What are your other plans?"

Alex glanced at me and shrugged. "Dinner out, maybe? We never talked about it."

Probably because I'd had my doubts that our date would happen. And I thought if it did happen, if I actually got to spend time alone with Alex, that by itself would be enough.

When we walked out to his car, Alex opened the door for me like he always did. "Thanks," I muttered as I slipped in and buckled my seat belt.

The passenger seat. It seemed I was here far too often these days, riding along with the consequences of somebody else's decisions. Mrs. Hastings threw a fit, so now I had to go to a family birthday party. Alex couldn't seem to tell his mother no, so I hadn't seen him in over a week. Alex didn't like being late, and so he had no interest in seeing where I lived.

When I was trying to make decisions, Kendra liked to ask me what God had given me to control, and right now it felt like the answer was "not enough."

Alex backed out of the driveway, and I looked out the window as Abraham emerged from his front door, his car keys in hand. I waved and he waved back.

"Who's that?" Alex asked.

"Abraham from my swim team. He lives across the street. You met him at the beginning of swim season."

"Well, great," Alex said, sounding like he didn't think it was great at all.

Silence descended in the car.

After a minute, Alex said, "So, I know that you're mad at me, but I don't want our night getting ruined because of the party. We'll be there for ten minutes, and then we can go do whatever we want."

"Whatever we want," I echoed. "Unless your mom decides we need to be at the party longer?"

Alex shot me an annoyed look. "That's not fair."

"How is it not fair? We had plans twice this week that you canceled because she'd made other ones for you. Tonight, we have to go to this party because she insisted."

"Of all people in my life, I thought *you'd* understand," Alex said through a clenched jaw. "Didn't you want to be there for your mom last fall when she was going through a rough time?"

"Clark is going away to college. That's not exactly the same kind of 'rough time.' And you didn't even plan anything for us to do tonight."

"Why am I in charge of planning things for us to do? All I cared about was getting to spend time with you."

His face was flushed with anger, and I found myself thinking about the photos of him and that dumb fifth-grade girls' counselor Amelia showed me at lunch, having goofy fun together. *I* wanted to have fun with Alex. This was my chance, and instead we were spending our time fighting. On Monday, he would go back to work with fun, beautiful Josie and maybe wonder what he was even doing with me. Because Alex having a fun, beautiful coworker was yet another thing God hadn't given me to control.

Tears threatened, and I turned to glare out the window instead. I refused to be manipulative with my tears the way Mrs. Hastings was these days.

Alex exhaled loudly. "I'm sorry, Tessa. I should've told her no and planned something fun for us to do. I'm tired and overwhelmed. I'm sorry."

I nodded but kept my face averted. My eyes still felt full of unshed tears.

"I didn't realize how tiring my work at OWC would be. And then I had my shift at Taqueria today, and I'm . . . tired." He chuckled dryly. "I can't even think of other words for 'tired'—that's how tired I am."

I swallowed hard and said in a stiff voice. "In the pictures I saw, you didn't look tired. You looked like you were having a great time at camp. You and Josie."

Nicely done, Tessa. Why not hold up a sign saying, "I'm jealous"?

"What are you talking about? Where'd you see pictures?"

I tightened my arms across my chest. "Josie posted all these pictures of the two of you at camp. Sure didn't look like it was 'so tiring' to work there."

"Are you friends with her?"

"No. Amelia is, and she showed me the pictures today at lunch. Josie's very pretty."

I couldn't bring myself to look at him. Why had I commented on how pretty she was? Angry, jealous, *and* insecure was never attractive.

"Tessa, don't do that." Alex sounded even more weary. "I'm *not* interested in Josie. And for what it's worth, we barely even see each other at work. The boys and girls are separate most of the day."

"That's not what it looked like," I muttered to my reflection.

Alex snorted a scoffing laugh. "And we both know that everything you see on social media is 100 percent true."

I swallowed hard and continued to not look at him. I didn't need a lesson on not believing everything I saw on Instagram, thank you very much. I didn't know what I needed exactly, but it wasn't that.

The car made an abrupt right turn into a parking lot. I braced myself on the door handle, and at least one vehicle behind us honked.

I forgot about being angry and swiveled toward him. "What are you doing?"

Alex screeched to a stop in front of an empty yoga studio and jammed the car into park. When he turned to me, his eyes were so earnest, I nearly broke down and cried. "I don't know why Josie posted those pictures on Instagram, but I'm not interested in her. I don't know what I need to say to make this clear, but you are the only person I want to spend time with tonight. I want to get to my cousin's birthday party so we can leave and enjoy time together. I don't care if my mom is stomping her feet and screaming on the driveway as we pull out, we are leaving after ten minutes. Okay?"

I nodded, not trusting myself to speak without crying.

He reached and took my hand in his own, weaving our fingers together. "Are we okay, Tessa?"

I kept my eyes on our entwined fingers. "You didn't want to come into my house."

I wasn't sure why it bothered me so much, but it did.

"I'm sorry." Alex's voice was husky, and he cleared his throat. "I was already feeling tired and cranky, and the idea of walking through your new house . . ." He sighed. "When I bring you home,

I will. And I *want* to. I also don't want to. I know that makes no sense."

The tightness in my chest loosened. I could understand that. If our positions had been reversed, it would've been hard for me to see Alex living somewhere else.

"I understand. And there's not much to see. I haven't even unpacked most of my boxes."

"That doesn't seem like you."

"Yeah, I know. But there's been a lot going on. I leave the house in the morning at six forty-five for swimming, and I'm not getting home until after five thirty." I squeezed his hand. "I'm tired too."

Alex flashed me a wry smile. "Maybe our big plans tonight can be dinner and a nap."

I grinned back. "We're really cool."

"The coolest."

Alex leaned across the seat to kiss me. His mouth was warm on mine and his fingers threaded through my carefully curled hair. Being close to him after time away felt wonderful. Maybe too wonderful.

I eased back from him. My whole body was tingling. "We'd better go."

His gaze skimmed my face. "Yeah," he said slowly. "I don't feel quite so tired all of a sudden."

"Yep." I giggled, feeling self-conscious as I settled back into my seat. "I couldn't agree more."

Alex took a deep breath and pulled out of the parking lot. I glanced at his profile and tried to trample the butterflies swarming in my stomach. What would it feel like to *not* have to do that? To not have to throw on the brakes?

That was a pointless line of thinking. Both of us wanted to wait for sex until we were married, and even if we *did* get married, that was years away. At least six. A lot could happen in six years. And even though it wasn't hard for me to imagine myself married to Alex someday, I knew love didn't come with a guarantee. If the last year had taught me anything, it was that.

"What'd you sigh about?" Alex asked.

"Just . . ." I considered how honest I wanted to be. "That I like you."

That I hope you don't break my heart.

"Well, thanks." He winked. "I like you all right too."

Chapter
12

LOGAN'S SMILE WAS MAYBE MY FAVORITE SIGHT in the whole world. Especially when I could tell he was smiling *because of me*. I had him on his play mat for tummy time, and even in the week and a half I'd been watching him, there was a noticeable difference in how strong he was. I stretched out on my belly, too, and put my head near his.

"Lo-gan," I sang.

He pushed himself up and grinned at me.

"Nice work, buddy," I said as he kept pushing up. "You're doing great."

Logan's smile turned to concern as he wobbled and rolled away from me and onto his back for the first time. The first time that I'd seen, anyway.

"Oh, Logan, good job!" I said as he burst into tears. "You don't need to cry, that was awesome." When I scooped under him, I found a wooden block beneath his head. "I bet that didn't feel too good, did it?"

"What's wrong?"

I jumped at the sound of Rebecca's voice. She stood in the open doorway from the garage, looking fiercely put together in a bright red dress and white flats. With my music on and Logan crying, I hadn't heard the garage door go up.

"He startled himself when he rolled over, that's all. He just started crying a couple seconds ago."

"He rolled over?" Rebecca zipped across the room. Logan stopped crying immediately and flailed at the sight of his mom. "Logan, Mommy is so proud of you! Oh, your diaper needs to be changed, doesn't it? It's so heavy. Mommy will change you."

Rebecca lifted him from my arms. Logan made a happy sound, and I felt weirdly betrayed.

"I was going to change him right after tummy time," I said as Rebecca carried him down the hall. I couldn't even tell if she heard me.

I paused my classical playlist—I'd read that classical music was good for brain development—and folded up the play mat to the soundtrack of Rebecca cooing at Logan and him cooing back. I gathered used bibs, tucked toys back into their baskets, and headed to the kitchen to clean the two bottles he'd used. The sink was still filling with soapy water when Rebecca reappeared, holding Logan outward. He gave an uncoordinated kick of excitement when he saw me, soothing my hurt feelings.

"Let's tell sister that you have a bit of a diaper rash that wasn't there this morning," Rebecca said in a sing-song voice, keeping her gaze on Logan. "She needs to be changing your diaper a little more often, it looks like."

I blinked at the top of Rebecca's head. "I changed him right after his bottle an hour ago."

"I could smell him as soon as I walked in the door." Rebecca smoothed his fuzzy hair. "He has sensitive skin. That's why I showed you the ointment that needs to be put on at every diaper change."

"I'm doing that," I said. "I don't know why—"

"I'll finish up the bottles," Rebecca said, stomping out the end of my sentence. She lifted Logan's arm and waved for him. "Logan, tell your sister bye."

Logan blinked at me with heavy-lidded eyes. Apparently rolling over for the first time had worn him out. I softened my voice and said, "Bye, Logan. See you tomorrow," but Rebecca turned and walked him away from me.

I physically left the house, but my mind didn't. As I walked out the front door, started my car, and drove the few blocks home, my mind churned through the conversation with Rebecca. Should I have said something different? *Did* I cause the diaper rash? I had put the ointment on him like she showed me. At least, I was pretty sure I had. It was possible I'd forgotten. But did one missed application cause diaper rash?

There was a white truck parked in our driveway that I didn't recognize. Probably a straggling parent from the afternoon art camp, which ended at five.

When I opened the front door, I heard Mom laughing in a warm, gentle way. Then, "Is that you, Tessa?"

"Yep."

"Phil and Kayleigh are here. Come on into the kitchen."

I wasn't exactly in the mood for small talk. I dropped my bags—my swim bag from the morning practice and my Kavu bag—onto the floor and skirted through the living room.

Mom, Phil, and Kayleigh were seated at our tiny round table, a box from Riverbend Bakery in the middle.

"Hi!" Kayleigh chirped at me. "Daddy brought cookies. You want one?"

"Sure, thanks."

I'd seen Kayleigh that morning as my practice wrapped up and hers began, but it was strange to see her in real clothes and uncapped. She wore pink cotton shorts with a tank top that was also pink, but not quite the right shade to go with the shorts. Her pale blond hair had a slight green tinge to it.

I smiled at Phil as I perused cookie options. "Hey."

Phil looked the same as I remembered. Receding hair, wire-rimmed glasses, and a thicker build. He had on a polo shirt that was a very Dad color of mint green. He smiled at me. "Hi, Tessa. Good to see you."

"You too."

Mom nudged the box of cookies closer to me. "I've never had Riverbend Bakery cookies before. They're delish, as you kids say."

Phil laughed.

"I've literally never said *that*," I said as I selected a chocolate chip cookie.

"*Literally* is another one too," Mom said to Phil. "The teens say it all the time."

Phil grinned. "Do they *literally* say it all the time?"

Mom laughed warmly and a look passed between them that left me feeling chilled. Were they *flirting* with each other? Right in front of their daughters?

I knew the answer to my question was yes when Mom glanced at me with a guilty-looking expression.

"Well, we'd better get going." Phil pushed back from the table. "Carrie, let me know about that lighting. Kayleigh and I are free most Saturday and Sunday afternoons."

"It's so nice of you to offer. I'm happy to pay."

Phil waved this away. "I think I still owe Tessa a favor." He winked at me and rested a hand on top of Kayleigh's head.

I felt myself blushing even though he was overselling what I'd done. Getting Kayleigh back in the pool hadn't been hard. She just needed to not be alone.

"That was no big deal," I said as Mom asked, "What'd Tessa do?"

"How about I tell you as I install those can lights?" Phil guided Kayleigh—still licking the lavender icing from her sugar cookie—toward the front door. "Would one o'clock this Saturday work for you?"

"The least I can do is provide lunch. How about you come at noon instead?"

Phil grinned. "Sounds great."

But to me his words sounded more like "It's a date."

Mom closed the door behind Phil and Kayleigh, then turned to me. Did she know how enormous her smile was? That she looked like a middle-school girl whose crush had said hi to her in the hallway?

"Phil noticed that the art room would benefit from a little additional lighting," Mom said, still grinning. "He's in construction and said it would be easy to do."

"Okay."

Her smile dimmed. "Tessa, don't look at me like that. He's a nice man who likes to help people out. He does these kinds of favors for a lot of people at church."

"Okay," I said again.

Mom rolled her eyes. "What are you doing home anyway?"

"It's five thirty."

"Oh, is it?" Mom asked, pulling out her phone. "Well, look at that. I haven't cleaned up the art room yet. Feel free to eat dinner whenever you're hungry."

That was her nice way of saying, "Because I'm not making food for anybody but myself tonight."

"Okay." As she jogged up the stairs, I called, "Careful, I hear the lighting is bad up there."

Her fading footsteps were the only response.

I looked at the box of cookies on the table. "You really want to do me a favor, Phil?" I asked as I selected another. "*Don't* date my mom."

—◆—

When Dad called, I was sitting on the back porch eating Kraft macaroni and cheese, waiting for it to be eight o'clock so I could talk to Alex.

"Hi, honey." Dad sounded tired. "How are you?"

I shrugged, then realized he couldn't see. "Fine. You?"

"Fine."

That's not how he sounded. "Are you sure?"

"Well, I need to talk to you about something."

I dragged my spoon through my bowl. "Okay. What's up?"

"It's about this afternoon with Logan," Dad said. "I'd like to hear your side of the story."

"The story?" I echoed. "What do you mean?"

"I'd like to know your point of view on how the afternoon went with Logan."

"Uh, okay. Logan was sleeping when I arrived. He woke up about thirty minutes later and had a bottle. He drank the whole thing, and—"

"I don't need *all* the details, Tessa." Dad's voice was sharp. "Rebecca said she came home and found Logan crying and badly needing a diaper change. Apparently, when she pointed these things out to you, you were defensive and unapologetic."

My heart pounded the same way it did when I stood on the swimming blocks, awaiting the signal to jump in the water. "Do you actually want to hear what happened? Because you asked me a question, but then didn't let me answer it."

"You knew what I was talking about, but then started with all these other details that don't matter."

"Dad, you said 'the story' like something big happened. But nothing big happened. Yeah, when Rebecca came home, Logan was crying. He'd started about ten seconds before she walked in the door because he rolled over, and his head landed on a block. I was lying beside him when it happened, and I picked him up right away. There's the story."

There was a beat of silence. Then Dad said, "She told me his diaper was sodden, and he had a rash."

Keeping my voice calm was a challenge "*Sodden* is a strong word choice, and he didn't look rashy when I changed him last."

"And when was that?"

I rolled my eyes. I'd never been on trial before, but I was guessing it felt like this. "I don't remember exactly, but probably four or so. I think it was about an hour before Rebecca got home."

"Did you use the ointment?"

"I'm pretty sure I did."

"You're *pretty* sure?"

Only the robins pecking at the lawn could see my scowl. "Yes. I'm *pretty* sure. I changed his diaper three times today; it's possible that I forgot the ointment once. But I'm *pretty* sure I didn't."

Another silence fell. I set the congealed remains of my dinner on the patio table.

"So," Dad said slowly. "Your version of the story is that Logan startled himself and had only been crying for a few seconds when Rebecca arrived. And that you'd changed his diaper an hour before."

My "version" of the story? Like the situation was so complicated. "That's what happened, yeah."

"And you told Rebecca this?"

"As much as I could. She didn't seem very interested in what I had to say."

More silence. Then a reluctant, "She said you were a little late today . . .?"

I scowled. "Yeah, it was five minutes after noon when I arrived. One of my kids at swim lessons got picked up late, but I got there as soon as I could. I explained that to Rebecca already."

"When you knew you were going to be late, did you text Rebecca?"

"No. I was driving."

"Next time, that would be a good idea. Not *while* you're driving, of course. But if you're leaving the pool late."

I clenched my teeth. Clearly, Dad wanted to find *something* I'd done wrong today. "Okay."

Dad sighed. "I don't know what happened because I wasn't here, but Rebecca has been upset all night and even talked about not going to her class tomorrow."

Because of a little diaper rash? "Okay."

"If what you're saying is true, today was the first day Logan rolled over." Dad pitched his voice low. "I think it's possible Rebecca's upset about missing that. This probably isn't about you."

If what I was saying was true? It *probably* wasn't about me? Thanks, Dad. "Okay."

"She's waited so long to be a mom, and she badly wants to be great at it. But she also cares so much about teaching and caring for other people's kids." Dad sighed. "Rebecca is such a wholehearted person, and I think she's struggling with the balance of both. That's not your fault. Sorry you got caught up in the struggle of it today."

"Okay," I repeated. "So, do you need me to come over tomorrow or is Rebecca staying home?"

"She needs to go to her class," Dad said. "And she's going to have to get used to this because she's returning to work in August. Plan on coming over, okay?"

"I will."

"I'll talk to her and text if things change. Love you, honey."

"Bye, Dad."

I poked at my macaroni and cheese and considered reheating it, but I wasn't hungry anymore. Instead, I opened up Instagram. Rebecca's post from this evening was at the top of my feed. She had one of those check marks by her name, verifying that she was the real Rebecca Simmons, kindergarten teacher celebrity.

She had a new picture posted of Logan sleeping in his crib. The lighting was so perfect, I wondered if she'd brought in her ring light. All the caption said was, "Rough day with this guy, but it all seems worth it when I look at his sweet face." He *did* have a sweet face, but what was she talking about "rough day"? Maybe a rough day for *her*, but Logan had been great when I'd been with him.

"Whatever," I said. I put my phone away and tried to not care.

Chapter

13

Dad: Logan's diaper rash is gone. I talked Rebecca into going to her class, so you can plan on being here this afternoon.

Tessa: Okay.

Dad: Since tomorrow is Friday, can you bring your stuff for the weekend with you? Doesn't make sense for you to drive home, get your stuff, and drive right back.

Tessa: Okay.

Dad: We're looking forward to having you again! Any requests for dinner?

Tessa: Nope. Whatever is fine.

Dad: Have you given any more thought to the wedding and if you want to be my "best daughter"? ☺ No pressure, but we're less than a month away, so if you don't want to, I need to ask someone else to stand up with me.

—m—

On Thursday, Rebecca said absolutely nothing to indicate any-thing unusual had happened the day before. There was no apology for accusing me of neglecting Logan, nor did she acknowledge that I arrived at eleven forty-five—a full fifteen minutes before I was supposed to. I thought maybe she'd bring it up before I left for the day, but nope. Nothing.

Not that I needed praise from Rebecca of all people, but it still grated on me. As did Dad's text from this morning. I'd talked to Kendra about the wedding at my last appointment, and we'd decided that attending was okay with me—not that I *wanted* to—but being an active participant wasn't. Agreeing to that felt too much like I was putting my stamp of approval on the marriage.

But I hadn't worked out how to communicate this to my dad. Yeah, I was mad at him, but I also didn't like the idea of saying, "I'll be there, but because I disapprove, I don't want to be your best man. And can I bring a friend? My therapist—who I see regularly thanks to your actions—thinks it would be a good idea."

No, thanks.

As I slipped my feet into flip-flops to walk to Grounds and Rounds and meet up with the girls, I hoped they would have ideas for how I should say what I needed to say. And that at least one of them wouldn't mind coming to the wedding with me. With our packed schedules, finding times we could all get together this sum-mer was hard. Even tonight, we were meeting for coffee because Shay had plans with her grandparents and Izzy had promised to help her neighbor with something.

When I stepped outside to walk to Grounds and Rounds, I was immediately greeted by a familiar voice calling out, "Hey, T."

Abraham was in his driveway with little Maxine clipped to her leash. I couldn't help smiling. There was something comical about Abraham walking a miniature poodle daily.

I waved back. "Going for a walk?"

"Yeah. You?"

"I'm meeting some friends at Grounds and Rounds."

"Cool. I'll walk with you."

I felt a hiccup of hesitation. But, why? I spent time with Abraham every morning at swim practice. "Okay."

I self-consciously tucked my damp hair behind my ears. Logan had been extra refluxy that afternoon, so a shower hadn't been optional.

"Are you still seeing that same guy?" Abraham asked as he fell into step with me. "Aaron or whoever?"

"Alex. Yeah."

"That's cool. I wondered because I never see him at your place. And I haven't seen pictures of him on your Instagram for a while."

I didn't love this line of conversation. I attempted a light-hearted laugh. "Um, are you spying on me?"

Abraham grinned. "Of course."

Abraham was the sort of guy who knew that he was good look-ing. While I wasn't immune to noticing, I wasn't into guys who had already dated half the girls on our swim team. And while at the beginning of sophomore year I hadn't minded Abraham flirt-ing with me, and had even flirted back, I didn't want to do so now.

I increased the amount of space between us on the sidewalk. "We don't feel the need to share everything on Insta. In fact, I don't think Alex has posted anything since January."

"Huh. Does he know Josie McClean? I think he was on her Instagram."

I inhaled sharply. I could feel Abraham looking at me, and I worked to keep my face as placid as possible. "Yeah, probably. They work together," I said in what I hoped was an unaffected voice.

"I thought that was him. She and I dated for a bit, you know."

It was all I could do to not beg Abraham for details. Had he seen multiple posts on Josie's Instagram about Alex, or were these the same ones I'd already seen? Could he tell from her caption if she liked Alex? But I let a silence fall.

"Didn't work out, obviously," Abraham continued. "Nice enough girl, but I got tired of feeling like a project to her."

"Mmhmm." My mind raced with follow-up questions, but instead, I said, "My legs still hurt from that drill this morning. Yours?"

There was a moment of silence during which I could feel Abraham studying me. He must've decided to let the subject change. "Yeah, I've been sore all day. Coach Shauna is pure evil to make us work like that at seven a.m."

Maxine sniffed the base of a streetlight and resisted Abraham's tug on the leash. "She does this every time we walk this way. C'mon, girl." He tugged again, and this time she resumed trotting. "So, my mom wants to have you and your mom over for dinner."

"Oh." I knew my mom had talked to Mrs. Mitra a handful of times, but I hadn't heard anything about dinner plans. "That'd be fun. I think my mom wants to put in a greenhouse because of yours."

"She wanted to have you over tomorrow night, but it sounds like you have to be at your dad's?"

"Yep." I offered a grim smile. "Every other weekend."

"At least your dad wants time with you." Abraham said this with a smile, but there was an edge to his words.

My stomach squirmed. I wanted to offer comfort or reassurance . . . but that sounded like a deeper conversation. Would a deeper conversation make Abraham think I was interested in him? Because I definitely didn't want to do anything that would suggest that. We'd reached Cherry, the side street that would take me almost straight to Grounds and Rounds. "Well, I'm heading this way, so—"

"Me too." Abraham tugged Maxine's leash, and she turned and trotted along the sidewalk. "So, who are you meeting?"

Had he rerouted to walk longer with me? I tried to put even more space between us on the sidewalk. "Some friends of mine from school. You met Izzy at my house."

"The girl with the wild hair and the cupcakes?"

"Uh, yeah. That's Izzy in a nutshell."

"A couple of my friends are coming over for a fire pit. You'd know a few from Blazers, like Derek and Lexi. You should come over. You could bring your friends too."

"We're meeting for a quick coffee, and then heading our separate ways. Thanks, though."

Abraham shrugged. "Okay, then just you."

"I'm pretty tired."

Abraham laughed loudly. "Tired? That's lame, T. If you don't want to, say that."

I grinned as if teasing. "Okay. I don't want to."

"Yeah, all right. I doubt your boyfriend would like the idea. Of course, he's spending a lot of time with Josie . . ."

Abraham trailed off and watched me as I weighed how to respond. Thankfully, I spotted Shay coming out the back entrance of Booked Up. Saved!

"Shay!" I called out.

She turned, her low, honey-colored ponytail swinging over her shoulder. "Hi!" She spotted Abraham's dog, and her face lit up. "Aww, hi."

Somehow Maxine knew Shay was talking to her. Her tail wagged and she pulled the leash tight as she surged forward toward Shay.

I considered how Shay would look to Abraham. Shay was pretty in an unassuming way. She nearly always looked like she was dressed for the barn—regardless of whether that was on the day's agenda—and I doubted she'd ever ventured into the makeup aisles at Target. She had bright green eyes that crinkled when she smiled, and Shay was nearly always smiling when there were animals around.

She crouched and greeted Abraham's dog like they were old friends, even letting Maxine lick her face. Gross.

"Shay, this is Abraham. Abraham, my friend, Shay."

"Hi." Shay looked up and actually made eye contact with Abraham. It was as if Maxine had made her forget that she was shy. "What's your poodle's name?"

"Maxine."

"Maxine," Shay echoed as she rubbed behind the dog's ears. "Hello, Maxine. You're a good girl, aren't you?"

Maxine's whole body wriggled with delight. Abraham looked at me and winked, and I wasn't entirely sure why. Shay's enthusiasm? Because winking was his MO? Whatever his reasoning, I didn't like how my body warmed. How my heart fluttered.

"We got to go, Shay. We'll be late."

"Okay. I have to go, Maxine. Good to meet you." Shay rubbed Maxine's haunches. "You like that, don't you?"

I tugged at Shay's sleeve. "C'mon."

"Bye, Maxine," Shay said as she stood.

"Bye, T." Abraham smiled at me, and I turned away. "I hope you change your mind and I see you later tonight."

"See you at practice tomorrow," I replied pointedly over my shoulder, and then hustled down the sidewalk.

Shay jogged to catch up with me. "His dog is *so* cute. How do you know him?"

"He's on my swim team. And now he's my neighbor."

"Oh, so he lives close, then? I wonder if I could do a doggie play date with him. Stanley needs more socializing. Does he ever go to the dog park?"

Shay's question was pure innocence and still made me nervous. "Um, I'm not sure."

"Will you ask him? I could meet him there sometime."

"I don't know that Abraham is the kind of guy you want to hang out with, Shay."

She blinked at me. "Why not?"

"He's . . ." I shrugged. "He's very flirtatious."

Shay frowned. "Maybe with you. I don't think he would be with me. And even if he was, I'd ignore it."

That was probably true. Maybe it was because last year I'd watched Izzy fall into a relationship rabbit hole, but I found myself feeling protective of Shay. Shay had never seemed interested in boys the way the rest of us were, so there was that. However, her innocence bordered on the naïve. Shay wasn't Abraham's type, so maybe hanging out at the dog park would be fine, but I didn't trust him either.

As Shay launched into a story about Stanley, I pulled up Josie on Instagram. I breathed a sigh of relief. There weren't any new pictures. Abraham must have been talking about the old ones.

"Are you even listening to me?" Shay asked, her words laced with irritation.

"Sorry." I tucked my phone in my back pocket. "I had to check something. Now I'm listening."

"Never mind," Shay grumbled as she pulled open the door for Grounds and Rounds.

"I'm really sorry," I said again. Shay was mostly quiet and easy going, but her flinty expression reminded me that I'd also seen her grow very angry, very quickly. It wasn't a pretty sight. "You said Stanley got into Aunt Laura's spice drawer?"

Her face softened slightly. "Yeah, and he was sneezing all afternoon."

"Poor guy," I said.

Shay's mouth quirked with a smile. "Yeah, but it was also kind of funny. He seemed so bewildered."

"You're laughing at his pain? That's so cruel of you."

Shay laughed, and I breathed a sigh of relief. I did *not* want to walk in already arguing with a friend like I had on Saturday at Taqueria.

Inside Grounds and Rounds, we found Amelia and Izzy standing at the pickup end of the counter chatting with Wilson. Wilson went to school with us and did theater, though he stuck to the tech booth. I felt a rush of affection whenever I saw him. Wilson had once witnessed me making a scene in the coffee shop and spilling my coffee everywhere. In my defense, I'd just learned on Instagram that Rebecca was pregnant. Without asking, he'd made me a new latte to-go.

I ordered an iced coffee and Shay ordered a lemonade. Then we joined the others, where Amelia was telling Wilson a story that involved lots of hand gestures while he worked the espresso machine. Amelia had never stated her feelings plainly, but I suspected she had a big crush on Wilson. This was completely understandable. In addition to being smart and a genuinely nice guy, Wilson had an adorable vibe going on, with messy dark hair and black rimmed glasses.

"Hi!" Izzy set her cup on the counter and threw her arms around Shay and then me. "Should we go get a table?" She lowered her voice to a whisper. "I think they're flirting."

I tuned in as Amelia made a rolling gesture with her hands, sloshing her drink in a way that made me nervous. "But then Mrs. Taylor stopped them and said if they were going to use that kind of language, she'd go find a bar of soap in the bathroom. I was completely shocked too. This is *Christian* theater . . ."

I raised my eyebrows at Izzy. "*This* is flirting?"

"I think so?" She shrugged. "Let's see if our table in the back is open."

We followed her to our favorite round table, tucked around the corner. "How are you?" I asked as Izzy flopped into a seat.

"Exhausted." She rubbed at her eyes. "I was up until three a.m. watching Marvel movies with Sebastian. Why do I do that to myself?"

"I have no idea," I said. "That seems dumb."

Amelia's big laugh reached us, and we all exchanged smiles.

Izzy stirred her drink, something icy and pink. "Tessa, tell me you have pictures of Logan you can show me. I need baby pics."

"I do, actually." I pulled my phone from my bag, closed out of Josie's Instagram feed, and opened my photo album. "You can swipe right forever, basically. They're all of Logan these days."

"Ohmygoodness." Izzy hugged my phone to herself. "He's the absolute cutest."

She was still oohing and aahing minutes later when Amelia joined us, carrying Shay's and my drinks.

"Sorry, girls. Theater business. Wilson is doing tech for *Annie*, and there's so much that needs to be done." Amelia passed me my coffee, but before I could say thank you, she rushed on, "Since it's a private theater company, I thought it would be run more efficiently, and that everyone involved would be 110 percent invested, but that's not the case. I mean, the girl playing Miss Hannigan? She only tried out because her brother and sister love to be in shows, and she knew she was going to get schlepped to practice anyway. She told me, 'I figured I might as well try out for a part.' Can you believe that?"

Amelia flopped in her seat. "What were you girls talking about? What are you looking at, Iz?"

"Baby Logan." Izzy used the same smushy voice that Shay had used with Maxine. "Look at him!"

Izzy turned my phone to Amelia.

Amelia arched her eyebrows. "Yep, he looks like a baby."

"Hey." I was surprised to find that I felt a little offended. "He's adorable."

Amelia took a long sip of her foamy mocha. "All babies are cute, Tessa."

"I think he's cuter than the average baby."

"Everybody thinks that about their baby. Anyway, I was telling Wilson that Mrs. Taylor—she's the stage mom—is clueless about how a real show should run."

And off Amelia went, gabbing nonstop about a show that none of us were in and that none of us—I was guessing—particularly cared about. Shay picked at her cuticles and Izzy kept scrolling Logan photos, but Amelia carried on undeterred.

When she wound down, I realized I'd been tuning her out and reached for a question that I hoped she hadn't already answered. "When is opening night?"

"Friday, July fifteenth." Amelia staged her coffee for a drink. "I have basically three more weeks to pull this thing together, and I'm not sure it's going to happen. You girls will be at opening night, right?"

Her opening night was the same night as Dad's wedding? Ugh.

"I can't go that night, sorry," Shay said. "There's some famous author doing a signing at the bookstore. We all have to work."

"Ooh, who is it?" Izzy asked.

Shay shrugged. "I don't know, but it's a pretty big deal. Aunt Laura is so excited."

Amelia groaned. "That's going to draw people away from opening night. I figured at least you'd be able to come, Shay. You never have anything going on."

Shay frowned. "That's not true. I have plans tonight, too, you know."

Izzy snorted. "Stars, this isn't my calendar." She passed my phone back to me and whipped out her own. "I *think* the fifteenth is when we're going back to Posen for Abulita's birthday, but let me check."

"What?" Amelia sighed and looked at me. "Tessa?"

I swallowed hard, surprised to find that I was close to tears. "I can't. My dad and Rebecca are getting married that night. I was going to ask all of you if you could come with me."

Amelia, astounded, tipped her chair on its back two legs. "So, none of you can come to opening night?"

Izzy sighed. "Yep, that's the day we leave. We'll be gone all weekend." She frowned. "I'm so sorry, Tessa."

"Sorry Tessa, but not sorry Amelia?" Amelia brought her chair down on all four legs.

"I'm sorry about missing the opening of *Annie*, too, but I can come the next weekend." Izzy gestured to me. "Kind of a big deal that her dad's getting remarried and none of us can go."

"Yeah, I know." Amelia looked at me. She seemed annoyed, but also like she knew it was uncool to be annoyed. "Why would you even go to their wedding? Tell him you're busy."

"I can't," I answered brusquely. "It's complicated."

"How is it complicated? He cheated on your mom with this woman. Why would you go?"

"Because he's my dad," I snapped. "Maybe I'll write a musical about it, and then you'll possibly care about what I'm going through right now."

Silence landed on the group like a weighted blanket. I took a drink of my coffee and avoided looking at any of them. I should say I was sorry, but I wasn't. Amelia was being self-absorbed, so if anyone should apologize, it was her.

"That's not fair," Amelia said, her volume low for once. "I totally care about your dad getting remarried."

"You only care about it because it's keeping me from being at opening night." I pointed my coffee at Izzy and Shay, both of whom were studying their phones as if doing so would keep them out of the conversation. "You got onto both Izzy and Shay for having plans, like we owe you an audience. It's not like you're even in the show."

As soon as the words popped out, I wanted to reel them back in. Amelia's face turned a splotchy red, like I'd slapped her.

I looked into my iced coffee. "I'm sorry, I shouldn't have said that."

Amelia took a deep breath and stood. "You know, some of my Aspire friends asked me to hang out tonight, and I'd told them I couldn't because I had plans with my besties. But I think I'd rather hang out with people who aren't ridiculing me for being fat or not being on stage."

"Amelia," I groaned. She was seriously bringing up that comment from when we were at Taqueria?

Izzy's gaze darted between us. "Amelia, nobody called you fat."

"Tessa did," Amelia said simply as she turned and began to walk away.

"No, I didn't," I called after her. "I never . . ."

I trailed off as she marched through the back door and out of earshot. The only other person back here was a guy in a suit typing away and wearing noise-canceling headphones; otherwise, I was sure we'd be being stared at right now.

I turned back to Izzy and Shay. "I never called her fat. And I wasn't *ridiculing* her for not being on stage." I took a deep, shaking breath. "But I know I shouldn't have said that."

Shay offered a weak smile.

"You didn't mean it," Izzy said. "I know you didn't."

My heart pounded frantically in my chest. Why did arguing with a friend make my body feel the same way as when I sprinted across the pool?

"Maybe I did a little bit," I admitted. "She was acting like *Annie* is the biggest thing going this summer."

"For her it is," Shay said. "You know how deeply it hurts her that she's not succeeding in theater the way she wants to."

Shay's condemnation cut deeper than Amelia storming out. I hung my head; the shame made it feel too heavy to hold up.

"It'll all be fine," Izzy assured me. "She'll cool off. You'll apologize. Everything will be okay."

I blew out a breath as I thought about what God had given me to control. "I'll apologize about the stage thing, but I did *not* call her fat. She's talking about when we were at Taqueria, and I said I thought she'd been joking about Shay being impatient and hungry. But what I said had absolutely nothing to do with her size."

Izzy frowned. "I don't even remember that."

"Clearly she does, though she has a warped perspective of what happened. I don't get why she won't trust me that I didn't mean what she thought I meant."

Izzy bit her lip as she considered me. "Want a hug?"

I smiled. "No, but thank you."

"My Aunt Laura says people see what they look for." Shay sipped her lemonade. "I think that's probably what's going on here."

"What does that mean?" Izzy asked as she drew a smiley face in the condensation of her cup.

"Like how when you're focused on something, you see it everywhere. You're hyperaware. Laura was dieting last month and said everywhere she went, she saw carbs."

"Oh," Izzy said. "Yeah, that happens to me."

"That makes sense," I said. "Kind of like confirmation bias? Amelia's sensitive about her weight, so she understood my comment differently than it was intended."

"Yeah, basically," Shay said.

Ugh, I couldn't control *that*. *God, why didn't You make it so that people could clearly see our intentions?*

A heavy silence settled over the table. I sighed and glanced at the back door. "I'll go see if I can find her."

Shay smiled. "Good idea."

"Good luck!" Izzy called after me.

But Amelia wasn't in the alley, nor was she within sight on Main Street. I pulled my phone from my back pocket and called her. No answer. Finally, I shot her a text. I feel really bad about what I said. I'm so sorry that I hurt your feelings and missed getting to hang out with you. I'd love to talk about this. I'm free all night.

But she never responded, and that was out of my control.

Chapter
14

BUTTERY LIGHT FILTERED THROUGH the sheer curtains. I reached for my phone and cracked open an eye to confirm what I suspected: It was still early—6:32 to be precise. I groaned and pulled Rebecca's white duvet over my head. Somewhere in the house, Logan babbled cheerfully.

If I were home, my room would still be dark, thanks to the blackout curtains Mom had hung. On Saturdays, I usually slept until at least eight. Sometimes even nine. Not at Rebecca's house, though.

I'd drifted back to sleep when someone—and I had a guess of who—started hammering something.

"Shh," my dad said. "Tessa . . ."

I couldn't hear the rest, but I had no problem hearing Rebecca's response. "I can't spend the whole morning tiptoeing around the house. This is when Logan's the happiest and I can get things done."

Dad responded, but I couldn't make out the words.

Rebecca replied with, "She'll learn that when she stays at our house, she can't stay up all hours of the night."

All hours of the night? I'd turned off my light at eleven thirty. And I'd been in my room since ten o'clock, reading. *I* knew how to be quiet and respectful of others' sleep.

I grabbed my phone to see if Amelia had responded yet, but she still hadn't. Gosh, she could be stubborn when she was mad. I'd sent her two additional text messages yesterday. What else did she want from me?

But I did have a Marco Polo from Alex. I opened it and grinned at the sight of him. He was in his room, the lighting soft and warm on his face. His skin looked even more bronze than when I'd seen him last Sunday.

"Hey, I hope you're sleeping and won't see this until morning. I know you're at your dad's this weekend, but there was a weird scheduling issue at Taqueria, so I'm only working the dinner shift. Plus—" Alex dropped his voice to a whisper. "Clark has been puking all day, and this probably makes me a terrible person, but I'm so excited that Mom can't even guilt me into family stuff tomorrow. I don't know if you're able to get away when you're at David and Rebecca's, but I'm hoping you're free because I miss you."

The video ended. Elsewhere in the house, more hammering was happening, so Dad had clearly lost the battle for my sleep. I wasn't going to send a Marco Polo back looking like this, so I texted Alex. *Yes, I'm free! And awake! Come rescue me!*

I stretched, pulled my Northside High hoodie over my tank top, and finger-combed my hair into a messy bun. I padded down the hallway and through the living room, where Rebecca was adding to her gallery wall.

She gave me a closed-mouth smile as I entered. "Good morning."

"Morning," I replied in a chipper voice. I didn't want to give her the satisfaction of being crabby.

Dad and Logan were in the kitchen. Dad had Logan tucked in the crook of his elbow as he alternated drinking his coffee and eating a container of Greek yogurt with the other hand. His smile held an apology. "Did we wake you up?"

"Yep."

Dad glanced at Rebecca, whose back was to us. In a low voice, he said, "I'm really sorry."

Which was funny considering my dad never apologized for the affair and leaving us, but he felt *this* was a situation that required a "sorry."

"I'm not here very often," I said with a shrug. "I can handle it."

Dad's brow furrowed. "I want you to feel welcome here."

How welcome did he expect me to feel? I was sleeping in a guest room full of pictures of Rebecca's family. The only thing in this house that I had any real claim on was him.

I took a banana from the fruit bowl because I didn't like rummaging around in the cabinets. "I know *you* do."

"She does too," he said softly. "It's new, that's all. This is only the second weekend."

From the living room, Rebecca called, "Does this look good, David?"

I had a feeling she would've used the same volume of voice whether I was still in bed or not.

"Looks great, honey."

Honey. Dad had never called Mom anything but Carrie. With my jaw clenched, I stood near Dad while he held sleeping Logan.

"Now that Tessa's awake, I'll change out those pictures in the hallway," Rebecca said as she gathered up her hammer and nails.

"So thoughtful of you to wait," I muttered as I peeled my banana. I was confident Dad heard me, but he didn't reply.

"Did you know Rebecca's family used to take in foster kids?" Dad asked.

"Uh, no. I didn't."

"Yeah, when I would go pick up Rebecca for dates when we were teenagers, I never knew who else was going to be living there. I think they had about fifty kids stay with them over the years."

Why was he telling me this? "Cool."

"Rebecca always knew she wanted to be a teacher, even when we were in high school. She knew there were so many kids who needed extra love."

Was the point of this that I shouldn't be mad at her for waking me up or having an affair with my dad because deep down she was a good person? I didn't know how to respond . . . so I took another bite of my banana.

"She won an award last year that recognizes teachers who go the extra mile for their kids. Like making sure they have food and clothes. That sort of thing. She's led the charge for making breakfast available for free to all kids at her elementary school."

When it was just the two of them, did he try to talk her into liking me too? *Tessa has straight As, you know. In middle school, her classmates voted her most likely to be president.* As great as it was to hear that hungry kids got fed at Trailwood Elementary, what I wanted was for her to not marry my dad. And to maybe wait until eight o'clock before she started redecorating.

I'd eaten half my banana when Dad said, "I'd still like for us to go to Iceland, you know."

I looked up at him, confused by the awkward transition, and found his focus pointed toward the photograph Rebecca had finished hanging in the living room. It was a large print from Blue Lagoon in Iceland.

Dad and I had started talking about the trip to Iceland when I was thirteen and obsessed with astronomy. I'd longed to see the aurora borealis, and my sixteenth birthday was set as the magical date when the two of us would go. What neither of us knew then was that months before our planned trip, he'd reconnect with his high-school sweetheart and begin an affair that would lead to the implosion of our family. Two months before I turned sixteen, Dad moved out. When I refused to go to Iceland with him, instead of cancelling the trip, he took Rebecca on a "babymoon." Because apparently *that* was a thing now.

It would probably hurt his feelings to learn I was going with Mom. Maybe I should keep that to myself for now? Although Dad had never told me he was taking Rebecca. I'd learned about it on Instagram. Same as how I'd learned about Logan's existence.

"Actually, Mom and I are planning a trip there."

Dad turned, the surprise clear in his eyes. "Oh. I didn't know that."

"Yep." I took a large bite of banana and pulled out my phone to have something to distract myself with.

He took a long sip of his coffee. "Well, I'm glad your mother is willing to do that." Dad's words were slow and stiff.

"Mmhmm."

My heart hammered in my chest. I scrolled Instagram but didn't see anything.

"She's not a nature person, you know," Dad said, as if this was news to me. "Your mom always wanted to take vacations to cities."

"There's nothing wrong with that."

"I'm not saying there's something wrong with it. It's . . . Iceland isn't her thing."

My heart raced as I looked him in the eye. "She's doing it for me. She's prioritizing the trip because she knows it matters to *me*." I looked back to Instagram. "Mom's really considerate."

Dad opened his mouth. Down the hall, Rebecca pounded another nail into the wall. He closed his mouth, perhaps thinking better of what he'd intended to say.

—∽—

While Alex was in the bathroom of Fortune Wok, I sent another text to Amelia. I feel awful about hurting your feelings. Can we get together so we can talk?

Almost forty-eight hours had gone by since I'd hurt her feelings, and still she wasn't responding to me. I'd texted Shay and Izzy to see if they'd heard from her. Shay suggested that Amelia might have lost her phone—not an unusual occurrence—but Izzy had heard from Amelia that morning.

I'd drafted a text to our group thread to complain about Rebecca hanging photographs at six thirty in the morning, but I hadn't sent it. Doing so would feel weird after what happened at Grounds and Rounds, like I'd be ignoring the elephant in the room.

I imagined Amelia saying, "So, now you're calling me an elephant?" and huffed a private laugh.

"What's so funny?" Alex asked as he slid back into the booth across from me.

"Nothing." I sighed and put my phone facedown on the edge of the table. "I was thinking about how Amelia seems determined to believe the worst about me and what I say."

Alex frowned. "She hasn't texted back?"

"Nope."

The waitress arrived with my orange chicken and Alex's Mongolian beef. After we assured her we didn't need anything else and she walked away, I picked the conversation back up.

"I definitely crossed a line with my comment. I know I shouldn't have said it." I speared chicken onto my fork. "But it seems a little harsh to ignore my apology attempts."

"Maybe she lost her phone. This is Amelia, after all."

"Izzy had a text from her this morning, so that's not it." I dragged my chicken through extra sauce and took a bite. After I'd chewed and swallowed, I said, "I know I need to apologize, but it's not like she was being some great friend. I mean, even after I told them that Dad and Rebecca were getting married that day, she wouldn't shut up about the musical."

"Hopefully she'll apologize too," Alex said as he tapped on his Google calendar. "What Saturday are they getting married?"

"It's not a Saturday. It's Friday the fifteenth."

Alex's gaze snapped to me. "*July* fifteenth?"

"Yep."

"Oh, man." Alex's expression turned from surprise to regret. "I can't be there. I'm so sorry."

I froze mid-bite. "Are you joking?"

"Why would I joke about that?"

"I don't know, I was hoping you were." I laid my fork down so I wouldn't stab anything other than food and tried to ask calmly, "Why can't you come?"

"Every Friday is bonfire night, so unless their wedding is at ten o'clock . . ."

I groaned and sank back into the booth. "That's right. I wasn't even thinking about that. Stupid OWC."

"I know. *And* it's my mom's birthday."

"Well, great." I picked up my fork and stabbed a carrot coin. It felt good. "So, even if you did get time off, it'd make her angry if you didn't spend the evening with her."

"I could figure that piece out," Alex said. "But OWC is pretty clear that counselors are to be there during camp hours unless there's an emergency. Girlfriend's dad's wedding won't cut it, I don't—" Alex cut himself off and broke into a smile at something behind me. "Hey, how are you?"

I turned and looked up. Josie.

There were some people, like Rebecca, who looked glamorous on social media and ordinary in real life. This wasn't true for

Josie. Or maybe it was because I'd only seen pictures of OWC Josie. Yeah, I could tell that girl was beautiful, but in a natural, outdoorsy kind of way. The girl standing beside our table was basically the opposite of summer camp Josie. Instead of a ponytail, her hair hung in loose, dark waves around her face, and almost immediately my attention went to her outfit. A loose cardigan over a cropped black top and short jean shorts. With her long legs and flat stomach on display, she looked like she was ready to shoot a music video.

I turned away, feeling dowdy in my running shorts and swim team tee.

"I thought it was you." Josie had a rich, warm voice. "What's up?"

"Enjoying some air-conditioning and eating something that's not a sandwich or a hot dog. What about you?"

"Same. I'm here with some girls from my church who I mentor." Josie pointed to a table on the other side of the restaurant. The table was full of giggly middle-school girls. "Audrey's family owns this place . . ."

"Wow. I'm amazed you do that on your day off." Alex's admiration made my stomach clench. He gestured to me. "This is Tessa. Tessa, this is Josie."

I managed to lift my gaze to look Josie in the face.

"Hi," she said with a smile. "Nice to meet you."

Because my throat was tight, my voice came out weird. "Yeah, same."

Josie turned her smile back to Alex. "I heard we both have groups of twelve next week."

Alex offered a good-natured groan. "Beth's heart is too huge. She can't seem to tell parents no."

I wanted to not notice that her legs went on for days and her toenails were painted a cheerful pink. Or that she had sounded warm and comfortable when talking to me, and I'd sounded stiff and awkward. Or that she looked like a pop star, and I looked like I was on my way to swim practice.

And if *I* couldn't help noticing, how would Alex not notice the disparity between us? Especially with Josie's bare midriff right at eye level?

"Well, see you Monday." Josie glanced at me. "Nice meeting you."

If I opened my mouth, I'd possibly start crying. "Mmhmm."

Josie turned and left. Was Alex watching her walk away? Was he looking at her longingly?

I peeked at him. He was gathering a bite of snow peas and beef on his fork.

"I'm amazed she's spending her Saturday like this," he said. "I'm sick of kids right now. But Josie's gifted with them. She wants to be a teacher to middle-school kids."

Amazing. Gifted. His tone was normal, but it felt like Alex was yelling at me about what an incredible person Josie was. Tears swelled behind my eyes. Or maybe not *behind* my eyes, because my plate of orange chicken had grown blurry.

"Tessa." Alex said my name low and warm, and it only made me want to cry harder. "What's wrong?"

I'm fine sat on the end of my tongue. I swallowed it down, but I couldn't think of any other way to answer.

"Tessa." He said my name even softer this time.

Was this the tone Alex would use when he broke up with me? He was a great guy. He wouldn't want to hurt my feelings. *Tessa, I'm so sorry to tell you this.* That's how he would start. How had my dad told my mom about Rebecca?

Alex reached across the table, as if to take my hand, but my hands were in my lap. "Is this about the wedding?"

I pressed my hands over my face. My cheeks were wet and probably lined with mascara. "I need to get out of here."

"Okay. I'll get to-go boxes. You can wait outside if you want."

134 || RIVERBEND FRIENDS

I didn't even respond. I grabbed my bag, and keeping my head down, rushed outside. In my imagination, Josie watched me leave with those Disney Princess sized eyes of hers. *She's no threat to me,* she'd be thinking. *All I have to do is tell Alex I'm interested.* Or maybe amazing, gifted Josie was so absorbed with her mentoring, she hadn't even noticed my exit.

Out on Main Street, I wiped under my eyes and paced the segment of sidewalk by Alex's car. I could survive a breakup. Hadn't I learned to live with Alex dating Leilani freshman year? If I could handle him being with a Hawaiian Barbie doll of a girlfriend, surely I could survive losing Alex to a Princess Jasmine look-alike. I was going to lose him to someone else eventually, right? Was there really a difference in losing him now to Josie than losing him months or years down the road to someone else?

Your thoughts are spiraling, the Kendra who now lived in my head told me. *We need to turn that around. What has God given you to control?*

"Not enough," I muttered to myself as I paced. "Not nearly enough."

"Hey."

I looked up to find Abraham walking by with Maxine. I wiped at my cheeks. "Hi, how are you?"

"Uh, better than you, it looks like." Abraham stopped and rolled Maxine's leash around his hand to keep her right beside him. "What's wrong?"

"Nothing, I'm fine."

Abraham chuckled. "Liar."

"It's not a big deal," I lied again. Maxine pawed at my leg, and I reached down to rub her head. "Shay will be jealous that I saw you, Maxine."

Abraham stepped closer and said quietly, "Seriously, what's going on with you? I've never seen you like this. Not even when your dad brought his new girlfriend to that swim meet."

"It's nothing," I said as Alex emerged from Fortune Wok with two plastic containers and our drinks in to-go cups. "Alex, you remember Abraham?"

Alex put on a polite smile. "Sure."

Abraham glanced between us; his eyes narrowed slightly.

Alex took my hand. "You ready?"

"Yeah." I smiled at Abraham without meeting his eyes. "See you Monday."

"See you, T."

Alex opened my door for me. "T?" he muttered. "Is your name too hard for him to pronounce?"

Inside Alex's car felt like a hot yoga studio. Even cranking the AC only blasted us with warm air.

"I'm thinking Founder's Park?" Alex said in a tight voice. "That okay?"

"Sure."

We rode in silence the few blocks there. Alex parked in a shady spot at the far end of the lot and rolled down all the Civic's windows before turning off the car. It was hot outside, but the shade and the breeze floating through the car made the temperature feel okay. And this was a lot more private than a park bench.

Alex handed me my to-go box and a plastic fork. "What happened?"

"Abraham was walking his dog. We'd been talking for less than a minute when you came out."

"I wasn't talking about that. I meant in the restaurant when you got upset and wanted to leave." Alex's hand closed around mine. "I want to understand what was going on."

Me too. I tried to sift through my swirl of thoughts.

"I mean . . . it was kind of like . . . it almost seemed as if you were jealous . . ." Alex trailed off.

I swallowed hard. "Yeah," I said, my eyes still shut. "I was. Or I am."

His hand squeezed mine. "But, Tessa, I've told you that you don't need to be. I'm not interested in Josie. She's nice. I like working with her. That's it."

I inhaled deeply. "If you *are* interested, it's okay. But I'd like to know now and get it over with."

The weight of his hand disappeared. Alex looked at me with a mix of bewilderment and something else I couldn't define. Something that had a sharp edge to it.

"'Get it over with?'" he echoed. "What's *it*?"

The part where you hurt me.

The words kept circling my head, but they felt too vulnerable to say. Why was I bracing for the impact of a breakup, despite Alex's insistence that he didn't like Josie?

"Do you believe me when I say that I'm not interested in her? You're the only girl I'm into, Tessa."

"For now," I whispered to my lap. "We both know these things can change. I mean, look at my parents."

In a quiet, steady voice, he said, "I'm *not* your dad. I will never do to you what your dad did."

A sob rushed out of me, and then another and another. They were so heavy, I could barely breathe. Because I knew Alex was right. This wasn't about him and kind, pretty Josie. This was about my dad. Or maybe about the realization that loving someone left me vulnerable. I couldn't control who Alex was attracted to, just like I couldn't control my dad picking Rebecca instead of my mom.

"I know you'd never *mean* to hurt me," I cried, taking the napkin Alex offered and wiped my nose. "But I don't think my dad meant to hurt us either. Yet here I am. Tired because his girlfriend felt like six thirty in the morning was a fine time to start hanging up pictures from a vacation that *I* was supposed to go on."

Alex's hand rested on the back of my neck. "I'll take you to Iceland."

His sweet, serious tone melted me. "Thank you." I leaned against him. "My mom and I are going to go. Someday."

"If that falls through, I'll take you."

Even though I was sweating from the heat, I let myself rest against Alex's shoulder for a few minutes. There was still something inside me that wanted to pull the plug on our relationship. Even though he was saying all the right things, even though I knew in my gut that Alex wouldn't lie to me, a tiny piece of me still thought that I could outsmart the pain of losing him if I ended things before he could.

Alex kissed the top of my head. "What was that sigh?"

"Just realizing that I'm a mess."

He chuckled. "Aren't we all?"

Chapter

15

It was only my second Sunday staying with Dad and Rebecca, but already I was noticing that Sundays had a different vibe than Fridays or Saturdays. By Sunday afternoon, we'd all run out of small talk and were ready for me to not be there anymore. *Maybe* Dad felt more conflicted and wanted me there, but Rebecca had been cranky all afternoon, and I assumed my presence was the reason. When Logan went down for his nap at three thirty, Rebecca claimed she had a headache and closed herself in their bedroom.

Dad smiled wearily at me. "Checkers?"

I wasn't in the mood, but it was still hours before I could leave. "Sure."

We were in the middle of our second game when Dad got a text. Because his phone was in the middle of the coffee table, it was easy for me to see the text was from Rebecca. All I could read was Just got off the phone with before Dad angled it away.

He frowned at his screen. "I'll be right back, pumpkin."

He disappeared down the hallway. I scrolled Instagram for a few minutes, and then decided it'd be better to spend my time working on my summer reading. I was behind and still had two books to read. In the room, as I rummaged through my backpack, Rebecca shouted, "But this is my wedding day, David! And she's ruining it!"

Me?

I moved to my doorway. I could hear Dad's tone of voice—steady and calm—but not his actual words.

"Does Rachel think I agree with every decision *she's* made?" Rebecca wasn't shouting anymore, but I had no problem hearing every word. "Of course not, but she's my sister. How dare she judge me. Judge *us*."

Okay, *not* about me, thankfully.

This time I could hear Dad. "I understand your feelings are hurt, but we don't want her at the wedding if she doesn't support us, right? We don't need that."

Now Rebecca's voice dipped too low for me to hear. As did Dad's response. After another minute of their quiet conversation, I tiptoed back to the living room and sat on the couch with my battered copy of Toni Morrison's *Beloved*.

On the end table was Rebecca's wedding planning binder, labeled *The Simmons-Hart Wedding* in fancy script. I'd seen the binder lying around the house, as well as pictures Rebecca had posted on Instagram weeks ago. (Complete with links to print out my own wedding planning templates. Eye roll.)

I peeked inside the cover and found neatly divided sections for florals, food, seating arrangements, and so forth. I hadn't realized the wedding was going to be *that* big of a deal. Stuck to the inside cover was a pink Post-it full of to-dos. Everything was crossed out except two things: *Talk to Rachel. Matron of Honor?* and *Tessa?*

I closed the binder and picked up my novel. I'd be pushed for my answer soon, probably. Rachel's picture was on the wall in the guest room. She looked like Rebecca, only she didn't smile as broadly. There was something in her expression that made me think she wasn't someone I wanted to mess with, but maybe that was her Air Force uniform.

By the time Dad returned, I had read two chapters.

"Sorry about that." He glanced from our game to the clock on the mantel. "Rebecca's feeding Logan now. I think I'd better start dinner."

I tried to not sound too hopeful as I asked, "Would it be better for me to go?"

"No, not at all, Tessa." He gave me a strained smile. "We'll eat dinner as planned."

"Okay. I can help."

There wasn't much to do. Dinner was a bagged salad and pasta with jarred pesto. Growing up, Dad had a few meals that he made—anything on the grill, pancakes, and tacos—but Mom did everything else. It was strange how at Rebecca's house, so far Dad seemed to be in charge of food.

By the time dinner was on the table, Rebecca had emerged with Logan. Her eyes were red and puffy, but it was helpful to know that it wasn't about me. Even still, I was ready to get out of there. I took small helpings of pasta and salad so I could eat faster. I could snack at home later.

Rebecca had left to change Logan's diaper and I had shoved my last bite of pasta into my mouth when Dad said, "Oh, Tessa, have you decided about the wedding? We need to measure you for your dress."

Thankfully my last bite had been a big one.

I gestured that I needed a minute, then chewed and chewed while my brain grasped for the best response. Should I say I didn't feel comfortable being in the wedding? Did I need to say that I disapproved or was that vindictive?

I swallowed and took a drink of water. Then another. I had to give a reason for why I was available to attend but not participate, didn't I?

"If you don't want to do it, you don't have to," Dad said in a gentle voice.

My glass was empty, otherwise I would've taken another drink. I pushed a shred of lettuce on my plate. "I don't want to," I said quietly.

"Okay." Despite what Dad had said, the word dripped with disappointment. "I understand."

"Okay," I said to my plate.

In my peripheral vision, I watched him poke at his dinner. "Is it . . . um. Did your mom . . ." He cleared his throat. "Why don't you want to, if you don't mind me asking?"

Surely it wasn't that hard for him to discern why I didn't want to be in the wedding. "Well. I mean, you are marrying the woman that you abandoned our family for . . ."

Why did *I* feel so uncomfortable? *I* didn't do anything wrong.

"Ah." Dad arranged his fork alongside his plate. Tweaked his water glass. "I guess I can understand why you'd view the situation that way."

I bit my lower lip, but the words popped out anyway. "You were married to Mom. You decided you wanted to be with Rebecca instead. How is there a different way to view this than you leaving us?"

"We don't need to discuss this anymore." Dad pushed back from the table. "Your no is sufficient."

He picked up his half-full plate and carried it to the trash can.

I pushed back from the table too. "Oh, I see," I said to his back. "You don't actually want to know how I feel."

"I'm saying it doesn't need to be discussed." Dad's words were stiff and cold. "There's no point."

"No point?" I scoffed. "You know, I'm in *therapy* because of what you did. Yesterday, I completely freaked out on Alex because

I'm convinced he's going to cheat on me. Not because of who he is, but because of who *you* are—"

Dad turned and speared me with a glare. "That's enough, Tessa."

I shook my head in disgust. "Good talk, Dad."

I turned and stormed through the living room, where Rebecca stood holding Logan. He grinned and flailed at the sight of me, a stark juxtaposition to the way Rebecca was skewering me with her narrowed eyes. I felt a wild urge to flip her off—which was crazy because I'd never flipped anyone off. I clenched my fingers into fists instead.

My swim and duffel bags were packed and waiting on the bed, like they had been since lunch. I grabbed them and stomped out the door without saying goodbye.

My brief drive home was spent rewinding and replaying the argument. Well, was it an "argument" when one of you talked and the other shut you down? And I'd have to see Rebecca tomorrow when I went over to babysit. Ugh.

I wanted to talk to Mom about what had happened, but she would probably be in a funky mood. She had been the last time I'd spent the weekend at Dad's.

As I parked my Camry in the driveway, a text came from Izzy.

Any luck with Amelia yet? I saw her today, but she refused to talk about you.

I blinked rapidly at the text. Amelia refused to talk about me?

I've sent her a ridiculous number of apology texts. I typed so fast and angry that I had to correct nearly every word. **I don't have the energy to keep chasing her.**

I shoved open the car door and slammed it shut. I grabbed my bags from the back seat and slammed that door too. I was sorry for what I'd said—I truly was—but Amelia needed to wake up and realize she wasn't the only one having a less-than-stellar summer.

My phone buzzed with Izzy's reply. **Don't give up!**

I hooked one bag over my left shoulder and one over my right so I could reply.

If we don't have the kind of friendships where we can make mistakes and be forgiven, then what are we even doing?

I jammed my phone into my back pocket and marched inside.

The smell of the house—rich and buttery—reminded me that I was still hungry. Mom's music was loud . . . or at least I thought it was her music. I had never, ever heard her listen to country before.

I lowered my bags to the floor and walked around the entry stairs. Last time I came home from Dad and Rebecca's, Mom had been in her yoga pants eating frozen pizza with the Property Brothers. Tonight, Mom's hair was up in an artfully messy top knot, and she wore a polka-dotted apron over her clothes. Which looked like clothes she would wear out of the house. She diced bright green chives and hummed to the music.

When she caught sight of me, she beamed. "Oh, hi! I didn't hear you." She turned the volume down on the Bluetooth speaker. "Did you just get home?"

"Yep." My phone buzzed in my pocket. Probably Izzy's response. "What are you doing?"

"Making dinner. I was in a cooking mood. We have shrimp roasting in the oven, brown butter mashed potatoes in the mixer, and an arugula salad in the fridge. Sound good?"

"Yeah." My gaze drifted to the speaker where a man's twangy voice mourned his childhood being over. "What's with the music?"

"I know. Not my normal tunes." Mom laughed and tucked a nonexistent strand of hair behind her ear. "Phil said he liked this album. So I'm trying something new."

Phil.

The combination of Mom's lipstick, fancy food, and open

mind about music had me feeling suspicious and irritable. "I'm going to go put my stuff away."

"Okay, dinner will be ready in a few!" Mom called after me.

I tromped upstairs and threw my bags on my floor. I should unpack them, but my room was still a mess of boxes anyway. What did it matter? I flopped onto my bed and pulled up Izzy's message.

I know you're feeling frustrated, and I get it. But I think she's feeling so down on herself. Yeah, she's being stubborn, but I think you should overlook it and keep trying. IMO.

Followed by a kiss-blowing emoji.

I wasn't even going to respond to that. How come all these people—Amelia, my dad, Rebecca, Mrs. Hastings—were acting like babies, and I was expected to suck it up and be the bigger, more adult person? When did I get to throw a tantrum and have everyone else cater to me and what I wanted?

I was still lying on my bed a few minutes later, staring up at the popcorn ceiling, when Mom called, "Tessa, dinner!"

I dragged myself out of bed and clomped downstairs. The music was now Ella Fitzgerald, and there was something weirdly settling about that scrap of normality.

My stomach growled as I scooped bright pink shrimp onto my plate. "How was your weekend?"

"Great! Phil got the lights installed upstairs this afternoon and the space looks awesome!"

The cute outfit and bright eyes made a little more sense now. As did the meal. Did a woman naturally grow a desire to cook nice meals and make herself look pretty when she noticed someone she wanted to attract?

Mom drizzled salad dressing over her greens. "After dinner, you'll have to come up to the attic and see. You won't believe what a difference the lights make."

For the second time in an hour, I sat down for dinner. The

mashed potatoes tasted incredible. Even if Phil was the reason for the gourmet dinner, I could maybe be okay with that.

"Dinner's really good," I said.

Mom beamed at me. "Thanks, honey. How were things at your dad's this weekend?"

"Not great. We fought as I was leaving."

Mom frowned. "What about?"

"He asked me to be in the wedding, and I told him no."

Her frown deepened. "Why would he have thought you'd say yes?"

I snorted a laugh. "I have no idea. He said it wasn't a big deal, but he was obviously upset. And then when I tried to explain why, he got defensive and shut the conversation down."

"I'm not surprised. Your dad struggles to have conversations when he's in the wrong." Mom collected a variety of greens on her fork. "He's a bit like you in that regard."

Irritation flared to life in my chest. "What do you mean he's like me in that regard?"

"When he's wrong about something, he tends to shut down and get defensive. That's all I was—"

"And you think I do that?"

"Tessa, honey." Mom gave me an affectionate smile. "I love you, but yes, you definitely do that. You *are* his daughter, you know. You have many similarities."

I wanted to push back and leave the table but remembered my dad doing the same thing to me probably no more than thirty minutes ago.

I swallowed hard and made my body stay in my seat. "I would *never* do what he did and betray my family. Never."

"Baby." Mom reached for my hand, and it took every ounce of my self-control to not defiantly pull away. "Of course you wouldn't. But I think it's important that you understand your dad and I didn't have a great marriage."

My stomach twisted into a hard knot. "That doesn't excuse what he did."

"Of course not. What he did to us was completely wrong. I made mistakes too—"

"There's a huge difference between 'making mistakes' and 'cheating on your wife.'"

Mom nodded. "Yes, Tessa, I agree. And I wish things hadn't happened the way they did, especially for your sake. But I feel awakened to how God works things out for our good. *All* things. I think even in this, He'll work everything out for my good and your good. Maybe your dad's good too."

"How can you possibly want things to work out for his good?" My hands trembled, and I laid my fork down on my plate. "After what he did to us?"

"Don't get me wrong, there's certainly a part of me that would relish everything falling apart for him and Rebecca. But I used to feel that way *all* the time, and now it's more like 50 percent of the time. Maybe I'm getting tired of clinging to my victim status." Mom shook her head. "For whatever reason, I can see now that I share some blame and that neither of us was genuinely happy."

"*I* was happy," I said, my voice strangled with unshed tears.

Mom reached for my hand again, but this time I pulled away. "I know you were, Tessa. My first choice would've been to fix the marriage, but I wasn't given that option. So now the choice before me is to either hold on to what happened or to let it go as best I can and look for how God is going to move."

A wild, restless energy pulsed through me, and I pushed back from our tiny table. "You're saying all this because of Phil."

Mom's mouth fell open. "That's absolutely not true—"

"Oh, really? Then it's a coincidence that suddenly you're talking about how you weren't genuinely happy with Dad anyway? How God's going to work it out for your good the same day a nice, single man comes over to help you around the house? Kind of sounds like a first date to me."

Mom's jaw clenched and then released. "That is uncalled for."

"Whatever."

I marched up the stairs to my bedroom and slammed the door. I intended to blare NF's "Leave Me Alone" and flop onto my bed, but I was too amped for that. Instead, I paced what little floor space I had as my thoughts spiraled all over the place.

The feeling in my chest was like that time after a swim meet when I couldn't find my parents. It had happened ages ago, before I had a phone, and as swimmers disappeared with their parents and the aquatic center emptied, I'd wondered why mine hadn't come for me yet. Had they left already? Without me? It was one of the few times in my life that I'd felt abandoned.

Dad could marry someone else. He *would* marry someone else in a few weeks. He'd have a new wife. A new family. And Mom would likely remarry. Maybe not Phil, but somebody. She probably wouldn't have any more kids, but she would still have a new husband, a new family. But I didn't have that option. I couldn't get new parents and rebuild my family the way they could. My family was broken forever, and it would never be whole again.

Chapter

16

THE TEXT FROM DAD WAS THERE WHEN I woke up in the morning.

No need to come today. Rebecca isn't feeling well and will stay home.

That was odd, especially considering that her health seemed totally fine over the weekend, but I didn't mind a break from being at their house. When my last kid was picked up from swim lessons, I headed to my car feeling achy from the morning's exertion but also elated as I considered the unexpectedly free afternoon that stretched before me. Maybe I could finally unpack my bedroom.

As I walked to my car, I scrolled Instagram. Amelia's latest post promoted *Annie*. I double-tapped to like it. Should I comment, too? That seemed weird considering she was freezing me out. I wanted to mend things. If I wasn't watching Logan this afternoon, I could go to the Bryans' instead and see if Amelia would talk to me. Knocking on her door would be harder for her to ignore than a text.

I was about to put my phone away when I noticed Rebecca's latest post. The picture had the warm tint of an older photo. It was a formal dance picture from high school, and Rebecca looked to be channeling Rachel from *Friends*, from the haircut to the dress to the smirky smile she was giving the photographer. At first, I didn't recognize the guy who had his arms draped around her, and then I realized with a jolt that it was my dad.

He had all his hair still, coffee brown like mine, and he looked strange without his glasses. Dad's smile hung the same way, but the suit didn't. He was tall and lanky in high school, and it was strange seeing him cuddly with not-my-mom.

I braved reading Rebecca's caption:

I stumbled upon this photo last night and it melted me. Look how cute my guy and I are! This was our senior prom, and in a couple months I would make the dumbest mistake of my life and break up with him. I thought I was doing the right thing. We were going to different colleges, and I thought this way we'd be able to focus on our futures as individuals.

But my choice broke both our hearts and cost us years of happiness together. In nineteen days, I have the chance to say "I do" and undo that mistake I made at eighteen. We'll never be able to erase all the misery of being apart for so long or the negative consequences of my choice, but God is so good, and we'll finally get the happily ever after we should've had twenty-five years ago.

I reread her caption several times, my heart pounding more incessantly with each pass. At some point, I had stopped walking to my car.

The negative consequences of her choice? Like *me*? She would prefer I not exist. Maybe that was fair. After all, I'd prefer *she* not exist. But I wasn't thoughtless enough to post about it on social media.

I jammed my phone in my back pocket and made a beeline

for my car. I tucked myself inside and started the engine but then sat there. My throat was tight with unshed tears as I dwelled on Rebecca's confident smirk, like she'd known even as a high-school senior that she'd ultimately win. Not only had she broken his heart a couple months later, but then years later, she'd shattered his family and had the gall to say how good God was for giving her a happily ever after.

Where was my mom's happily ever after?

Knock, knock, knock.

I jumped at the rapping on my passenger window. Abraham. He smiled at me and popped open the passenger door.

"You scared me," I said.

"Sorry about that. You okay?"

"Yes, I'm fine."

He slid into the passenger seat without an invitation. "Really? Because you're sitting in your car and scowling."

"I'm fine. I finished up lessons and was . . ." My hand fluttered as I searched for the right word. "Thinking. What are you doing here?"

"I'm pretty sure I left my phone in the locker room. At least that's what I'm hoping, because I can't find it."

"Oh, okay. Well, good luck."

I released the parking brake and put my hand on the shifter, hoping this was enough to indicate that I was done with this conversation.

Abraham studied me; his head tilted slightly. "I'm worried about you, T. Every time I see you these days, you look upset."

I put on a smile. "Not true. You saw me at practice this morning."

Abraham didn't smile back. "Is it your boyfriend?"

"No. Alex and I are great."

"Because when I saw you on Saturday, things looked not-so-great."

I'd forgotten about that. "That was because . . ." I struggled for the right phrasing. *Because I was freaking out that he was interested in Josie* wouldn't send the message that everything was "great" between Alex and me. "That wasn't about Alex. We're fine."

His eyebrows arched. "Fine? What happened to 'great'?"

I rolled my eyes. "Don't you have somewhere to be?"

"I'm just saying, if he's not treating you well, there's no reason to put up with that."

I looked away. Even though I knew Abraham was a player, it was hard to not feel flattered by his concern. To feel a zip of connection. Of attraction. "Alex treats me *great*." I punched the word. "I wasn't upset because of him on Saturday, and I'm not upset because of him now. Okay?"

Abraham chuckled. "You're a terrible liar, T. And this is why I don't do serious relationships. Not worth the trouble."

I leaned back and leveled an assessing look at him. "That makes no sense."

"I think what *you're* doing makes no sense. Handing all that power to someone else? No, thank you. I start things. I end things. Total control."

"You've never had a girl break up with you?"

"Nope. I keep things as casual as I can, so there's no breaking up involved. I stop responding to texts or ignore their hints about wanting to get together again."

Even the teeny-tiny bit of attraction I'd felt for him vanished. "That sounds like a sad way to go through life, Abraham."

He snorted. "Sorry, but which one of us was crying on Main Street on Saturday?"

"I'm not saying having a serious boyfriend makes me happy all the time. Yeah, sometimes we have problems, but at least it's a real relationship."

Abraham raised his hands, as if surrendering. "That's fine if it works for you. You have your real relationship. I'll keep my total control."

"But it isn't total control," I argued. "Because you can't control how they feel, right? Not every girl you're interested in is going to be interested back. Hasn't that ever happened to you? You like a girl but she's oblivious that you exist?"

"I like to think it's impossible to be oblivious of my existence."

I rolled my eyes. "Of course you do, but I'm saying there's only so much in our control. Even when you like somebody, they may not like you back. They're never going to like you back and you have no power to change that."

"Ouch, Tessa." Abraham feigned that I'd wounded him by placing a hand over his heart. "I get it. You don't like me back."

I groaned. Of course he'd make a big joke out of our serious conversation. "Whatever. Go find your phone."

Abraham laughed and put a foot outside my car. "If you decide you want to talk, you know where I am."

"I'm fine, thanks."

I shifted my car into drive as soon as he closed the door. Once I was sure I wouldn't run over his foot, I pulled out of the spot. My stomach had a sloshy, guilty feeling. Maybe because I thought Abraham's lifestyle was morally wrong . . . and yet I understood the appeal. After Alex and I had resolved the Josie issue on Saturday, hadn't I felt that temptation to end things anyway? Not because I wanted my relationship with Alex to be over, but because I wanted the control.

God, I'm a mess, I confessed with a groan. Instead of pulling all the way out of the parking lot, I grabbed my phone and after a moment's hesitation, I called Shay.

"Hey, Tessa," she answered, sounding surprised.

"Could I come talk to you about something or are you at work?"

"Yes to both. I'm getting ready to groom Blaze. Something wrong?"

"I'll tell you when I get there."

———∿———

The barn smelled like manure. Which made sense, being a barn and all, but I hadn't expected the aroma to be so strong. Shay stood in the aisle with some kind of specialized brush, rubbing down a large reddish-brown horse that was strapped into position for grooming. Shay had a content smile on her face, but this was about the closest I'd ever been to a horse, and I felt nervous.

"It sounds to me like Rebecca is trying to justify the whole situation," Shay said as she worked the brush thing in a circular motion. She seemed unperturbed by how much dust the brushing stirred up. "Like, 'We were supposed to be together and that's why this is all okay.' I think she feels guilty for what happened."

"But she's always going on about how obviously God is blessing them. I don't think she sees anything wrong with what they did."

Shay cocked her head at me. "You don't think maybe she keeps going on about God's blessings *because* she feels like she did something wrong? Like she's trying to pretty everything up?"

I frowned and considered this. "I suppose it's possible. But if I was in her situation, I wouldn't be posting about how miserable they'd both been and how bad the consequences were if the dude had a whole other family. It's not like my dad was crying all the time because of her, right? Otherwise, he and my mom would've never fallen in love and gotten married." My mind flitted to Mom's confession the night before, how they hadn't been happy in a long time. "Right?"

"I don't know. I wasn't there." Shay sidestepped to a new section and resumed brushing. "I'm sure it wasn't all miserable. You're here, after all."

"Oh, ew, Shay. Don't go there."

She blinked at me and then reddened. "I didn't mean *that.* Gross. I meant that I'm sure both your parents are happy to have

you even if the marriage overall wasn't happy. Which I'm not saying it wasn't. I don't know."

The horse studied me with one of his big eyeballs. I leaned
back, even though I knew it was impossible for him to reach me.

"I feel like he's going to bite me."

Shay giggled. "How would George possibly bite you? Besides,
he's a sweetheart and you're not an apple."

Elsewhere in the barn, a horse whinnied.

"Hi, Ava," Shay called in a gentle voice. "Don't worry, you're
next."

There were at least a dozen horses in here. How could Shay tell
that whinny belonged to Ava?

"You're really good at this," I said.

She grinned and shrugged. "Yeah, I know."

The barn was clearly her happy place, same as the pool was
mine, the kitchen was Izzy's, and the stage was Amelia's. Only the
stage didn't get to be pure happiness for Amelia, did it? Recently, it
brought insecurity instead, as she faced the fact that she might not
get to occupy it the way she wanted to. She'd been so deliriously
happy after *Peter Pan* was over. She'd had the thrill of performing
one night when Teresa was sick, the joy of succeeding as stage
manager, and the hope that all of it would make a difference this
summer when she auditioned for *Annie*.

And yet here she was again, shunned from the spotlight. Which
I'd thoughtlessly called attention to in a moment of frustration.

"Have you talked to Amelia recently?"

Shay paused brushing for a moment. "Yeah. Last night."

I felt a twinge of envy. Shay was so easy to get along with.
Unless you were hurting horses or pushing some specific buttons
of hers, she was chill. Why couldn't I be more like that? Did I have
even an ounce of "chill" in me?

"I've texted her so many times, but she isn't responding. I'm
thinking about going over to her house this afternoon."

Shay's circular brushing paused. "I think that would be effective."

"You don't think she'll slam the door in my face?"

"No." Shay gave me a sympathetic look. "Amelia likes big gestures like that, whether she realizes it or not."

"Guess I'll head over there then."

"Sorry you have a lot of hard relationships right now." Shay resumed brushing. "You should consider a pet. They're much easier than people."

I snorted. "Yeah, maybe."

At the rate I was going, Kendra and I might need to meet *two* times a week.

—◌◌◌—

The Bryans' house was in a comfortable, established neighborhood with lots of minivans parked in driveways. The houses weren't old enough to be charming or broken down, and even when they were first built, I doubted the neighborhood had been flashy. They'd probably always been common-sense houses for practical, Honda-driving families.

I hadn't spent much time at Amelia's house, but according to her, their place was a revolving door of church members from River of Life Community Church. They came for Bible study, for counseling, and probably other things too. I liked Mr. and Mrs. Bryan okay, but I also felt uneasy around them. Amelia once told me they thought those who got divorced did so because it was "easiest" and that there was "never" a good reason. I understood black-and-white thinking like this—I used to have the privilege of thinking of life the same way—but some of us had to live in the gray whether we wanted to or not.

As I walked up the driveway, I wondered which of her neighbor's houses belonged to Josie. My money was on the extra cute white one with the bright red door.

I forced my focus off Josie and back to rehearsing what I was going to say to Amelia.

Mrs. Bryan answered the door with a pleasant smile. "Oh, hello. It's Teresa, isn't it? How are you, dear?"

"Uh . . ." Should I correct her? "I'm good. Thank you."

"Come on in." She stepped back from the doorway. "Are you here to see Millie?"

Well, Mrs. Bryan was now oh-for-two on our names, though in fairness to her, Amelia had gone by Millie until sophomore year of high school. A lot of people still called her Millie, just not people who cared about what she wanted.

"Yeah, is she around?"

"She is." Mrs. Bryan turned and called up the short staircase that led to the bedrooms. "Millie? Teresa's here to see you!"

Yikes, that was awkward. I should've corrected her about my name.

She smiled placidly at me. "How's your summer going?"

"Fine, thanks." I shifted my weight. No sign of Amelia approaching. "How about you?"

"It's been nice. Kind of different. Last summer we were planning Josh's wedding and Maggie was home. This summer, Josh is married and Maggie stayed in Bloomington for an internship."

"Mmm," I said, unsure of how to reply.

We looked at each other for an uncomfortable moment.

"It's sure been warm out," Mrs. Bryan added. "I saw the heat index is supposed to be over a hundred on Saturday."

"Yeah, it'll be really hot."

This was the smallest of small talk. I glanced up the stairs and Mrs. Bryan did the same.

"She might have her headphones on," she said. "I'll go check."

I released a breath I hadn't realized I was holding and listened as Mrs. Bryan walked down the hall and rapped on Amelia's door. "Millie?" Her voice was pleasant, but in a way that made me wonder if that tone was because of me. After a few seconds, she rapped louder on the door and said a louder, "Millie?"

"What?" Amelia's voice carried easily.

"Teresa's here to see you."

"Who?"

I could feel my face turning red. Geez, this was awkward.

"Teresa? Your friend from school?"

"Okay . . ." Amelia said, clearly having no idea who her mom was talking about. Maybe that would work in my favor. Maybe Amelia wouldn't have come down for Tessa but would come down for mystery Teresa.

The door opened. My heart clattered in my chest as Amelia's footsteps drew nearer.

When she saw me, she burst into laughter. "Mom! It's *Tessa*." Amelia rolled her eyes at me. "The only Teresa I could think of was from *Peter Pan*, and I couldn't figure out why she'd be showing up at my house."

"Oh." Mrs. Bryan laughed awkwardly, her cheeks pink. "I'm so sorry."

"It's fine," I said.

Her mistake was possibly a blessing. It was hard to imagine another scenario in which Amelia saw me in her entryway and actually smiled.

"C'mon up to my room," Amelia said as she turned.

I slipped past Mrs. Bryan with a smile and followed Amelia down the hall.

Her room was very Amelia. There was lots of stuff everywhere and zero color coordination. She had posters for *Hamilton*, *Dear Evan Hansen*, *Newsies*, and *Wicked* taped to her walls and a bookshelf that was home to an odd assortment of playbills and devotionals.

She sat in her desk chair and cleared a spot on the edge of her bed for me. "Sorry about my mom. I talk about you girls all the time, so she should know your name. It's so typical of her to not pay attention."

I shrugged. "It was a mistake."

"It's a pattern." Amelia said, unyielding. "Her mind is always somewhere else when I'm talking to her. She probably thinks my best friends are Teresa, Sasha, and . . . I can't think of a replacement for Izzy."

"Lizzie?" I offered.

Amelia laughed. "Yes, Lizzie."

"And you're still Millie, I noticed."

Amelia pushed back against her desk chair, and it gave a loud squeak of protest. "Forever. I will forever be Millie to her."

"That could be the name of your one-woman show on Broadway someday." I offered a tentative smile. "Forever Millie."

Her own smile turned strained, then wobbled. She gave a humorless laugh and looked away. "Yeah, right."

"Amelia, I am so sorry about what I said." My words emerged shaky from nerves, but I pressed on. I did *not* want to be like my dad and be unable to admit when I'd done something wrong. "It was a thoughtless, stupid comment, and I regretted it as soon as it came out of my mouth."

Amelia nodded but kept her gaze on her hands. "But you weren't wrong. I'm *not* in the show."

"That's Aspire's loss," I said fiercely. "I mean it. You're an amazing actress. I thought you were a better Mrs. Darling than Teresa the night you subbed in."

Amelia's smile hung appreciative but unconvinced. "That's because you're my friend."

"No, it's because you're *really* good. I was shocked when you didn't get a part in *Annie*, because I don't understand why they can't see what I see."

"My audition wasn't very good," Amelia said with a resigned

sigh. "I thought this time I wouldn't be so nervous, but I was, and it showed."

I thought about what Izzy would do if she were here and reached across the gap to hug Amelia. It felt a little weird.

Amelia sniffled against my shoulder. "It seems like everybody else is so successful at what they love to do, and I'm not."

I pulled back. "When you say 'everybody' who do you mean?"

"You, Izzy, and Shay."

"So, us three? We're everybody?"

Amelia chuckled. "Yes. Y'all are 'everybody' in my world."

"Okay. But how are we 'so successful' at what we love?" I leaned back, relaxing now that the conversation had steered toward logic and away from hugs. This I could do. "Because I don't see that."

Amelia fluttered her hands. "Let's start with you. You're such a good swimmer."

"Thank you, but I'm not the best or the fastest or anything. I didn't even make the podium at state."

"But you got to go to state. That's success on its own."

"I did go to state," I admitted. "I was middle of the pack in most of my heats. I DQ-ed on my breaststroke. Does that sound successful to you?"

Amelia rolled her eyes. "Okay, look at Izzy."

"Okay," I said slowly. "Let's look at Izzy."

"She's such a good baker."

"That's true."

"Those cupcakes she made on my birthday with the opera glasses? Ah-mazing. Or did you see her *Hamilton* cupcakes on YouTube last week? She's so gifted."

"She is," I agreed. "But how does that make her more successful than you? Because I watched you do incredible things on stage all year long. It's no different. It's not like Izzy is some teen baking celebrity. She's doing what she loves right where she is, same as the rest of us."

"Shay has that great job at the barn," Amelia said with a sigh. "Great for *her*, I mean. The owner keeps giving her more and more responsibility because she's so good with the horses."

"Amelia, you're stage director and understudy. That's a lot of responsibility that they gave you. And they gave it to you because *you're* so good."

"I wanted this audition to go better." Amelia plucked at the hem of her Ramones T-shirt. "How am I going to show my parents that this is a legitimate career path if I can't even get a small part?"

"I think you're putting too much pressure on yourself. You have lots of time," I said. "We're heading into junior year. I have no idea what I want to do when I grow up. A lot of us don't know."

"Maybe you're right," Amelia said slowly. "Mom and Dad were so complimentary when I got to play Mrs. Darling that night. So, when I got the email from Mrs. Taylor asking me to be a stage manager again . . . they don't get it. They don't understand theater at all."

"Well, they're parents. I think 'not getting it' comes with the job."

Amelia laughed, and then picked at her already chipping nail polish. "Thanks for coming over. I know you've tried to reach out a couple times and I ignored you."

"You felt hurt. Understandably. I get it."

Amelia heaved a sigh. "Yeah, I know, but still. Shay laid into me a little bit last night, saying you're going through stuff, too, like your dad getting married again, and I blew it off." Amelia peeked at me from under her lashes. "I'm sorry too."

"It was fine. I didn't handle things great either."

Amelia flung her arms around me and released a relieved breath. "I'm so glad you're my friend."

The hug didn't feel so bad this time. I even squeezed back. "Same to you."

Chapter

17

WHEN MY PHONE BUZZED AND Dad's picture lit up my screen, my instinct was to let the call go to voicemail. It had been a little over twenty-four hours since our fight, and I'd already mended one relationship today. *C'mon, God, that's enough for one day. Right?*

But I was sitting on the back patio painting my toenails. Not answering the call now only delayed the problem.

"Help me, Jesus," I murmured before tapping the green phone icon. "Hi, Dad."

"Hi, Tessa. How are you?" he asked in a brisk voice. Like we were colleagues passing in the hallway.

"Fine. You?"

"Good. I'm calling to let you know that we do need you to come tomorrow to watch Logan."

"Okay." I should ask how Rebecca was feeling. That would be the polite response. After debating a few seconds, all I tacked on was, "I'll be there."

There was a lull. I pulled the phone away from my ear to be sure the call was still connected. It was. "Well . . . bye."

"Actually, I have something else to discuss with you."

Of course he did. I dipped the brush into the cheery pink polish to start my second coat. "Okay."

"Last night, what you said was pretty hurtful to both me and Rebecca."

I waited for Dad to elaborate, to specify what was hurtful or maybe to say something about understanding why I was upset. He didn't. "Okay."

"I thought by now, things would be better. I thought you would've gotten over what happened."

My jaw clenched as I efficiently and evenly ran the brush over my big toenail. "I see. What you're saying is that you think less than a year is sufficient time for me to have gotten over you cheating on my mom and having a baby with your high-school girlfriend?"

"I understand that this has been a big change, and there's a lot to adjust to. I'm not saying that it shouldn't bother you at all. I'm saying that you still seem very angry."

Was he expecting some sort of apology from me because I still had strong feelings about what had happened? Because I was not apologizing for that.

"That's true," I said after a lengthy silence. "I am still angry."

"That's fine, but, Tessa, if the fit you threw Sunday night was an attempt to keep the wedding from happening, that's not going to work."

"A fit?" I echoed with a harsh bark of a laugh. "That's an exaggeration. And no, I didn't have some grand scheme. I was answering your question about why I don't want to be in the wedding."

"Okay." The word sounded dismissive. "If I'd realized you were still struggling so much, I wouldn't have asked you to watch Logan this summer."

"I like watching Logan." My words came out stiff. "But if you'd rather I not, that's fine too."

I'd earn my Iceland money in a less emotional way, thank you very much.

"I'm not saying that because we want to change things. And you do a great job with Logan. It's not that."

So, what was it? Did they want my blessing on their marriage? Because that wasn't going to happen, and I'd never done a single thing to indicate that it would.

My phone beeped with an incoming call. Alex.

"Dad, I got to go. I'll be there tomorrow."

"Okay. I love—"

I took a perverse satisfaction in ending the call before he'd finished.

—⁓—

Please come 15 minutes early. Thank you.

By the time I got back to the locker room where my phone was—and where Rebecca's curt text was waiting for me—it was eleven thirty. She always acted like I had complete control over my arrival time, no matter how many times I told her that I couldn't leave until all my swim lesson kiddos were picked up.

My last kid was just picked up. I'll get changed and head your way as soon as I can.

"Like I always do," I muttered as I headed for the showers.

I pulled up in front of Dad and Rebecca's on time. When Rebecca answered the door, her smile was full but lacked warmth. The house was quiet.

"Hi, Tessa. Come on in."

I stepped inside, dropped my bag to its usual spot in the entry, and slipped out of my flip-flops. The air-conditioning made me shiver because I hadn't taken the time to dry myself off well.

"Logan's sleeping," Rebecca said in a hushed voice, "but I wanted to have a talk before I leave for my class."

A talk? That didn't sound great. "Okay," I said with a casualness I didn't feel.

I followed Rebecca into the living room. She had on a long floral skirt and a ruffled sleeveless shirt, both of which I could imagine Ms. Larkin wearing. She sat primly on the couch, and I perched on the edge of an armchair. The wedding binder was on the coffee table between us. Had she crossed me off her list on Sunday?

"I feel like it would be beneficial for us to discuss some of the things you said Sunday night." Rebecca gazed at me with an expression that I imagined she used in parent-teacher conferences. The your-kid-is-a-pain kind of conferences.

She didn't expect me to start, did she? "Okay." I rubbed the goose bumps on my arms. "Sure."

"I know you and your dad talked some last night, but . . ." Rebecca didn't finish her sentence. Instead, she gave me that I'm-concerned-and-caring smile. I instinctively almost smiled back. "You know, your father and I have known each other for a very long time. We were high-school sweethearts."

What, exactly, was she hoping I'd say to that? "I know."

Rebecca tucked a nonexistent strand of hair behind her ear. "We dated for two years in high school. The only reason we broke up was because we were headed to different colleges."

Again, she looked at me as if expecting a response. "Uh, yeah. I know. I saw your post."

Rebecca blinked rapidly, her confusion obvious.

Seriously? That post had *wrecked* me yesterday, and she didn't know what I was talking about? There was an edge in my voice as I said, "The dance picture you posted on Instagram. The one where you said I was a negative consequence of you breaking up with my father?"

Rebecca laughed, but it was forced and uncomfortable. "Oh, Tessa, I never said you were a negative consequence."

Did she *laugh* at that? "You absolutely did. Should we read it together?"

She uncrossed and recrossed her legs, the concerned-but-caring teacher face gone. "You seem intent on making me the bad guy in this situation—"

I huffed a disbelieving laugh. "Who do you think is the bad guy? My mom?"

Her face flushed, but she took several breaths before saying calmly, "Nobody needs to be the bad guy. There's no need to blame anybody. It's time for all of us to move on."

Immature responses bounced on my tongue, eager to escape. *I hate you. You're an idiot. I hope my dad leaves you like he left my mom. I hope you have to figure out how to "move on."*

Instead, I repeated the words softly, looking at my lap. "Move. On." They were laughable words coming from her, so why did they make me want to cry?

"Yes. I think it'd be so good for all of us. I know you have a serious boyfriend. As hard as it may be to believe, you may be in my position someday."

My jaw tensed as I glared at the goose bumps dotting my legs.

"Say Alex broke up with you, and you were heartbroken, but you decided to move on with your life. And you started dating someone else. Things were fine, but not like they were with Alex. Well, say Alex became an option again. Is it so hard to imagine that in that situation, you'd realize that you'd never gotten over him? Or that, by trying to start a relationship with someone else, you'd veered from the path God had intended for you all along. In that situation, would Alex *really* be the bad guy?"

I looked up from my knees to Rebecca's face. She peered at me with such confidence, her lies and justifications filling her with a false self-righteousness. What could one say in the face of such gross delusion? That she would dare to minimize the sins she and my dad had committed to those of a hypothetical high-school breakup.

"My parents weren't dating when you came back," I said slowly. "I shouldn't even have to say that. They'd been married long enough to have a teenager when you and my dad started messing around."

Rebecca's face looked as though she'd tasted something sour. She fidgeted with the pendant on her long necklace. "If what your father and I did was wrong, it was wrong in the name of love—"

"It didn't feel loving to me." My temper boiled over. "If you and my dad are too stupid to understand that what you did was wrong, and that what you did deeply and profoundly hurt my mom and me, then I don't know what else I can say."

Rebecca's face went white and hard with anger. She stood slowly, scowling down at me as if I were some wayward kinder-gartner that she could intimidate. "I refuse to be called names in my own house. Get out."

I marched to the entry, jammed my feet back in my flip-flops, grabbed my bag, and stormed out the door.

—⁓—

"It sounds to me," Kendra said slowly, "like Rebecca is unhealthy."

As soon as I'd gotten home from Dad and Rebecca's, I'd texted Kendra about what had happened. Her assistant had called me ten minutes later to see if I could come during a cancellation at four o'clock. Her office was in downtown Riverbend, upstairs from the dry cleaner, and less than a five-minute walk from my house. That was probably good, seeing all signs pointed to me needing therapy for years to come.

I liked her office. Two of the walls were exposed brick and the other two were painted a warm shade of sage. She always sat in the same chair, and I had the option of the loveseat or a squashy navy-blue chair, which is what I always picked.

"She would have to be, right?" I said, pulling my sweatshirt sleeves over my hands. I'd felt chilled ever since I'd left Dad and Rebecca's. "To think she could explain to me why she's not to blame in this situation? And to pretend it's the same thing as if Alex and I broke up? As if my parents were only dating when she and my dad were having their affair."

Kendra pursed her lips and watched me pick up one of the squishy balls from the basket of fidget toys she kept on the coffee table. I squeezed it hard and stared at it as it slowly began to retake shape.

"I feel like *this*." I squeezed hard again and opened my palm to show her the deformed ball. "This is what the divorce did to me, and now everyone wants to know why I'm not back to being a regular ball yet."

Kendra had a way of smiling that looked sympathetic and kind. Maybe they taught that in college when you were training to be a therapist. "That's valid, Tessa. Have you talked to either of your parents about what happened this afternoon?"

"Mom's been teaching, so no. And Dad called me twice, but I haven't answered. Based on the conversation I had with him last night, I think he's inclined to agree with Rebecca. That I'm overreacting. That I should 'be the ball again' by now." I held up the not-quite-right ball I'd crushed with my hand. "It doesn't seem to matter how calmly or rationally I say what I'm feeling. They can't understand why I'm so bothered."

"Tessa." Kendra leaned forward in her seat. "You're expecting a healthy response from unhealthy people. If they're not healthy, then they're incapable of responding to you in a healthy way."

I exhaled slowly. "But this seems so obvious. Shouldn't even an unhealthy person get that a divorce is traumatizing for a kid?"

"That's how it is with unhealthy people. You feel like you're saying two plus two equals four, and they're giving you a puzzled look and saying, 'No, two plus two equals Q.' You can't expect a healthy response from an unhealthy person."

I leaned back in the chair and looked up at the painted tin ceiling. In my cupped hand, I could feel the ball reinflating, or whatever process it went through to turn back into itself. "That's very frustrating," I finally said.

"I know." She paused. "We have about ten minutes left, by the way."

"You're going to ask me to think about what God has given me to control, aren't you?"

Her smile widened. "You know me well."

The ball was back to its spherical shape, and I didn't have the heart to undo all its work, so I just rotated it in my hand. "I don't have to babysit Logan."

"You don't."

"But legally I do have to go there every other weekend."

"That's true."

I considered this. "But when I'm at their house, I can control how I act. I can talk or not talk. Be kind or be rude. Make plans with friends or stay in my room."

"Yep."

I inhaled deeply. Exhaled. "Rebecca thinks of me as this spoiled teen, I'm pretty sure. If I were to be rude and stay in my room the whole time, it'd only make that worse. I don't want to add fuel to her fire—if you know what I mean."

"I do."

"But God didn't give me control over what she thinks of me."

"No, He didn't."

"Or what she posts on Instagram."

Kendra snorted and adjusted her weight in her chair. "If only! Have you mentioned that post to your father?"

"No. He'd probably think it was fine and that I was overreacting."

Kendra arched her eyebrows. "Can you control his reaction?"

"I guess not."

I watched as a cardinal attempted to land on the window ledge of Kendra's office, several times, and then flew off. I wish the solutions to my problems were so easy and obvious. *This ledge is too small. I'll go elsewhere.*

"The whole thing feels so exhausting, you know?" I shifted my gaze from the window back to Kendra. "Growing. Forgiving. Relationships. Even my mom has started saying more things about moving on and seeing what God has for us in this new season."

Kendra nodded slowly. "Healing is not a race, Tessa. It's okay to go slow. It's okay to lie down on the track and take a nap if you like."

"That does sound pretty good."

Kendra grinned and stood, her gentle way of saying that our time was up. "You can't change how healthy they are or aren't— you can only become healthy yourself, so take some time to think through what you can control. And if you have time in your schedule next week, let's meet then."

I thought about making a joke about her getting one of those rewards systems like at Grounds and Rounds, where you got a free coffee after you'd bought ten, but I decided against it. It was a depressing joke.

Alex: Sorry I missed your call. One of the parents had a flat tire so this poor kid didn't get picked up until after nine. Listened to your message. Sounds like you had a rough day.

Tessa: It was kind of the worst. It's never a good sign when your therapist squeezes you into her day and then recommends you come next week too.

Tessa: When Rebecca started in on how she wasn't the bad guy, I couldn't believe it. How is this my life?

Tessa: I understand we all tend to gloss over certain sins, but this one seems so obvious.

Tessa: Are you still there? Where'd you go?

Tessa: Okay ... not sure what happened, but it's late and I need to go to bed. Can we get together tomorrow night?

Alex: Apparently I fell asleep and slept through your messages coming in. I think I can make tomorrow night work? (Or tonight, I should say. Hopefully this message doesn't wake you up.)

Chapter
18

Wednesday afternoon I had successfully parallel parked near Pizza Guy, where I was meeting the girls for lunch, when Dad called.

I scowled at my phone and—as I always did these days—considered not answering. He'd called several times yesterday after Rebecca had ordered me out of the house, and twice this morning while my phone was in the locker room at the pool.

"Hi, Dad." I kept my voice flat.

"Hey, kiddo," he greeted me. "You got a minute?"

"I have *a* minute." I checked for traffic before popping open my door. "I'm meeting up with friends."

"I'd like to sort out this situation with Rebecca. Do you want to do that now or schedule a time for later?"

"Now's fine."

Not like it would take long for me to tell him what happened and for him to tell me why I was overreacting or misunderstanding the situation.

"She said you called us both stupid and then stormed out of the house yesterday."

Dad relayed this in a neutral tone, and I followed suit. "That's pretty close but skips the part where she said she refused to be called names in her own house."

"I see," Dad said. In the background, I could hear Logan chattering away and my heart lurched. I missed that guy. I hadn't seen him since Sunday. "Tessa . . ." Dad sighed. "You're not the only one feeling stressed right now, okay? I think it'd be helpful for you to know that two of her sisters aren't coming to the wedding because . . . well, for complicated reasons. So, Rebecca's feeling extra sensitive right now, and I'm sure she didn't mean to imply that you're unwelcome at our house or that we don't want you watching Logan anymore."

I'd arrived at the red and yellow striped awnings of Pizza Guy. Through the window, I could see Amelia, Izzy, and Shay debating pizza options.

"Are you also having a conversation with Rebecca about how she's not the only one feeling stressed right now?" I asked. "Or just me?"

"That's none of your business, Tessa."

I rolled my eyes and leaned against the brick wall. "Look, Dad. I miss being with Logan. I would have loved to watch him yesterday, but the stuff Rebecca said about how I need to get over what happened isn't okay. I will walk out the door 100 percent of the time that she says that."

"Okay," Dad said after a pause. Even in that simple word, I could hear how exhausted he was. "There's one and a half weeks left of this. I think I can get permission from my boss to work from home in the mornings through then. That way, when you arrive, it'll be me here. And I'll be sure to leave work right on time so I can get home before Rebecca. How does that sound?"

Ridiculous.

"Yeah, that'd be fine," I said.

"So, you'll come today?" Dad asked.

"Well, I already arranged to eat lunch with friends, but I could get there around one."

"That'd be great." Dad sounded relieved. "Thanks, Tessa."

I thought about Kendra encouraging me to tell Dad about Rebecca's Instagram post, but I was ready to get off the phone, so I said, "See you in a bit."

I set a timer on my phone to remind me to leave, and then pushed open the door. Inside Pizza Guy were two of my favorite smells on the planet—rising dough and Parmesan cheese. The classic rock music was loud, but not so loud that I couldn't hear an employee singing along as he generously covered a pizza with mozzarella.

"Hey!" Izzy pranced over to me for a hug. "Who were you on the phone with? Your boyfriend?" She sang the words, like we were in middle school.

"No, my dad."

"Oh." Izzy wrinkled her nose. "That doesn't sound as fun. Something wrong?"

All three of them looked at me. I considered briefly spilling about the whole thing, but honestly it felt exhausting to go through all of it again. "Just the usual stuff," I said. "I'll head over there once we're done."

"We went ahead and ordered," Amelia said as she gave me a squeeze. "We know you're not picky."

"Not about pizza."

"That back booth is open." Shay pointed. "Let's grab it."

Our hour together passed pleasantly, which felt like a relief since our last two get-togethers had been busts. Shay glowed as she talked about Green Tree Farm, as if the barn was some new crush of hers. It was adorable. Amelia had turned the corner on her feelings toward *Annie*. Instead of mourning not being on the stage, she complained with delight about how much work was to be done in the next seventeen days.

"And as if I don't have enough going on with fixing the blocking in act three, Lydia still can't get through most of her scenes, so what else can I do but drop everything and run lines with her?" While all Amelia's words were complaints on the surface, the light in her eyes and her big smile made it clear that she adored every minute of rehearsal. "What are you up to this week, Izzy? Your art lessons are over, right?"

"Yes, they were so fun!" Izzy smiled at me. "Tessa, your mom is delightful. I love her! I have so many ideas now for both cupcake designs and my YouTube channel. I need to get some new content made for that, but it probably won't be this week because Mrs. Kirby is teaching me to sew."

"Mrs. Kirby? The chicken-lady neighbor?" Amelia asked.

Izzy nodded.

"I love chickens," Shay said as she grabbed another slice of pizza. "Can I come help sometime?"

"Of course!" Izzy clapped and looked at Amelia and me. "Do you want to come help too?"

"Absolutely not," Amelia said at the same time as I said, "Hard pass."

My phone vibrated on the table as my timer went off. "Ugh, I got to go, girls."

"But we hardly talked about you, Tessa!" Amelia said as I downed the last of my Coke. "How are you doing with the wedding coming up so fast?"

"Uh, it's complicated," I said. "Too complicated to rush through in the next few minutes."

"I'm so sorry. I wish I could be at the wedding with you." Amelia looked like she meant it.

"Same here," Shay echoed.

"Yeah, me too," Izzy said. "Alex will go, right?"

"No, the wedding is on a Friday." I preoccupied myself with getting my phone in my bag so they wouldn't see any traces of irritation on my face. "Friday nights at OWC are a big deal. There's a bonfire and that kind of stuff. He doesn't wrap up until nine. And it's his mom's birthday."

"Ugh," Amelia said. "All Josie's pictures make it look like the funnest place to work, but it would be annoying to never get a free Friday night during the summer. Did you see that picture she posted yesterday of Alex? Where they both have Cool Whip all over their faces?"

My stomach did that twitching thing, like it always did at the sound of Josie's name. But Alex and I had already talked about this. No need for me to be jealous.

"Uh, no. I didn't."

"It's a riot." Amelia did a big sweeping scroll on her phone. "You have to see."

I felt Izzy watching me, and I sent a fake smile her way. "Okay, but I got to go—"

"Here it is." Amelia shoved her phone in my face. "Aren't they hilarious? I had no idea Alex could be so fun. We could use more guys in theater. Think he'd audition?"

I blinked at the selfie. As Amelia described, both their faces were covered in Cool Whip or shaving cream, like they'd each taken a pie to the face. I had no idea what had happened because stupid Josie didn't say anything more than "@RunAlexRun makes me LOL every day." Why was that all she said? Didn't she know I needed all the details of what had happened so I knew precisely what level of freaked out I should be?

I handed the phone back to Amelia, who was inexplicably listing off the names of guys who had been in *Peter Pan*.

"You okay?" Shay asked.

"Yep." I put on a smile. "I'm totally fine. See you, girls."

As I walked out of Pizza Guy, I told myself all the reasons why

I didn't need to freak out about this. Alex said they hardly saw each other during the day, no matter what the pictures looked like. And didn't I know firsthand how Instagram pictures didn't tell the whole story? What about last September when I posted pictures of Abraham and me hanging out at a swim meet, and Alex thought we'd started dating? Or Izzy, who'd had a fake nude photo show up on Snapchat? There was no reason to panic.

Maybe I should bring up Alex and Josie and my jealousy at my next appointment with Kendra. I had a dumb amount of stuff to talk about with my therapist these days.

"It'll be fine," I told myself as I got in my car. "I'm fine."

I pulled up my text thread with Alex, which was still the text from this morning saying that he was hoping to come over to my house on his way home from work. We could talk then. I would bring up the picture. He would tell me I didn't need to worry. That would be that.

I shot Mom a quick text updating her that I would be watching Logan after all. I was sure she'd have a strong opinion about that. She'd been irate when I told her what had happened yesterday with Rebecca, even though I'd given her as few details as possible.

Dad opened the door, holding Logan in one arm. Logan grinned and flailed at the sight of me. I couldn't resist returning his smile and taking one of his hands.

"Thanks for coming." Dad sounded weary as he handed Logan to me. "He barely napped this morning and was super fussy. He's about ready to go down for his nap."

"Not yet," I cooed to Logan as I took him from Dad. "I just got here, buddy."

He made a cooing noise back at me that made my heart feel like it was going to burst from joy.

"He's on a schedule," Dad said gruffly as he wiped at something crusty on his shoulder. "The schedule is important."

I barely resisted rolling my eyes. Why did they hire me to

babysit Logan if they felt like everything had to be explained to me constantly? "Dad, I know about his schedule. I've been doing this for over two weeks now."

"Right," Dad said. "Yes, of course. I think I'll have to change my shirt. Excuse me."

For five minutes, Dad rushed around the house gathering his things for work. Finally, he strode across the room to us and leaned to kiss Logan on the forehead. "Bye, Logan. See you after work."

Then he turned and walked toward the garage.

Oh. No goodbye for me, apparently. Just for Logan.

Dad must've realized this too. He froze mid-stride and turned. I could almost see the debate raging in his head. Walking back would be an awkward admission that he overlooked me in the first place.

"Call if you need anything," he said slowly, as if this was his purpose in stopping. "I have a meeting with my boss at three, but otherwise I should be able to pick up."

"Okay." I tried to keep the hurt out of my voice. I was sixteen. I didn't need my dad to hug me goodbye before he left for work. I'd spent the last year avoiding talking to him or touching him. What right did I have to be hurt now when he'd forgotten me? No right at all.

Dad offered a strained smile. "Bye, honey."

Then he turned and left. Logan seemed indifferent to his departure, and I wished I felt the same.

—◠◡◠—

At eight o'clock, as soon as Alex's OMW text came, I went out front to wait on the porch. I paced back and forth until his car pulled into the driveway behind mine.

Alex looked dead on his feet when he got out of his Civic. "This group of fifth graders is going to be the death of me."

I smiled. "Are they that much worse than your week two campers?"

"Yes. Week two was a mischievous group." He closed his door and walked with dramatic heaviness toward me. Maybe Amelia was right and he *should* audition. "This week's group is all fist fights and pranks."

"Fist fights?"

When Alex hugged me, he put an unusual amount of weight on me, and I stumbled backward a few steps, laughing. "@RunAlexRun makes me LOL every day" played in my head.

"Your fifth-grade boys are having fist fights?" I asked once he helped me stand up straight again. He smelled like sunscreen and bug spray.

"Mostly just two of them." Alex lifted his Chicago Cubs cap, adjusted his hair, and resettled it on his head. "Was I obnoxious in fifth grade? Is that why you wouldn't go out with me until last year?"

My laugh felt wooden. I sat on the porch steps, and he took the seat beside me. "No, that was because you weren't interested in me."

"Ugh. So, even if I wasn't obnoxious, I *was* as dumb as these fifth graders." Alex grinned at me, and then it faltered. "Something wrong?"

I hesitated. Should I bring up the Josie thing right away?

"That's a yes." Alex instantly looked more awake. "What happened? Rebecca?"

"Not exactly."

Alex frowned. "Did I do something?"

Again, I hesitated.

His frown deepened. "What'd I do? Is this about falling asleep last night when we were texting? I felt really bad about that—"

"No, that's not it," I rushed to say. "It's nothing, really. Maybe.

I'm trying to not jump to conclusions, but it's been bothering me all day."

"Just say it, Tessa."

I looked at my toes and wiggled them. The words came out in a rush: "Josie posted a picture of the two of you with whipped cream on your faces."

I didn't know what Alex's face looked like, because I wasn't brave enough to look him in the eyes.

"It was shaving cream, but yeah, I know what you're talking about." He paused. "That bothered you?"

"Yeah." I tightened my ponytail. "Maybe it shouldn't. Maybe I should be fine with it, but it made me feel . . ."

Alex caught my hand in his. "If you keep doing that to your ponytail, you're going to start losing hair," he said in a gentle voice. "If it bothers you, that's all I need to know. I can talk to Josie about it."

"Ew, no." I leaned back to look him in the eyes. "Don't do that. Then she'll know I was weirded out by it."

Alex's laugh sounded hollow. "Tessa, help me out here, then. What do you want me to do?"

Don't decide that you like her more than me. Don't hurt me.

Insecurity felt like ice running through me. I tucked my knees against my chest and wrapped my arms around them. "I don't know. Nothing. I guess I wanted to know if . . ."

I couldn't finish my sentence. It was too humiliating.

"Tessa." Alex rested his hand on my knee. "We had shaving cream on our faces for, like, thirty seconds. She snapped the picture. That was it. You're making something out of nothing."

"Okay." I nodded hastily. "Yeah, I figured. I just . . . wanted to check. She keeps posting these pictures, and it seems like she likes you . . ."

"I get it." Alex smiled a sleepy smile at me. "It's not a big deal, but it would probably look like that to me if the situation was reversed. I'll try to stay off her Instagram."

"Okay, thanks."

But it wasn't that I wanted him off her Instagram. I wanted an oath that he would never think of Josie as anything besides a coworker. That he would like no one else but me. That he wouldn't hurt me. I wanted to control this. So. Badly. But God didn't give me Alex's feelings to control.

Alex squeezed my knee, bringing me back to the twilight and the porch. "Can we talk about something else now? Something that's not related to OWC?"

"Sure."

"Did you ever talk to your dad?"

I filled him in on everything with Dad and Rebecca, but my mind kept drifting to that stupid Instagram post of Josie's. She got fun, goofy Alex during the day. They laughed, played wacky games with kids, and took pictures together. When was the last time Alex and I had taken a picture together?

After about thirty minutes, Alex headed home, and I kept sitting out on my porch. I watched the night sky grow darker and the stars shine brighter. I thought about being a kid and setting up my dad's telescope on clear nights like this. I hadn't thought about that in ages. Would he do that with Logan when he got old enough? Would he take Logan to Iceland when he was sixteen?

My phone buzzed. The text was from Abraham. Hi.

I looked up. He was in the doorway of his house, backlit by the light. He waved. I waved back. I could see him typing again.

A new message came through. Still going to tell me everything is great with Alex?

I sighed. Things are fine. Just a miscommunication.

Is it about this? A screenshot of Josie's post appeared.

I was glad he couldn't see my face because I flinched. Nope. He's allowed to have friends who are girls.

I stood and went inside my house. Otherwise, I was afraid Abraham would decide to come out and talk with me in person about this.

Inside, I could hear the creaking floors as Mom moved around in her studio, cleaning up and prepping for the next morning. She was on the phone with someone and kept laughing. As I pulled a jar of salsa from the refrigerator, I overheard her say, "Kayleigh cracks me up. I love her dry sense of humor."

She was on the phone with Phil? Why?

Another warm laugh reached my ears and chilled me on the inside. My phone vibrated with another text from Abraham. **Josie isn't a "just friends" kind of girl.**

I hesitated a moment and then decided to power off my phone. *God, You're not giving me much to control, are You?* I muttered as I abandoned my snack and opted to go to bed early instead.

Chapter
19

THE NEW ROUTINE OF DAD PASSING LOGAN OFF to me and then coming home before Rebecca took nearly all the stress out of baby-sitting Logan, and the next week flew by. Even on days when Logan was a little grumpier or pooped as if he'd been saving it up special for me, it all felt easier since I didn't have to interact with Rebecca.

Although it was my weekend with them, I signed up for a Friday/Saturday swim meet and volunteered to help in the church nursery Sunday morning, which I thought might give us all an easy excuse for me to stay home. And the weekend after that was their wedding. I was pretty confident that I'd be home that weekend too.

I looked at my phone. Logan was taking an extra-long nap. Tomorrow and Friday were my last afternoons to watch him before Rebecca's class ended, and I'd spent more time today catching up on Netflix than being with him. It wasn't my favorite—I'd much rather spend time with him. I kept looking at his monitor, hoping he'd stir.

I was about to go wake him up from his nap—for the sake of his schedule and absolutely not because I was missing him—when Amelia called. I blinked at the screen and tried to remember the last time Amelia *called* me instead of sending a Snap or a Marco Polo.

I turned off the TV. "Hey, what's up?"

"Hey, Tessa." Amelia's tone made my heart rate spike. "I need to talk to you about something important."

Alarms clanged in my head. Were her parents getting divorced? Did someone die? Whatever she was calling about sounded intense. "Okay . . ."

"So, you know how Josie is my neighbor?"

Oh. *That's* where this was going.

I blinked rapidly at the Blue Lagoon picture Rebecca had hung up a few weeks ago. My heart seemed to be pounding right in my ears. "Yeah."

"Well, she came over last night because she was feeling confused and stressed about something. Um, something to do with Alex."

I closed my eyes. My brain flooded with options. Josie liked him. She'd kissed him. She was going to ask him out.

"Okay," I said. "Go on."

"I'm so, so sorry . . . but she said Alex has been flirting with her, and it makes her uncomfortable because she knows he has a girlfriend."

I felt my breath hitch in my chest and worked hard to take a deep breath. That didn't make sense. That simply didn't make sense. Alex wouldn't do that to me. He'd *said* he wouldn't do that to me.

Logan's monitor lit up as he awoke with a yowl. I turned the monitor down. Sometimes he did this and then put himself back to sleep. Rebecca had told me to always wait a couple minutes before going in.

"I'm heartbroken for you, Tessa." Amelia sounded like *she* was on the verge of tears. "Josie said that this was happening last week. She hoped having some space between them over the weekend would help, but I guess he texted her a few times over the weekend and . . . well, she said he's been even more persistent this week . . . I'm so sorry."

"Okay." The word came out as if I'd been punched in the stomach. On the monitor, I watched Logan thrash out of his swaddle. "She must be misinterpreting a situation or something. Because Alex wouldn't do that. It's not who he is?"

My statement curled into an unintentional question. It wasn't who I thought my dad was either . . . until I learned differently.

"Did Josie say anything specific?" My voice pitched high and strained. "Like specific things Alex said or did that made her think he was flirting?"

"No. She said she didn't want to gossip or speak poorly about him since she knows I'm friends with him. Josie would never want to say a mean thing about anybody, so I know it must be real bad if she was this worried and came to me."

"Mmhmm," I said tightly. Logan was full out screaming. I wanted to join him. "Um, I have to go because my brother woke up."

"Okay. Tessa, again I am *so, so* sorry—"

"Yeah, I know. We'll talk later."

I hung up and sat there with tears brimming in my eyes. And then streaming down my cheeks. "This is fine," I whispered to myself. "This is all going to be fine."

Because this was a mistake. A miscommunication. Alex had told me he didn't like Josie like that, and I trusted him.

But I had trusted my dad, too . . .

Alex wasn't my dad though. He'd promised he wouldn't do

anything like that to me. That he would take me to Iceland someday.

My gaze roamed to the Blue Lagoon picture. Of course, my dad had promised that too. And both Amelia and Alex had said Josie was a nice girl. Hadn't I seen firsthand that she was the kind of person who mentored middle-school girls from her church on her day off? Did I really think a girl like that was making all this up?

I thought of Abraham's text from a week ago that I'd never replied to: Josie isn't a "just friends" kind of girl.

Did he mean that Josie wasn't good at being just friends with boys . . . or that boys weren't good at being just friends with her?

Logan's wails grew louder, and I pushed myself off the couch. I would *not* overreact. This was most likely a misunderstanding, and Alex and I would clear it up tonight when he was off work.

If he had time for me.

Alex had cancelled our plans twice in the last week. It keeps happening. Was it really to do family stuff? Or was he creating space in his schedule to secretly spend time with Josie? Who he'd been texting over the weekend, apparently.

Family, Tessa, I told myself firmly. *He was spending time with his family. Stop this.*

I nudged open Logan's door and could instantly smell why he was so angry. His face was red from crying, and even when he spotted me approaching his crib, he didn't do his usual happy kicks. Instead, he wailed louder, as if explaining to me what had gone wrong.

"I know." I leaned into the crib and lifted him out gingerly. His clothes were still clean, so the diaper had done its job, at least. "C'mere buddy, it's okay."

I held Logan against me as I opened his curtains.

Maybe Alex had been flirting a bit to try and subtly test the waters. Like he didn't want to break up with me if Josie wasn't interested, but he wanted to know if she was a possibility.

And funny how *none* of his work stories ever involved her. I heard about lots of other people at OWC, but never her. Coincidence?

Logan scrunched his body and let out a cry, and I realized I'd been standing there at his window, doing nothing.

"Sorry, Logan."

I shoved away worries about Alex and Josie. I would ask him after work, so there was no point thinking about it now. All I had now was a warning from Amelia, who had vague details from Josie. I needed to speak directly to the source.

I laid Logan on the changing table and peeked at my phone. Five minutes to three. So, in about five hours, I could talk to Alex. This would be fine. It was a misunderstanding.

Logan yowled his disapproval, and again I realized I'd been standing there, staring off into space.

"I know, let's get that diaper off you quickly. Then we'll play, okay?"

I used five baby wipes to get him fully clean, then sang loudly over his cries as I put a thick layer of ointment on his booty and washed my hands.

"Now you're all clean, and I'm all clean." I cooed in his ear as he screamed. "I'll hold you now."

After thirty minutes of Logan fussily sucking down his bottle and then protesting every activity I tried to engage him in—from the swing to tummy time to reading—I said, "Let's take you outside."

Being outside was like pressing a magic button to make Logan happy. Usually, I walked him around in the backyard, but Amelia's phone call had me feeling antsy. The stroller was already set up in the entryway, so I nestled Logan down into the infant carrier and tucked a blanket around him.

"Shh," I said as I pushed the stroller back and forth in an effort to create a rocking sensation. His complaints quieted. Then stopped completely. He watched the swinging motion of a bright monkey toy that dangled above him.

"See?" I said. "It's not so bad, Logan. And we're not even outside yet."

I opened the front door and finagled his stroller out over the threshold and onto the patio. The sun blazed bright, and I realized that not only had I left my phone inside—probably on the couch where I'd been sitting while he drank his bottle—but my sunglasses were in there too.

"One sec, buddy. I'll be right back."

I dashed inside, leaving the front door cracked. When I scooped up my phone, I saw I had a text from Amelia. **Let me know when you talk to Alex. I'll be home tonight and happy to talk. Hugs.**

I swiped to text back a quick "thanks" when I heard a loud sound out front. Like something big had fallen.

"Logan?" I called as I sprinted for the door, as if he could answer me. "Logan!"

The stroller was no longer on the patio. Instead, it was in the flower bed, upside down, one of its wheels still rotating slowly.

"Logan," I whimpered as I ran down the front steps.

My baby brother lay helplessly in the decorative stones that surrounded a bird bath. He'd fallen out of the infant carrier and was facedown in the mulch. Hadn't I buckled him in? I pushed the stroller aside and helped him roll over. There was blood on top of his head—he must have hit something—and his eyes blinked groggily at me.

"Oh, Logan, I'm so sorry." I clutched him against me and rocked, relief and regret coursing through me. He was breathing. He was blinking. But how could I have been so irresponsible? How had I not realized the stroller wasn't in a safe place? How had I forgotten to lock the wheels? How had I not buckled him in? How could he be bleeding because of *me*?

"I'm so sorry," I said, my throat tight as we rocked. "I'm so sorry. I'm so sorry."

Shouldn't he be crying? Why wasn't he crying? I pulled him back from me so I could study his face. Blood had begun to ooze from the gash on top of his head. Why did he look so unfocused? Something went cold inside me. This was serious.

Jesus, help me, I prayed as I pulled up Dad's number and listened to the phone ring. *Jesus, let him be okay. Please let him be okay.*

Dad's cheerful, "Hi, you've reached the cell phone of David Hart," greeted me. I hung up and tried again. Two phone calls in a row had always meant "It's serious, pick up now." But Dad didn't pick up.

"It's okay, Logan," I said, stroking his cheek. "We're going to call your mom. It'll be okay. She'll know what to do."

Logan's eyes slid shut and panic clawed at my chest. I'd seen behavior like this only once before, when a girl at swim team had dived into the pool and hit her head. "Logan," I said in an urgent voice, and his eyes opened again. "Hi. Stay awake, buddy. We got to stay awake."

Could babies get concussions? Surely they could, right? They were probably more susceptible than adults, considering their skulls weren't fully formed.

"Stay awake, Logan," I chanted as Rebecca's phone rang and rang and rang. I rocked harder and tickled under his neck. Finally, Rebecca's voicemail picked up. "Rebecca, you have to pick up," my voice was pitched high and hysterical. "You have to pick up, I need you."

The next time I dialed, it didn't even ring. It went straight to voicemail. Tears streamed down my cheeks and splashed on Logan. Whose eyes were closed again. I tickled under his chin. "You have to wake up, Logan. You have to stay awake."

His eyes opened and landed on me, but still he wasn't crying.

"It's going to be okay," I said as my finger poked the three numbers that had been repeated to me my entire life, but that I'd never dialed.

"911, state your emergency."

How was this real? How was this happening?

I swallowed hard and said, "I'm babysitting my brother and he hit his head." A sob broke through. "I need an ambulance."

—⚏—

Inside the ER of Riverbend General, a man with a phlegmy cough was taking an eternity at the front desk.

I jumped when my phone buzzed. It was Rebecca. I saw you called while I was taking a test. Do you need something? My thumbs fumbled over my response. At hospital with Logan. I forgot to lock the stroller and he fell out. We're in the ER now. Tears blurred my eyes as I considered the words. Should I add that I was sorry? That it was my fault?

"Can I help you?"

I hit *send* and stepped up to the counter. "Hi, my brother was brought in by ambulance."

"Name?"

"Logan Hart." I bit my lip. That was right, wasn't it? He wasn't Logan Simmons-Hart or anything?

The receptionist clicked several things with her mouse. "Do you have his insurance card?"

I shook my head. "I texted his mom. She should be on her way soon."

"And what's her phone number?"

I pulled my phone back out and rattled the digits off to her. A text came in from Rebecca. OMW.

"Okay . . ." the receptionist clicked several more things. "Okay, honey, why don't you take a seat? The doctor will be out in a bit."

I bit my lip for a second. "Can't I go back and be with him?"

"I'm afraid not. The doctor will come out and update you as soon as he finishes. Go ahead and have a seat."

I hesitated, then turned and did as she said. I sank into a chair and stared at an abstract painting that looked like it had been on the wall since before I was born. There had been no returned phone call from either of my parents yet. I'd tried Mom on my drive to the hospital, even though I knew she was teaching a class and never had her phone on her then. And what would I have asked? For her to come be at the hospital with me?

Minutes clicked by. I watched each one pass on a white-and-black schoolhouse clock. Was Logan still crying? He'd been wailing by the time the ambulance arrived and they'd loaded him inside. "It's a positive sign," one of the EMTs had reassured me.

I'd clung to those words the whole drive over.

The double doors pushed open, and out strode a man who was clearly a doctor. He caught my eye and gave me a half smile. "Are you Logan's big sister?"

"Yessir." My hands trembled in my lap, and I clutched them together. "How's he doing?"

"Let's go back here to talk, okay?" He pushed open one of the doors and held it open for me. "First room on the right."

I thought it would be Logan's room, but it was, instead, a much smaller waiting room, with a couple of chairs facing each other and a box of Kleenex and outdated magazines on an end table.

"Can you tell me about what happened?" he asked, taking a seat across from me.

I wiped my sweaty hands on my legs. I'd already gone through this with the EMTs, but I presumed he wanted to hear it from me. "He'd been real upset since he woke up from his nap. He loves being outdoors, so I put him in the stroller—" I bit my lower lip to try and keep my whole face from crumpling. "Only I guess I didn't buckle him up. I had a light blanket over him."

I pushed hair out of my face with a trembling hand.

The doctor handed me a Kleenex. "What else?"

I wiped my eyes. "We got outside, and I realized I'd forgotten my phone, so I went back in to get it. I didn't know . . ." The sobs pressed heavy against my chest, straining to get out. "I didn't realize that the stroller would roll off the porch."

"How big of a drop was that?" the doctor asked quietly.

"I don't know." I kneaded the Kleenex with my fingers. "It's maybe a foot and a half off the ground? There's a garden right there, and Logan fell in the mulch. Except he must have hit his head on something too. There are some decorative stones around a plant."

A sob escaped, but I held back the others.

"You didn't lock the stroller?"

I shook my head. "I'm so sorry," I whispered.

"It's very important to lock strollers and to buckle babies in." The doctor's voice was stern. Serious. "That's crucial to their safety."

I nodded. "I'm so sorry," I barely managed to say before another sob snuck out.

"Your brother can't keep himself safe. *You* have to do that for him."

"I know, I know. I understand."

There was a lull during which I did everything I could to not dissolve in front of him.

"The front desk told me Mom is on her way. I'm going to have you sit tight in here for now. A social worker is going to come get you in a few minutes to talk about what happened. It's standard in injuries with nonmobile babies."

A social worker. I'd never be allowed to watch Logan again, would I? And how could I argue with that? Dad and Rebecca had trusted me with Logan's safety—God had given me that to control—and I'd failed.

"Okay," I said meekly.

"We're done with the staples and the head CT," the doctor said quietly. "I've ordered a skeletal survey to be sure, but I don't anticipate finding other injuries. Calling the ambulance was a good idea."

I stared at the Kleenex crumpled in my hand. I shouldn't have even had to call the ambulance, because the accident never should've happened in the first place. The doctor left, and I sat in the little room for a while—three minutes? Ten minutes?—before a woman who didn't look much older than me came in holding a slim computer under her arm.

"Logan's big sister?"

I nodded.

"I'm Bethany. Nice to meet you."

"You too." My voice had a graveled, unused sound to it.

She took the same chair the doctor had and smiled without showing her teeth. "Pretty rough day, huh?"

I nodded again.

"Why don't you tell me what happened?"

I went through the whole thing for a third time. How Logan had woken up fussy. How I hadn't buckled him. How I'd left him on the front porch with the stroller unlocked. How it was completely my fault that my brother had staples in his head and was getting all kinds of scans.

"While it does sound like this was an accident, it's still considered negligence," Bethany said slowly.

Negligence. That was such an ugly word.

When Bethany handed me another Kleenex, I realized I'd begun weeping again.

"I'll have to talk to your parents, too," Bethany said in a soft but firm voice, "and see what concerns they have. Your mother's here with Logan, I think."

"She's not my mom," I said with a raspy voice.

"Oh, I see. Well." Bethany considered this information. "I think we're done, but why don't you sit tight for a bit?"

Minutes ticked by. Finally, Bethany popped back into the room. "Tessa? You're free to go. I have your phone number and might have to call with some additional questions, but we don't need anything further from you."

"Oh. Okay." I wanted to ask to see Logan. I also *didn't* want to see Logan. Not with staples in his head that *I'd* created the need for.

Feeling alone and wretched, I gathered my bag and pile of used Kleenex and walked out of the room.

Only to hear Rebecca calling my name.

I turned. Her eyes were red, puffy, and furious as she strode toward me, Logan swaddled and clutched against her. I couldn't see the staples.

"I'm so sorry," I said, tears churning up again. "I can't believe that I—"

"I've put up with a lot of spoiled, childish behavior from you," Rebecca said in a voice like a dagger.

"I'm so sorry," I whimpered. "I never meant—"

"You will do anything to sabotage my relationship with David, won't you? But no more. You are no longer welcome in my home, and you are forbidden to spend time with my son."

She was already walking away from me. "You're safe now," Rebecca said to Logan. "Mommy has you."

I turned and walked away without offering any kind of defense. What would I even say? I was irrefutably in the wrong this time.

Chapter
20

IN THE PARKING LOT OF THE HOSPITAL, I wept and screamed and pounded my fists on anything within reach. My legs, the console, the car door. What kind of awful sister didn't buckle her baby brother in? What kind of idiot didn't lock a stroller? Why had I so stupidly left Logan outside in the first place?

I didn't even know what time it was when I finally started my car and drove numbly through town back home. When I turned into the driveway and reached for the garage door opener, it wasn't there. I blinked at my visor for a few seconds. I could still see the indentation on the fabric where the opener had been, but . . .

I groaned. I'd driven to my old house.

I had pulled into my old driveway and was trying to get in my old garage, and I didn't have my opener anymore because it belonged to Liz and John. Now *they* got to live in my perfect house and have a perfect life.

I backed out of the driveway so quickly, my fender scraped

the curb. I sped past Alex's house, past the park where I'd played several terrible seasons of soccer. Past Amelia's neighborhood, where Josie lived. Perfect Josie who would never do something so stupid as leave her baby brother unbuckled in a stroller without the brakes on.

When I finally got to the right house, there was a white truck hogging the driveway. I pulled alongside the curb. It felt like I'd lived an entire lifetime since I left that morning at six fifty for swim practice.

What time was it, even? My car dashboard said it was three minutes after five. If it was a normal afternoon, I would have a few more minutes with Logan until my dad arrived. But it wasn't a normal afternoon. My whole body ached, from a pounding headache down to my curled toes. I trudged up the driveway, dreaming of a bubble bath and a nap, but also feeling like I didn't deserve such comforts.

I swung open the front door and nailed my mom's shoulder. "Oh, sor—"

I cut my apology off as she and Phil sprung apart. They'd been kissing.

Mom wiped her mouth and looked at me with the expression of a kid who'd been caught sneaking a piece of candy. "Hi, honey. How are you? How's Logan?" She cleared her throat and tried to smile. "You're home early."

Phil's face was bright red, and he kept his gaze focused on our fireplace.

Kayleigh bounded down the creaky steps, her blond hair in two bouncy pigtails. In her left hand, she held up a mobile project Mom did with her elementary kids. "I found it!"

"Great," Phil mumbled. "Let's go. Bye, Carrie." He nodded curtly to me, "Tessa."

I stepped aside so they could get through the door, and then stood there with my mom. I felt like that ball in Kendra's office, and that my afternoon had squeezed everything out of me. Unfaithful boyfriend, a 911 call because I'd hurt my brother, being dressed down by Rebecca—and deserving it—and now watching my mom officially "move on."

"I don't even know what to say, Tessa." Mom's voice was low and husky. "I'm so sorry you walked in on that. I had no idea it was going to happen, but we were standing there and . . ."

"It explains why I've called you multiple times and you never answered." My voice was scratchy from hours of crying.

"No, that's not it. I tried calling you back—"

"I needed you, and you weren't there for me." My words trembled as they rose into a full-on yell. "I screwed up and Logan got hurt, and no one was answering their phones."

"Oh, Tessa, honey." Mom took a step toward me, her arms wide open, and I put up a hand to stop her. I absolutely did not deserve comfort.

Mom wrung her hands together. "What happened to Logan? Is he okay?"

I shook my head. "He's in the ER. He fell out of the stroller and cut his head on some rocks, so they had to do staples, and it's entirely my fault."

"Oh, baby, I'm sure it's not—"

"It absolutely is. And Rebecca said she'll never let me see Logan again, and I can't even blame her for it. I had to meet with a social worker, Mom. A *social worker*. Because I was negligent."

"Accidents happen even to the most careful of—"

"Don't excuse me!" My words emerged as a shriek. "I wasn't careful. I hurt him. *I* hurt my baby brother. It was a situation completely in my control, and I botched it."

"Tessa, I'm sure things feel bad right now, but Rebecca will calm down and it'll be okay."

"Even if they try to pay me, I can't accept their money now." I wrapped my arms around my chest and rocked back and forth.

"Not that I'm going to need the money for Iceland anyway. You won't want to go anymore. You won't want to leave Phil, or you'll be planning a wedding or—"

"Tessa, no." Mom reached for me again. "I realize you're emotional, and you walked in on a confusing situation, but this thing with Phil and me is . . ."

I didn't know if she kept talking, but I stopped hearing her as I thundered up the staircase to my bedroom. I gave the door a firm push shut and locked it.

Mom followed me and knocked at the door. "Tessa, honey, please let me in."

I answered by turning on NF's "Leave Me Alone" and cranking the volume. I flopped on my bed and stared blankly at the boxes pushed against the wall. I'd never unpacked them, because I'd never wanted to move here. Was anybody living in my old room? Had they put the baby in there, or was it a spare bedroom now?

My phone buzzed and lit up with a DM from Izzy. **Saw Rebecca's post. Is she talking about you? What happened?**

With a trembling finger, I tapped on the Instagram post Izzy had sent. The image was a black-and-white filter of Logan asleep in her arms. There weren't as many staples as I feared, but they were stark and ugly on his scalp. My breathing felt shallow even before I read the caption.

PSA: If you suspect the person taking care of your baby is lazy and irresponsible, listen to your gut. Say something, no matter how awkward it might be. Maybe if I'd spoken up about my concerns, I wouldn't be sitting in the ER holding my baby and waiting for results from a battery of tests.

Shame streamed through me as if I'd swallowed a glassful of it. Comment after comment was about how Rebecca shouldn't blame herself and stories of women having to fire incompetent childcare providers. Lots of praying hand emojis.

I froze when I got to the comment from Jamie543. **David's bratty kid??? I hope you finally gave her what she deserved.**

This was one of the few that Rebecca had responded to. **Finally. Even David is furious.**

I powered off my phone and pressed my palms against my eyes. I couldn't believe this. Not only had I screwed up in a way that I would regret forever, but now Rebecca was *posting* about it. And I didn't even have the right to be mad, not when everything she said was completely true.

I pulled my weighted blanket over my head and squeezed my eyes shut, but I couldn't get rid of the image of Logan with staples in his sweet head, or the sound of Rebecca forbidding me from seeing him, or the reality that I'd irrevocably screwed up.

My Bluetooth speaker powered off.

I pulled back my blanket to find Mom standing in my room with my doorknob in one hand, a drill in the other, and a face full of concern.

"Tessa, I've just gotten off the phone with your father. I need to understand what's going on." Her voice was surprisingly calm considering the measures she'd taken to break into my room.

"I was going to take Logan for a walk." My voice sounded like I'd rubbed it with a cheese grater. "I didn't buckle him in, and I didn't lock the stroller, so when I ran back inside to grab my phone, the stroller rolled off the patio, and he fell out. I couldn't get ahold of anyone, so I called 911."

Mom sat on the edge of the bed, one of her knees popping with the action. She rested a hand on my back. "That must've been scary for you."

"He cut his head." I clenched my teeth until the threat of tears passed. "And he didn't look right. He had this unfocused look."

"Then it sounds like 911 was the right thing to do."

I didn't answer. The right thing to do would have been buckling him in. The right thing to do would have been locking the stroller. The right thing to do would have been taking him with me when I went in to get my phone.

"I'm sorry about missing your call." Mom pushed strands of hair back from my face. "I was in a class."

"Yeah, I figured." My room was full of bright sunshine, which felt wrong. "Was Dad mad?"

Mom's hesitation was all the answer I needed. "He's only heard Rebecca's side. He'd like to talk to you, but he said you're not answering your phone."

"I turned it off."

"That's fine." Mom rubbed a figure eight over my back, and then retraced it. "Sometimes unplugging is the best thing we can do."

I laid there silently and let Mom think she was soothing me. I held myself stiffly. I didn't deserve to feel better.

"Everybody makes mistakes, Tessa," Mom said softly. "Once, I drove across town to your grandma and grandpa's and realized I'd never buckled your car seat. It was a cold day, and I tucked a blanket around you and . . . forgot. I couldn't believe I'd done that. And there were at least two times that you rolled off the couch as a baby. These things happen. Kids get hurt sometimes."

This was different. I squeezed my eyes shut as the black-and-white photo Rebecca had posted came to mind, with Logan's stapled head. "This whole time I thought Rebecca was being so overprotective, but she wasn't. I proved her right. I couldn't be trusted."

Mom took in a deep breath and released it. "Baby, nobody is saying you can't be trusted."

"Rebecca is. She did a whole post on social media about how she'd known all along they shouldn't trust me, and now Logan's the one paying for it," I said through the swell of a sob. "And she's not wrong."

Silence. Mom breathed fast and even, like she did when she got angry but wanted to keep a lid on it. "She posted about this on social media already?"

I sniffed and nodded. "Izzy sent it to me. There were all these mean comments on there. I don't even know why I read them."

"Well, that's not okay." Mom's voice pitched higher. She pulled her phone out. "I can't believe she posted about it. Why would she do that? How does that help the situation?"

"It's fine. I deserved it."

"Nobody *deserves* having their mistakes aired on Instagram, Tessa Rae. She should know better. She's a grown woman, not some preteen girl." Mom's thumb moved down the screen and then she audibly gasped. "How could she post this? This is cruel."

"Nothing she says on there is factually wrong."

"Even if it were true—which it's not—this is an extremely immature thing to post. Especially considering she's talking about the daughter of the man she supposedly loves. I'm calling your father right now."

"Don't call Dad." I made a half-hearted grab for her leg as she stood. I didn't have energy for anything else. "I don't care if she leaves it up."

"Tessa, love, I understand you being upset about what happened to Logan. I understand you blaming yourself and feeling wretched for your part. That's fine. But it's absolutely not okay for her to use this as part of building her dumb Instagram brand— Hi, David. I need to talk to you." Mom stomped off down the hall, but her voice carried for a while. "Are you aware of the slanderous remarks Rebecca made about our daughter on Instagram?"

By the time Dad had replied and Mom resumed talking, she was downstairs and out of earshot. I heard her voice, not the words themselves, and I didn't even care to listen in. I pulled the blanket back over my head and laid in the darkness. I relived my afternoon on repeat. Putting Logan in the stroller. Rolling him outside. Replying to Amelia when I should've been outside with my brother. His bleeding head. The social worker saying I'd been negligent. Rebecca calling me spoiled and childish.

Again. And again.

Eventually, I heard Mom coming back upstairs, her footsteps heavier and slower than normal.

"Hey, kiddo."

Not Mom, but Dad.

I pulled back my blanket. Dad's face was already creased, but the creases deepened when he saw me.

"I'm so sorry," I said in my scratched-up voice, and then the tears came. I couldn't believe there was any moisture left in my body. "It was an accident."

"I know, baby." Dad crouched on the floor, lining his eyes up with mine and resting a large hand on my head. "All the tests came back clear. Logan's going to be totally fine."

My eyes slid shut with relief. He was okay. Logan was going to be okay. "I'm still so sorry."

"I know you are." His thumb caressed my temple. "I know you care a lot about Logan."

"I do." Saying so felt like a confession. "I love him so much."

Dad wiped away each tear that fell. When I finally slowed down, he said, "I'm sorry about what Rebecca said. Both online and, I suspect, at the hospital."

I shook my head. "I'm not. I deserved it all. And more."

"You didn't. That post was awful, and I'm so sorry you saw that. She's taken it down now. And, Tessa, regardless of what she may have said, you are *always* welcome at our house—"

"But I'm not." When I blinked, I could still see tears clinging to my eyelashes. "You keep saying that, and you might want that to be true, but we both know that I'm really not."

"You're my daughter." Dad's eyes, dark brown like mine, turned glassy. "You are always welcome in my house."

"She doesn't want me there. She doesn't like me, Dad. And neither of us can control how she feels."

"This is new for all of us," he said. "Rebecca's angry now, but she'll calm down. I promise."

"She won't let me babysit anymore."

Dad didn't refute that, just reached an arm around me and squeezed. "I love you, Tessa. This doesn't change that. Not one bit."

I thought with longing of my afternoons with Logan. The feel of his head against my shoulder. His wide smile when he saw me. The way he'd kick with uncoordinated delight if I left the room and came back. All that was over now. Because even if Rebecca hadn't ended it, Logan would never look at me the same way again.

Chapter
21

"ALEX CAME BY LAST NIGHT, but you were already asleep," Mom said as we sat at the table together eating breakfast. I couldn't remember the last time we'd done that.

When I'd told her I wasn't going to swim practice—I couldn't remember the last time I'd done that either—she'd walked downtown to grab us a box of donuts. I normally loved donuts, but I didn't feel hungry.

I sipped the herbal tea Mom had made to help with my scratchy voice. "Did he say why?"

"He said he'd called and texted several times and you weren't answering. He was worried." Mom selected another donut from the box. "I gave him a few details about the events of the afternoon and told him you'd turned off your phone."

"Okay, thanks."

I nibbled my chocolate-sprinkled donut. He'd probably been trying to reach me for the usual reasons—we normally talked on his drive from OWC to Riverbend. But did he come to the house because he was worried or because he had something important to tell me? Like that we were breaking up?

It was a little after eight thirty, and I still hadn't turned my phone on. I was afraid to, though I couldn't totally pinpoint why. I wanted a break from the world for a little longer.

"Mom, did you suspect Dad was cheating on you?"

Mom's eyes widened. This apparently wasn't where she'd expected our conversation to go.

"Well, that's challenging to answer." She laid her blueberry-lemon donut on the plate and dabbed her mouth with a napkin. "I knew your dad was distracted. He'd started working late and participating in happy hours with coworkers, which he'd never done before. He wasn't interested in . . ." Mom's cheeks turned pink. "Um, romance."

Oh, geez. I looked at my tea and felt my face flush as well.

"So, while I hadn't suspected him specifically of cheating, when he finally told me the truth about Rebecca, I wasn't entirely surprised. There was this piece of me that said, 'Yes, *that's* what my subconscious was picking up on.'" Mom peered at me. "I don't know if that makes sense."

"Yeah," I said on a drawn-out breath. We sat in silence for a moment and then I added, "I was completely surprised."

Mom sighed sadly. "I know."

"I had always thought of Dad as someone with so much character, you know? He never seemed like the type to do something like cheat on his wife."

Mom nodded but didn't reply.

I went back to nibbling at my donut, my thoughts sifting through the phone call with Amelia yesterday afternoon. I hadn't felt what Mom did—that this confirmed something I'd suspected. Did that mean anything? I didn't think Alex would *purposefully* flirt with Josie while he had a girlfriend, but it wasn't hard for me to imagine his friendliness blurring into flirtation. Josie's beauty was obvious, and she must be a person of great character if she'd been bothered by Alex flirting with her. Better character than me if I was honest. Back when Alex was dating Leilani, I would've relished him flirting with me.

"You look like something is weighing on you, Tessa," Mom said softly.

I kept my gaze on my plate, wondering if I should start with Amelia's phone call or my conversations with Alex about Josie.

"I'm sorry you had to walk in on Phil and me like that," Mom said.

Oh. She thought this was about *that*.

Ordinarily, walking in on my mom kissing a guy would've been a top-of-mind issue. How crazy that it was, like, number three on my list of serious concerns.

"Yeah . . ."

"I should've talked to you about Phil." Mom spoke slowly, as if explaining a challenging concept to me. "But it felt complicated."

"Is he your . . ." I trailed off. *Boyfriend* sounded like the wrong word to describe a man in his forties who'd already lost a wife to cancer.

"We've gone out a couple times—"

"Oh." I put my elbows on the table and my face in my hands. "And you didn't tell me?"

"I didn't want you to get worked up over nothing. Like if the date was a bust."

I looked up. "Was it a bust?"

Mom shook her head.

I didn't know how to answer. These days, it felt as if life was like running on a treadmill cranked to full speed, and I was the only one who couldn't seem to keep up. Couldn't seem to get back on without being flung off.

Mom clearly wanted *some* kind of response from me. She kept looking at me as she rotated her coffee cup in quarter turns. "We're obviously aware of how this would impact you and Kayleigh." Mom swept nonexistent crumbs off the table and onto her empty plate. "Phil thinks Kayleigh would be excited about the idea, but obviously she's a lot younger and it's . . . different for her."

Mom looked at me again. I sipped at my tea. Did she want me to volunteer an answer to the question she wasn't asking? *Actually, Mom, I'd prefer you being happily single because currently Dad's situation is taking up all my mental space for "parent drama." Thanks for understanding.*

"And who knows that it would even go anywhere," Mom continued as she stood from the table. "We might go on a few more dates, realize the relationship wouldn't work out, and that'd be that."

I wasn't feeling that lucky. With the way my life was trending, it seemed more probable that they'd decide to elope this summer. We all attended the same church, they both had one child, both their daughters swam, and—I was guessing—they were both pretty lonely. That seemed like a lot of compatibility right off the bat.

"You don't have to say anything right away." Mom turned away and wiped her hands on the dish towel. "Maybe think about it. Process your feelings with Kendra tomorrow or whatever. I'm glad you have an appointment with her already scheduled."

"Yeah." Though I probably needed a double appointment to work through all my junk.

Mom offered me a strained smile. Couldn't *one* thing stay the same? Couldn't my mom be happily single for a few more years? Was that such an unfair thing to want?

I could hear Rebecca calling me spoiled and childish at the hospital. Asking my mom not to pursue happiness for herself because I didn't want to share her clearly aligned with Rebecca's accusations.

"I better get ready to go," I said. I could blow off my own practice, but not swim lessons.

"Okay," Mom said. "Me too."

And even though we'd sat and talked for longer than we had in weeks, it still felt like we'd left thousands of words unsaid.

—⁓—

I didn't turn on my phone until after I'd gotten home from teaching swim lessons. A flood of notifications competed for my attention, and I immediately wanted to shut it off again.

From Alex alone, I had two voicemails and five texts. All his communication sounded as though he didn't have anything specific to talk to me about, just that he was concerned when he couldn't get ahold of me. That is, until I read the text from this morning. **Hope you're doing better today. I'll come over after work, okay? We have a lot to talk about.**

A lot to talk about. Maybe he meant what had happened with Logan.

Or maybe he meant something else. Dread turned into a rock in my stomach.

My dad sent a text that Logan was acting like his normal self today and to not worry. He included a picture of Logan grinning which I swiped away from immediately. The thought of Logan being afraid of me and never smiling at me like that again was too heartbreaking right now.

I scrolled through the texts from the girls. There had been some normal chatter—Shay sharing a story about one of the riders she'd helped, several pictures of Izzy's Fourth of July cupcake creations from a few days ago, and then there was an abrupt change in the tone. Had Amelia DMed them about her conversation with Josie? Had Izzy sent them Rebecca's post? I wasn't sure, but the messages shifted to **Tessa, we're here for you**, with lots of praying hand emojis, and an actual prayer text from Izzy. **Lord, help Tessa through this challenging time. Help her to know what's** hers to take responsibility for and what isn't. Fill her with peace. Amen.

I knew I should respond. I typed out, Thanks, girls. It's been a rough 24 hours. But I couldn't think of anything else to say, and that seemed too short of a response considering how many words they'd flung around since last night.

Finally, I sent the inadequate text to my friends, along with two others. Sorry to worry you. See you tonight, to Alex. Thanks, glad he's doing well, to Dad.

Izzy responded immediately, and I shut my phone off again.

I surveyed my room. The unpacked boxes still lined the wall. Books I'd never arranged on my shelf, stacked haphazardly. The pile of photographs and posters that I'd never hung. I'd never really moved into this room. Sure, I slept here, and my stuff was in here, but I'd never settled in. As if some miracle might happen that would plunk me back into my old room, my old life.

I'd resisted—maybe even *rejected*—that God might have something here for me. Something good. Something I actually wanted. Or needed.

The noise of Mom's afternoon art camp was my soundtrack as I emptied boxes, arranged books, and unpacked my desk. Hours later, when parents arrived to pick up their kids, I heard Mom speaking in a low voice with one of the fathers. I was pretty sure it was Phil. I had barely eaten—my stomach had been too tight for me to eat much, yet I still felt queasy.

My weekends at Dad and Rebecca's were always so awkward, even before I'd completely screwed up and hurt Logan. I survived my time there by knowing it was just forty-eight hours every couple weeks, and that afterward I could relax in the house with Mom. That would look very different if she married Phil. Would he and Kayleigh move in here? Or would *we* move in with them? Would I be moving into their guest bedroom and sharing a bathroom for the first time in my life? If so, then I wouldn't feel like I had a home anymore. I'd feel like a guest no matter where I was.

—〰—

I resolved to face the issue head-on with Mom at dinner that night—I didn't need Kendra's help knowing that I had a lot of fear about Mom dating Phil—but then she told me she was having dinner with the ladies from her Bible study. So instead, I mixed a bagged salad with tomatoes and chicken and half watched a *Friends* rerun while I ate.

Eight thirty came and went with no Alex. I reluctantly turned my phone back on, and my heart plummeted at the two texts he'd sent.

Josie asked if I could talk after work, so I'll be a few minutes late. And then, later, he'd sent a simple, **Leaving now.**

I had managed to eat about half the salad, but I couldn't eat the rest now. I put the bowl on the coffee table. Already, what I'd eaten wanted to come back up.

I thumbed through the other texts that had come through. My dad said he thought it'd be a good idea for the three of us—him, Rebecca, and me—to get together and talk things through. Mom could come, too, if I wanted. I knew he meant that comment to be soothing, but the thought of Mom and Rebecca in the same room was enough to make me sweat. Maybe I'd wait to respond to that until after my appointment with Kendra.

As I heard a car pull into the driveway, I noticed a text from Amelia. **Did you talk to Alex? Josie came over again last night. I'm so sorry this is happening now. If Alex breaks up with you, he's an idiot.**

I laid my phone facedown and made myself take in a deep breath. And then another. Okay . . . he was maybe breaking up with me. Now I knew. I could be prepared. I could stop worrying about when Alex was going to break my heart and get on with the work of healing from it. I took another deep inhale and released it. Now I wouldn't turn into the screaming, crying girlfriend. I would listen, I would nod. I would say, "Thank you for your honesty" and "I hope we can still be friends." I could preserve my dignity, and then I could cry later in my room. Those were all the things God had given me to control in this situation, and I'd have to trust Him that it was enough.

There was a knock on the door.

You can do this, I told myself as I stood on trembling legs and crossed the entryway. I closed my eyes briefly. *Jesus, give me strength.*

I opened the door to find Alex standing on the front porch, the sun descending behind him in a blaze of red and orange.

"Hi," he said softly.

My heart hammered painfully. I was going to miss so much about him. "Hi."

His smile appeared strained. Alex was a good guy. He wasn't looking forward to this any more than I was. "Sorry I'm late. Just in time for the sunset, though. Want to sit outside?"

He didn't realize my mom was gone. He was suggesting this so we'd have privacy while he broke the news to me.

"Sure."

I sat on the front steps and so did Alex. He sighed as he sat, like my grandpa sometimes did. "Sorry I'm late. I don't know if you got my message, but Josie asked to talk."

Despite knowing what was coming, the sound of her name was painful.

Alex started to put his arm around me, and I slid away. "Look, I already know why you're here." My voice was strangled with tears. So much for dignity. "Let's get this over with."

Alex blinked at me. "Get what over with?"

"The breakup. Amelia texted me. I already know." I wiped

away the dumb tears that had gathered on my eyelashes. *You can control this, Tessa.* "Let's not drag this out, okay?"

"I'm so confused right now." Alex pushed his hair off his forehead. "Amelia said I was breaking up with you? What would make her think that?"

"I guess she heard it from Josie. It's okay." I wiped away even more tears. "I understand."

There was a brief silence and then, "I'm *not* breaking up with you, Tessa."

I risked a glance to find Alex with his elbows on his knees and his forehead in his hands, his fingers threaded into his hair. "This is such a confusing mess. Same as I told you last week, and a couple weeks ago, I'm *not* interested in her. I'm interested in *you.*"

Alex was saying all the right things, and yet I felt no sense of relief.

"But that doesn't make any sense. Because Josie told Amelia that you were flirting, and Amelia texted that she was sorry and if you broke up with me you were an idiot."

He looked baffled. "I don't understand how Amelia got involved in this."

I tucked my knees to my chest and wrapped my arms around them. "She's Josie's neighbor."

"Yeah, I get that, but she's making some wild assumptions." Alex's voice was hard. I rarely heard him this angry. "And I can only imagine that Josie has helped her with that. But it makes me mad that Amelia felt the need to dump all this on you and worry you when nothing was going on."

"Well, something was going on," I said in a small voice. "Right?"

"Apparently in Josie's brain." Alex turned and looked me square in the eye. "As far as I can tell, here's what happened. Her aunt had been sick with cancer and died. Josie was upset, obviously, and I said if she wanted to talk about it more, we could get together over the weekend. I was *not* flirting, just . . ." Alex's hands flailed. "Trying to be nice. Trying to be supportive. Trying to be a friend."

"Okay."

"And then last week, her dog died. Also upsetting. So, when I stopped for Starbucks the next morning on the way to work, I picked up a coffee for her, too. Again, not flirting. Trying to encourage her."

Alex looked at me, assessing. I nodded, prodding him to go on.

"Then tonight, she asked if we could talk. I told her I only had a few minutes because I had plans with you, and she said all this weird stuff about how I'd made my interest in her really clear, but that she wouldn't feel right about anything happening during camp since we signed those contracts."

"What contracts?"

"Everybody has to sign a thing promising to not date anyone else at OWC. They're junk. Half the counselors are dating each other. But anyway, she said that to me, and I was completely shocked. I thought, *What does she mean, 'I've made my interest clear'?*"

"And did you ask her?"

"I did. She said I asked her out and brought her gifts, which I have to assume is related to the two things I told you. And she said I'm always asking about her evening plans, and that there are always fifth-grade girls who ask if I'm her boyfriend." Alex made a disgusted noise in his throat. "I told her that was friendly conversation. I asked Connor and Eli about their evening plans, too, and certainly not because I want to *date* them. And that I didn't even know what to do with the fifth-grade girls' comments."

I inhaled deeply. Exhaled. I wanted to believe him, to trust him. And logically I knew that he'd given me zero reasons to doubt him. And yet there was my dad . . .

I kept my arms wrapped around me, like a protective shell.

Alex's knee bounced fast, like a vibration. "I don't feel like I can read you very well right now. Do you not believe me? Are you mad? What's going on?"

"When Amelia told me you were coming here to break up with me—"

"Which infuriates me, by the way. Why would Josie talk to her about that except that she knows you and Amelia are friends? Was she *trying* to cause problems for us?"

"I don't know. Amelia acts like Josie's on the track for sainthood."

Alex shook his head. "Josie's not without her flaws."

"Neither am I," I said. "I feel like I'm more flaws than anything else right now. And here's beautiful, perfect Josie who wants to be with you . . . what am I supposed to think? Why would you ever pick me over her?"

Alex rested a hand on my knee. "Because you're *you*. It's not like I'm sitting here with this list of boxes that need to be checked, and if a girl checks off more boxes than you, I'm going to change my mind. Nobody else is *you*."

"But nobody else is my mom, and my dad still left her. Left *me*."

"Tessa." Alex put his arm around my shoulders, and he kept it there, even though I held my body stiff, distant. "I know everything with your dad makes this feel so much scarier. I know there's probably nothing I can say that'll make that fear of yours disappear. But for me there's nobody else like you. Nobody else knows me like you do, sees me and encourages me like you do. I have more fun with you than anybody else and when anything happens to me, the first thing I want to do is call you and tell you about it. Besides," he nudged me, "there's no other girl who suffered through my multiple Lightning McQueen birthdays as a kid. Like I said, nobody else is *you*."

I giggled. It wasn't quite "relief" that I felt, more like a cousin of it, but my knees eased away from my chest. I glanced at Alex and released a breath I'd been holding. "Okay. And I think you came to at least one Cinderella-themed birthday party, so we're even."

A smile bloomed on his face, and he rested his hand on the back of my neck. "I'm so sorry this was worrying you on top of everything else you had going on. Your mom told me some of what happened with Logan, but I'd like to hear about it from you."

I sighed. "Yeah, yesterday was basically the worst."

When Mom got home thirty minutes later, we were still sitting on the front steps in the dark, fireflies blinking off and on around us. My knees were no longer up against me, but rather were bent toward Alex.

Maybe Alex would break my heart someday. Or maybe I would break his. Or we'd drift apart. A lot could change, I knew that. And I knew this likely wasn't the last time my insecurities would flare up.

But I also knew that having complete control in a relationship came at a cost too. I didn't want to live the way Abraham did. Yeah, maybe he had the control I craved, but the cost was missing out on *this*. Somebody knowing me, seeing me at my lowest, and sticking with me even then.

Chapter
22

I WAS SLICING AN APPLE WHEN MY PHONE BUZZED with a text from Shay to me and Izzy. Amelia said the dress rehearsal of Annie is tonight. I feel bad none of us can be there Friday. Want to help me surprise her?

I slid my phone back in my pocket and resumed slicing. Amelia had texted me a few times since last Thursday. I'd mostly ignored her, except when she texted: Talked to Josie. She said it was a misunderstanding??? That's great! Let me know if you want to talk. Then I had texted back a simple, Thanks.

I guess I could understand why she'd told me about what Josie said, thinking she was protecting me, preparing me. Maybe I would've done the same thing in her position. But if she hadn't called that afternoon, I wouldn't have been so distracted and taken such poor care of Logan. Not that my negligence was Amelia's fault. That was mine. But still, her part in it grated on me. As did her assumptions that Josie liking Alex meant he liked her and was breaking up with me.

So, no, I didn't want to go to the dress rehearsal. I had enough going on today. I was heading out the door for an appointment with Kendra, and immediately after that I was meeting Dad and Rebecca at Starbucks. Dad said Rebecca wanted to apologize and "clear the air" before the wedding in three days.

After all the heavy lifting my emotions were going to do this afternoon, I was pretty sure all I'd have energy for tonight was taking a bath and eating ice cream.

My phone buzzed with Izzy's reply. I'm in! No ride though. Tessa?

Going tonight was probably the right thing to do, wasn't it? Ugh. I was so sick of not wanting to do stuff and feeling like I should anyway. Like meeting Dad and Rebecca this afternoon, or going to Amelia's show, or telling Mom that I was fine with her dating Phil when I felt anything but fine about it. Not that I had done that last one yet, but I knew it was probably the right thing to do.

I typed, Maybe. I have to meet Dad and Rebecca for coffee at 5:15. I'm not sure how long it'll take. I'll text when it's over but may have to meet you there.

How are you feeling about that? Izzy replied.

I smirked and sent back the nauseated emoji followed by the puking emoji.

I'll be praying for you! Shay wrote back. Izzy echoed that she would be too. Hope to see you at 7! she added.

—m—

The closer I got to Starbucks, the tighter my body became. I kept having to release my grip on the steering wheel, uncurl my toes, and unclench my teeth. My eyes were puffy from an intense session with Kendra, which had been a lot of me pacing in her office and crying while she handed me Kleenex.

We'd talked about what an acceptable apology looked like, that Rebecca's post crossed a line, and it was my job to make sure she understood that. Kendra said I should own what was mine—the accident—but nothing else.

"You have a tendency to want to make life easier for other people," Kendra had said. "Especially your mom. You're not responsible for how they feel."

Kendra thought it was a good idea to bring Mom to my meeting with Dad and Rebecca, that the only reason I wasn't bringing her was that I was trying to protect her. "Rebecca will have your dad there. I want you to feel like you have an ally too."

But I was forced to ignore that advice. Mom had art classes until five. I'd briefly considered asking Zoe, my favorite youth pastor at church, but I hadn't been to any of the youth group summer events and other than a few "checking in" texts, we hadn't spoken since school let out. The situation felt like too much to dump on someone during the ten-minute drive to the Starbucks by my dad's office.

"So, it's just You and me," I murmured to God as I wedged my Camry between two oversized SUVs.

Inside Starbucks, Dad and Rebecca were at a small booth in the back, sitting on the same side. Kendra told me that if I arrived first to choose a round table so that nobody was on anybody's physical side. Apparently, they hadn't considered this.

I ordered my iced coffee, lingered at the counter until it was ready, and then made my way to Dad and Rebecca. I kept my gaze averted as I took my seat across the table from them.

"Hi, Tessa, thanks for coming," Dad said.

My hand trembled slightly as I brought my straw to my mouth. "Mmhmm." I wondered where Logan was but didn't dare ask.

"With the wedding on Friday, we thought it'd be good to clear the air."

"Okay," I said to my coffee.

"We'll go first." Dad leaned forward and rested his elbows on the table. "We know that what happened with Logan was an accident. We know watching a baby his age is complicated. There's a lot to keep track of and a lot to do. We shouldn't have rushed you into a job that you weren't ready for."

Shame spilled over me. I wanted to deny what he'd said, but I knew that my negligence was what led to Logan being in the ER. How could I argue that I'd been ready for the responsibility?

"We also know that Logan matters a lot to you. We want you to have a relationship with him. But right now, we're only comfortable with supervised visits."

Supervised visits were more than I thought I might get for a while. I should feel grateful. "Okay."

There was silence across the table, and then Rebecca cleared her throat. "And I'm sorry for any pain my post on Instagram might have caused you."

Another silence followed.

Was that it? Was that the apology? I looked at the two of them. If Rebecca was searching for words, I couldn't tell by her facial expression. She wore a hard mask, her lips clamped.

Dad glanced from Rebecca to me. "She didn't realize you would see it."

As if that made it okay. I exhaled a disbelieving laugh, causing Rebecca's gaze to sharpen. "You know I follow you."

"I didn't use your name," Rebecca said in a hard, quiet voice. "I protected your privacy."

"Not really," I said slowly. "One of my best friends saw and knew you were talking about me. And in the comments, someone asked if you were talking about David's daughter—"

"We don't need to linger on this, do we? The post has been taken down. I'm sorry for the pain it caused."

What happened to Logan was 100 percent mine to own, and I had. The social media post, however, was 100 percent Rebecca's, and she needed to own that. Not just that it had caused me pain, but that it had been wrong to post at all.

"How would you feel, if instead of apologizing for what happened to Logan, I only apologized for how it made you feel?" By some miracle, I kept my voice gentle. "If I took no responsibility for what I'd actually done?"

"My Instagram post is not the same as your blatant neglect," Rebecca snapped. "Logan has staples in his scalp. We had to meet with the social worker. I thought she might take Logan away from us. All because of *you*."

Dad put a hand on Rebecca's back. "Tessa isn't denying that what she did was wrong. What she's saying is that you posting about it was also—"

Rebecca pushed his hand away. "Stop defending her. You're supposed to be on my side."

"Honey, she's my daughter," Dad said. "The way you feel about Logan? The way *we* feel about Logan? I feel that for Tessa, too. And you attacking her on Instagram, even without using her name, was inapp—"

Rebecca snatched her purse and scooted out of the booth. "I'm not listening to another word of this."

"Rebecca," Dad said with a groan as she stalked away. He half stood, and then glanced at me. He looked to her one more time and then sat. "I wanted that to go differently."

He pushed his glasses up and rubbed the bridge of his nose. I wanted to tell him that it was okay—but it wasn't okay. I could hear Kendra in my head. *You're not responsible for how they feel. God hasn't given you that to control.*

Dad repositioned his glasses and offered what was probably supposed to be an encouraging smile. "She'll get there. She'll apologize."

I sighed. Who was he trying to convince? "Dad, she may not. You can't make her apologize. Just like you can't make her like me. You can't make her want me in her house. Those are her decisions to make."

Dad's jaw tightened. I wondered if he ever regretted the decision to choose Rebecca over Mom. Did he wish he'd invested more in his first marriage, as imperfect as it was? Did he understand any more clearly that the ripples of his decision would go on forever?

"I know what the custody papers say," I said quietly. "But I don't think weekends with you and Rebecca are a good idea right now."

Kendra had told me that if I needed her to, she could say something to a judge if Dad wouldn't accept the reality of Rebecca's feelings toward me.

But he nodded and said a gruff, "You're probably right."

He looked away from me and touched his eye . . . as if he was *crying.* I'd never seen him cry. "I'm sorry, kiddo." He looked at me, his eyes brimming. "For everything."

I didn't know if the umbrella of "everything" included the last year or if he meant the last fifteen minutes at Starbucks, but something in my heart softened. I'd said I was sorry so many times since last Wednesday, and I could see in his eyes what I'd felt in my own soul. The torture of trying to forgive yourself when you knew you didn't deserve it.

I placed my hand over his. "We all make mistakes."

His eyes widened. Softened. "Yes," he murmured. "We certainly do."

Chapter
23

I'd kind of hoped that my coffee with Dad and Rebecca would go so long, there would be no way I could make it to the dress rehearsal for *Annie*. But I had plenty of time, even with picking up Izzy. I considered making up an excuse for not going, but my conscience lit up at that. Even if I stayed home, I wouldn't be able to enjoy myself, because all I'd be thinking about was that I'd lied to my best friends.

I finished up early. Shay, you want to walk to my house now-ish and then we'll leave to get Izzy?

Izzy sent back confetti emojis.

I wished I agreed with Izzy's sentiment. I left my phone on my bed and went clattering downstairs to grab a quick dinner.

"Perfect timing," Mom said as she turned off the burner and slid two grilled cheese sandwiches onto plates.

"Wow, it's like you read my mind." I took the plate she offered me. "Thank you."

"There's more of that fruit salad in the fridge from last night," Mom said over her shoulder as she rinsed the skillet.

"Okay, great. I need to eat quickly because Izzy, Shay, and I are going to surprise Amelia at her dress rehearsal tonight."

"Aww, that's sweet of you girls."

"It's very sweet of us," I said dryly.

At the table, Mom prayed a succinct blessing over our food, and then I took a huge bite of grilled cheese.

"How was your appointment with Kendra?" Mom asked.

I'd already given her the basics on what had happened with Dad and Rebecca, but we hadn't covered my appointment yet. She didn't normally ask.

I chewed and swallowed. "Fine. Helpful."

"Yeah? You felt like she prepared you well for your conversation?"

"Yeah. I seemed better prepared than Rebecca, anyway."

"I would say so since she stormed out. Fruit?"

I shook my head. "I don't think I have time. Shay will be here in the next ten minutes."

Mom rolled her eyes and gave me a scoop of fruit salad. "That's plenty of time, especially with how you're snarfing your sandwich."

"I'm not snarfing."

Mom smiled. "It's a relief, actually. It made me nervous last week when you were barely eating."

I made a show of taking a tiny bite, which made Mom smile more.

"Anything else from your time with Kendra?"

Even after my first appointment, Mom didn't grill me this much on what happened. Why was she—

Oh. She was hoping I'd talked to Kendra about Phil and had an update for her. And that gleam in her eye made me suspect she was hoping I would say it was fine with me. If I said no, she'd stop smiling like that.

Kendra had told me that God didn't put me in charge of how my parents felt, but why did it *feel* like I was in control of that sometimes?

"We talked about Phil some, if you're wondering." I poked a chunk of apple and put it in my mouth. "I guess it'd be fine with me. If you guys continued dating or whatever."

Mom received this with a nod and a smile that was clearly a muted version of what she was really feeling. She didn't want to freak me out with her enthusiasm, it seemed. "Okay, well, that's nice to hear. I promise everything will move slow, but it's good to have your blessing."

I nibbled at my sandwich, and then worried Mom would notice that I was eating differently. I made myself take a large bite.

"Thanks, Tessa." Mom smiled warmly at me. "I appreciate it."

The doorbell rang.

"That's Shay," I said, slipping away from the table and away from the conversation.

"Have fun, honey!" Mom called after me.

It wasn't that I was taking responsibility for Mom's feelings, I argued with the version of Kendra that lived in my head these days. It was just that I liked doing things that made her happy.

That wasn't the same, was it?

—m—

"And then Dad left to go home to try and smooth things over with Rebecca." I pulled into a parking spot outside the community college theater. "That happened, like, an hour ago, so now you're all caught up. Let's go cheer on Amelia."

I unclipped my seat belt and popped open my door. Both Shay and Izzy exited slower.

"That's so much, Tessa," Shay said as she climbed out of the passenger seat.

"Yeah, I don't even know where to start responding," Izzy closed the back door. "With a hug?"

She wrapped her arms around me and squeezed.

I tried to seem comfortable and patted her back a couple times until she released me. "Thanks."

"My sister hit me in the head with a golf club once," she said sincerely. "I still love her."

I looked away. "Okay, thanks. We'd better get inside."

Aspire held practices at a church downtown but rented the community college's theater for its performances. Izzy had been there a couple times to see shows, and she led the way inside.

"I feel nervous, and I don't even have to get on stage," Shay muttered to me as we entered the theater.

I nodded my agreement. "I'm definitely happy drama class is over."

The theater was nicer than I expected, with cushioned seats that sloped toward the stage and soft lighting. There were a few grown-ups on stage tweaking the set placement, but any of the pre-show chaos must have been contained to backstage. Or maybe you didn't have pre-show chaos in private theater groups.

"There she is," Izzy whispered. She pointed toward the sound booth. Amelia was easy to spot as she walked with her long, distinct strides toward the stage.

"Should we go sit in the first row?" Izzy whispered. "Surprise her when she turns around?"

"First row?" Shay groaned. "But that's so close to the stage."

"Well, the other option is—"

"Girls!" Amelia's shriek echoed in the theater. She ran across an aisle, her arms open for a hug well before she got to us. "What are you doing here?"

Izzy gladly followed suit and ran to hug Amelia back. "Surprising you! We felt bad that we couldn't come on Friday."

"You girls are literally the best." Amelia released Izzy and turned to Shay, and then finally to me. "Hey, I've been meaning to call you, there's been no time with the show and everything." She squeezed me in a tight hug. "I'm so glad things worked out with Alex," she said in her loud theater voice.

I could feel Izzy and Shay's curiosity radiating off them. I hadn't mentioned any of the Alex stuff in the car. I'd assumed that Amelia had been keeping them in the loop, since she'd shoehorned herself into the whole situation.

I faked a smile and looked away.

"Wait, things *did* work out, right? I mean, Josie said—"

"I don't want to hear any more secondhand information from Josie, but thanks." I hadn't meant to say that *so* sharply.

Amelia looked at me like I'd slapped her. In a quiet, not-Amelia voice, she said, "All I was going to say was that she said Alex made it very clear that he likes you—"

"I said I don't want to hear it. I wish you hadn't called me in the first place because nothing good came from that phone call."

"I'm . . . I'm really sorry, Tessa." To her credit, Amelia truly sounded sorry. "I thought if it was my boyfriend, I'd want to know . . ."

"Amelia?" someone called from a gap in the curtain.

Amelia turned. "Be right there!" She looked back to me, her eyes round with an apology that I didn't want to see. "I'm so sorry I hurt you, Tessa. I never meant for that to happen. I thought I was helping."

"Amelia?" A different voice called.

She swallowed hard. "I have to go. I want to talk about this more later, though. Intermission, maybe?"

I gave her an indifferent shrug.

Amelia hesitated, then turned and walked toward the stage, her shoulders hunched forward as though she carried the weight of our argument with her. I could feel Shay and Izzy looking at me.

"I probably shouldn't have come," I muttered. "You guys go ahead and get seats. I'll be right back."

I turned without looking them in the eyes. I'd come tonight because supporting Amelia seemed like the right thing to do. But just like when Rebecca attempted apologizing to me, doing the right thing with the wrong heart didn't work so well.

Funny how I had finally gotten what I had wanted all summer. Someone—Amelia—had behaved kindly and graciously while I threw a fit. It didn't feel nearly as good as I had imagined.

—m—

I considered leaving, but I didn't want to strand Izzy and Shay. Also, I had a feeling I'd regret that decision. Instead, I paced along the sidewalk, took some deep breaths, and tried to sift through what was mine to control in this situation and what wasn't.

When I went back into the theater, the show was underway. I was surprised to recognize the song "It's the Hard-Knock Life" being belted out on the stage by a group of boys and girls who looked like they were in middle school. Amelia sat center stage, several rows back, and scribbled notes on a clipboard. Izzy and Shay sat beside her. Izzy swayed and bounced to the beat of the music, while Shay sat still. There were several grown-ups scattered about in various seats, but mostly it was just us.

A few weeks ago, when I was the one chasing Amelia down trying to apologize, I'd told Izzy, "If we don't have the kind of friendships where we can make mistakes and be forgiven, then what are we even doing?" I'd been so annoyed that Amelia seemed bent on believing the worst about me, that she wouldn't trust that I hadn't called her fat and that I deeply regretted what I'd said about her not being in the show.

But now, I was doing the same thing. Didn't I believe that Amelia wanted what was best for me? That she'd told me what

Josie had said because she cared about me? That she thought she was helping? Even if I felt Josie's motives were a little sus, I didn't think that about Amelia, did I?

I didn't.

I walked down the aisle and shuffled sideways along the row to get to my friends. They saw me coming and all three of their faces looked wary. I attempted to smile at Amelia, but it wobbled as regret and grief stirred in my chest. Her whole face softened, and she opened her arms as I took the seat beside her.

I hugged her back for real this time. "I'm so sorry."

She squeezed me extra tight. "Me too."

Her forgiveness allowed me to breathe more deeply and to fully enjoy the fruit of Amelia's hard work from the last six weeks. *Annie* was a great show, but the coolest part was seeing the respect the cast members and adults had for Amelia. Even from the sidelines, that much was clear.

"Thanks for making sure we came," I said to Shay as we left. "I wouldn't have wanted to miss that."

On the ride home, Izzy chattered about her favorite parts in the show and how excited she was to take Drama 2 this next year at school. Shay and I exchanged several glances in the front seat. Whatever gene Amelia and Izzy had that made them love the stage, neither of us had it.

"Think she'll sleep tonight?" Shay asked as we watched Izzy skip up her driveway.

"Not for a while, anyway." As soon as Izzy was inside, I pulled away. "Feels super quiet without her."

"It does." Even without looking, I could tell Shay was smiling. "I used to feel kind of intimidated by how loud both of them were, but now I like it."

"Yeah." I smiled. "Loud can be good. Quiet's nice, too, though."

A few minutes later as I pulled alongside Booked Up, Shay said, "I think it was brave of you to come back into the show tonight.

If it was me, I might've been stubborn and stayed outside." She sighed. "As you know, I can be a little hotheaded."

I grinned. "Who, you? Only in specific situations."

She chuckled and unbuckled her seat belt. "Thanks for the ride."

"Anytime."

I watched her disappear into the dark store and continued home. Watching *Annie* with my friends had been surprisingly relaxing. I felt as though I'd been lifted out of the stress of my life for a few hours, like a mini vacation of sorts where I got to leave my ordinary life behind. I drove the short distance home feeling less stressed than I had in days.

At home, Mom was up in the attic studio painting. Dizzy Gillespie played on the speakers, and an oscillating fan combatted the hot air that always gathered up there.

"Hi, honey," Mom said as I came up the stairs, but she didn't turn around. "Did the show end early?"

So typical. I chuckled. "It's ten o'clock, Mom."

"What?" Now she turned and checked the clock. "Well, look at that. I had no idea it was so late."

I pulled out one of the stools from the table and sat. "If I hadn't come home, at what point in the night would you have noticed?"

"Maybe three?" Mom grinned. "Four? Guess I'll clean up for the night. How was the show?"

"It was really good. We should get tickets and go this Saturday or next weekend."

"That would be great. Phil was telling me the other day that Kayleigh loves theater stuff. Maybe they'd want to go with us."

The tension I'd felt release while watching *Annie* crept back into my shoulders. "Mmhmm."

Mom must've noted the change in my tone. She'd been gathering her brushes and now looked up at me. "Would that be okay?"

I hesitated. Then shook my head no.

Mom looked crushed. "Oh."

"I'm sorry. I know I said earlier that I was okay with you and Phil, but . . ."

"No, that's fine, honey," Mom said, feigning a brightness she clearly didn't feel. "That's totally fine. I'm glad you're being honest."

"I don't have any problems with Phil specifically, I'm . . ." Why couldn't I seem to complete my thoughts? "I'm not ready."

Mom nodded. "Thanks for telling me."

"I might be ready later, but I'm not there quite yet."

"I understand. Really." Her smile looked forced. She made a show of looking around at her art supplies. "I'm going to finish cleaning this up, and then I'm heading to bed."

"Yeah." I stood. "I think I'll get a snack and do the same."

"Okay. I love you."

I leaned in for a quick hug. "Love you too."

Everything in me wanted to take it back, to make her happy. I wanted to say that I was totally fine with Mom dating Phil. But I didn't. Because I wasn't.

I walked down the two flights of stairs to the kitchen and listened to Mom moving around in her studio. This was what the house would sound like when I was gone in a couple years. Mom, puttering about by herself, while a few blocks away Dad got on with his new life and new family. All because Mom had been considerate about my feelings and Dad hadn't. That didn't seem fair.

But not being ready *now* for my mom to start dating didn't mean I wouldn't be ready *ever*. I could work on it.

Chapter
24

FRIDAY MORNING, I POPPED AWAKE at five and blinked at my dark ceiling. My brain churned through scenarios for the wedding that night. What if I wasn't allowed in the church? What if Rebecca threw a fit when she saw me there? Dad had texted me the day before to say Rebecca felt badly for how things had gone at Starbucks and that we'd try again after the stress of the wedding had passed, but I wasn't convinced she actually felt that way.

At six thirty, I got out of bed and dressed for swim practice.

When I called Alex, he greeted me with, "I thought you weren't going this morning. I thought you wanted to sleep in."

"That was my plan." I broke off a piece of granola bar and shoved it in my mouth. "My brain had other ideas and started working at five."

"Ugh. Wedding stress?"

"Apparently. I couldn't stop thinking about it."

"Maybe swimming will help. Running always helps me when I'm stressed."

"Yeah, maybe."

Alex sighed. "I wish I could go with you tonight. I hate that you have to go alone."

I did too. Kendra and I had talked about it and decided there was nothing to be done about it. "Sometimes in life there are things we have to do alone," she had said. "But we know from Scripture that God never leaves us. He'll be there with you."

We'd looked up a verse that I could memorize and recite to myself, but even still my stomach knotted painfully every time I thought of walking into that church by myself. But Alex couldn't help that he couldn't go, and I didn't want him to feel any worse than he already did.

"What's on the schedule for Forced Family Fun this evening?" I asked.

"Well, seeing as it's Mom's birthday, I'll probably have to watch some kind of girl movie, and my dad will grill something. I won't even be home until after nine, so my job is to show up and be present, really."

"That's my job tonight too," I said glumly as I turned into the aquatic center parking lot. "I think I'm also supposed to act happy? Or at least not cry."

"You can do it," Alex said softly. "I'll be thinking about you and praying for you. And we're still on for tomorrow morning, right? Donuts and a bike ride?"

"I wish I could fast-forward to that." I put my car in park. "Maybe I'll catch some kind of crazy twenty-four-hour flu and have to spend the whole day sleeping."

Alex chuckled. "We can hope, I guess."

The whole day had a funky vibe. I didn't know what your dad's wedding day was supposed to feel like, but I wasn't lucky enough to catch any kind of flu, so I spent the whole day with one eye on the clock. Which seemed to be moving toward six o'clock way faster than a regular day.

When I came downstairs to leave for the wedding, Mom was sitting in the living room knitting a raspberry-colored scarf as she watched an episode of *Fixer Upper* that even I'd seen twice. I didn't know how the average person spent their ex-spouse's wedding night, but this didn't seem like the best option. Maybe she'd had plans with Phil that she'd cancelled because of me.

Mom looked up from her scarf and tilted her head as she studied me. "This is what you're wearing?"

I looked down at my black dress, which I'd worn to the Valentine's dance at school. It had a swishy skirt that I liked, and a high neck so I didn't have to feel nervous if I leaned forward. "What's wrong with what I'm wearing?"

"I don't think you're supposed to wear black to a wedding."

"I think it's fine." I looked down and considered my choice. It's not like anybody had volunteered to take me shopping for tonight. This was the nicest dress I owned. "And it's more like a funeral anyway, right?" I grinned at Mom, and she gave me a look that said, *that's amusing, but don't say that.*

"What are you going to do with your hair?"

"This. I brushed it. And it's not in a ponytail."

"Okay," she said with that high pitch that meant she disagreed but wouldn't push.

"I put on a necklace." I ran my thumb down the long chain. "That's effort enough, right?"

Mom chuckled. "Sure. I hope you have a not-miserable time."

"Thanks. Not-miserable is the exact bar that I've set for myself tonight. What are you doing tonight?"

"Basically this." She must've seen the disapproval on my face because she smiled. "I'm fine. I had two rambunctious art classes today on top of a quick coffee with Amanda Hastings, so I'm looking forward to some quiet tonight."

I leaned against the couch. "You had coffee with Mrs. Hastings?"

"Yep. It's a birthday tradition for us. And it was great." Mom rested her knitting needles on her lap. "She helped me see that you won't live here forever—" Mom's voice wavered slightly "—and that I should take advantage of the time with you now and wait on dating for a while."

Guilt sloshed in my stomach. Though I wasn't surprised this was Mrs. Hastings's counsel.

"Your happiness matters a lot to me," I said. "And I don't want you to be alone. It's just with everything going on right now . . ."

Mom reached over the back of the couch and squeezed my arm. "When I put myself in your shoes, I know I would feel the same way. And learning to be content without a man is important to me, so I'm fine with this. Really."

Mom's smile didn't quite reach her eyes.

I leaned over the couch to hug her. "Thank you," I whispered.

She squeezed me close. "Don't cry or you'll ruin your makeup."

"I'm not wearing makeup."

Mom sighed. "Oh, to be sixteen and naturally gorgeous."

I rolled my eyes, but with a smile on my face. I put on my heels that I'd last worn in February and double-checked that my wristlet had the essentials. Then I could put it off no longer. "Well. Guess I'll see you in a few hours."

"We'll have cereal when you get home," Mom said.

I smiled. "Sounds perfect."

When I pulled into the parking lot of the old church, there was an open spot beside my grandparents' Buick. I hadn't considered that they would be here. Maybe my aunt, uncle, and cousins from Indy would be here too. Were these the kinds of communication breakdowns that happened in divorced families?

Even though it was 5:55, I hesitated to get out of my car. "This is going to be fine," I said aloud. I tried to remember the verse Kendra and I had picked out for me to memorize, so that I could recite it to myself as I walked in alone. But I couldn't recall a word of it. Instead of heading inside the church, I opened my Bible app and scrolled, as if I would magically stumble upon the right verse.

It was now 5:58. I took one more deep breath and got out of the car.

My phone buzzed with a text as I locked my car. It was Amelia. Praying for you, friend. Here it was almost six o'clock, nearly time for the curtains to rise on opening night of *Annie,* and Amelia had thought of *me.* Was praying for *me.*

Thank you, I swiped with my thumb as I walked as fast as possible across the parking lot. That means more than you know. Hope Annie goes well tonight! Can't wait to see it for real next weekend.

And as I opened the door to the church, the verse floated through my thoughts. *Sovereign Lord, my strong deliverer, You shield my head in the day of battle.*

I'm not in control, I thought. *But You are, and You shield me. That's enough.*

Chapter
25

I SAT IN THE BACK PEW, surrounded by strangers, and listened stoically as my father made vows to Rebecca that he'd made to my mother and broken. I couldn't see Logan, but I could hear him chattering up front with whoever was holding him. My heart twanged with sadness.

I turned away during the "you may now kiss the bride" part of the ceremony. I'm not sure who decided we needed that in wedding ceremonies, but . . . *ew.*

The pastor, who I also didn't recognize, said with a broad smile, "It's my pleasure to introduce to you for the first time, Mr. and Mrs. Hart."

As others around me clapped, the words cut into my heart. Mrs. Hart. That was my mom's name.

The new Mrs. Hart turned to the audience and raised both her arms. One hand grasped my father's and the other her bouquet. She looked as though she was declaring victory. *You shield me*, I thought desperately, blinking away the threat of tears. *You're sovereign, and You shield me.*

Piano music filled the church. Everyone around me stood and clapped as my dad and Rebecca marched triumphantly down the aisle. My dad scanned the crowd as they walked, and I instinctively shrunk behind the man who'd been sitting to my right. Maybe that was childish, especially considering I would see him in a few minutes at the reception, but I wanted to delay that interaction for as long as I could.

"The bride and groom have invited us all to the back lawn for dinner and dancing," the pastor said into a microphone that he didn't seem to need. "If you're family, please keep your seat for a few pictures. Everyone else should go around back where food is waiting for you."

Everyone around me shuffled out, loudly expressing their approval to each other that they didn't have to wait for pictures to be over to start eating. "That's the perk of second weddings," one man joked to his wife. "You've been to enough that you know how to do it right."

I knew glaring at him was unfair of me—he'd been joking—but I couldn't seem to hold back. For nearly everybody else here, this was just another wedding. A Friday night commitment they had to find a babysitter for. In an hour or two, they'd leave full of roast chicken and wedding cake and go on with their normal lives.

As the rows around me emptied, I pulled out my phone to avoid looking as awkward as I felt. Both Izzy and Shay had added on to Amelia's message. **Eager to hear how tonight goes!** Izzy had said with lots of praying hand emojis. And Shay. **Wish we could be there with you.**

Thanks, girls. Ceremony is over. Now I'll smile a few times, eat some cake, and get out of here.

"There you are!"

I looked up at the sound of my grandma's voice. "Hi, Grandma."

She smiled at me as she shuffled down the row. She wore a bright, floral dress and had gotten her hair done for the occasion. Maybe my mom had been right about my dress.

But Grandma said, "Don't you look lovely?" as she bent to hug me. "We saved a seat for you up front."

"Thanks. I got here a little late."

She made a show of looking around. "Were you sitting by yourself? Where's that boyfriend of yours?"

"He had to work tonight."

Up front, Logan screeched. A woman with a bob of silver hair paced the front of the sanctuary, bouncing him in her arms. "Rebecca's mom," Grandma said with a sour expression as she followed my gaze. "I've never been a fan."

I couldn't see Logan very well, but his tiny hands grabbed at the hat he wore. Probably to hide the staples. My thumb ran along the chain of my necklace. Would I get to hold him tonight? Even if Dad and Rebecca were okay with that, would Logan even come to me, or would he cry?

"Come on up front," Grandma said. "We'll suffer through these pictures together."

As she said that, the church doors swung open. Dad and Rebecca entered with their photographer trailing behind them. Dad's gaze locked on me, and he grinned as he walked toward me.

"Hi, pumpkin." He fit an arm around me and squeezed. "Glad you're here. You look beautiful."

"Thanks," I murmured, giving in to the hug. The fabric of his jacket rubbed against my bare arms. I couldn't remember when I'd last seen him wear a suit.

Up front, Rebecca reclaimed Logan and used her teacher voice to arrange the family. "We'll do my side first," she told the photographer. "Mom and Dad, stand over here. David?"

"I'm coming." Dad smiled at me one more time and strode up front.

I trailed behind my grandma to where Grandpa and Aunt Jana sat in a pew close to the front.

"Look who I found skulking around the back," Grandma announced a bit louder than I would've liked.

Grandpa smiled and motioned for me to hug him—he wasn't getting up apparently—and Aunt Jana offered me a tight smile that made me feel not so alone. None of them looked thrilled to be here either.

"Your cousins had to work," Aunt Jana greeted me. Then in a low voice she added, "And your uncle said he had already come to one of David's weddings."

I laughed. "Can't argue with that. Where are Jeff and Katie working?"

As we chatted about jobs, I heard the photographer repeating Logan's name. "Logan," the photographer said in a sing-song voice. "Over here, Logan. Logan."

I glanced over. Dad held Logan turned toward the camera, but Logan had different ideas and was craning his neck to look behind him. When our eyes met, Logan broke into a drooly smile and cooed.

"Hi, Logan," I said reflexively.

He flailed his arms and legs and made his "ooh" sounds even louder. He was looking at *me*. That grin was for *me*. That excitement was for *me*.

Dad must have realized it, too, because he stopped trying to redirect Logan's attention and instead made a full body turn toward me. "Oh, that's what the problem is. Do you see your big sister, Logan?"

Dad held Logan out as he approached me. Logan's eyes grew wider, his grin broader, and his arms and legs spazzier the closer they got to me. I reached for him, grinning and tearful all at once. The camera clicked repeatedly as Dad planted Logan in my arms.

"Hi, buddy." I rested my forehead against his and felt tears spill down my cheeks. "I missed you."

Now that he'd gotten to me, Logan was way more interested in my necklace than anything else. He grasped it with both fists, yanked, and snapped it right off my neck all within a second.

There was a collective gasp of surprise, and a couple echoes of, "Oh, no."

Logan looked up at me as I laughed. He looked so pleased with himself.

"It's okay." I unwound the chain from his fingers. "Accidents happen."

—m—

Thankfully Logan stopped fussing with his hat, because any time it came off, whoever was around him would instantly say, "Oh, dear, what happened to his head?"

Finally, he dozed off while Rebecca's mom carried him. It felt unfair that he got to be oblivious as Dad and Rebecca shared their first dance, tossed the bouquet, and fed each other cake while the rest of us had to pay attention.

"Lucky Logan," Aunt Jana whispered to me. "I wish it was socially acceptable for me to close my eyes and go to sleep."

"They're pretty militant about his schedule," I said. "Surely they'll want to get him to bed soon."

"I wouldn't count on that. I've known Rebecca Simmons a long time and she's always struck me as the 'I only get to be a bride once' kind of gal."

A few minutes after the dance floor opened up, Rebecca's mom sashayed over to me. "You mind holding him for me, honey? Mr. Simmons wants to hit the dance floor, and you don't look too interested in dancing."

I cradled Logan on my lap. "Just with this guy, but I don't think he's in the mood."

Mrs. Simmons laughed like I'd said something truly hilarious, and then wobbled across the grass in her tall heels where a pudgy man with gray hair waited to sweep her onto the dance floor.

I sat content at the small round table, gazing at Logan as he snoozed under the glow of the twinkle lights. He was unperturbed by Sister Sledge's "We Are Family" blaring on the speakers, the raucous laughter, and the significance of the event.

"How nice for you, Logan," I said softly as I stroked the back of his hand.

Out of the corner of my eye, I caught sight of Rebecca's billowy white skirt approaching me and looked up. Her smile was thin, not the victorious grin the newly minted Mrs. Hart had worn earlier.

She took the seat beside me and looked at Logan. Was she going to demand him back?

"He obviously loves you." She moved her gaze to me. "That was pretty obvious in there."

I looked away to Logan's chubby cheeks. "I really love him too."

I could feel her gaze on me as she said, "I finally got up the courage to watch the Ring cam footage from his accident." She swallowed hard. "The stroller was nowhere near the edge of the patio. I think I've left it there without locking it, honestly. And how you cared for him afterward . . ."

Tears gathered on her eyelashes, and she blinked them away.

My heart pounded as the memories of that awful afternoon condensed in my mind. Logan's unfocused eyes. The wail of the approaching ambulance. The social worker using the word *negligence*.

"I've never regretted anything more," I told Rebecca in a strangled voice.

She responded with a sad smile. "I believe you. And I shouldn't

have reacted by posting about it on Instagram. I . . ." She shook
her head. "I don't know why I did that. Habit, maybe."

"I forgive you," I said. And I meant it.

Rebecca's smile still hung thin. "My class is over," she said
slowly. "But pretty soon I'll need to get my room ready for next
semester. Would you consider watching Logan for me?"

I tried to not look too ecstatic. "Yeah. If you're okay with that,
I'd love it."

Rebecca's gaze shifted to someone behind me. "Hi," she said,
in a voice that made it clear that whoever this was, it wasn't a guest
she recognized.

"Hi."

Alex.

I turned as his hand fell warm on my shoulder. Not just Alex,
but Alex in a suit, with a tie and everything. "What are you doing
here?"

"I made arrangements," he said with a casual shrug. Then he
shifted a polite smile to Rebecca and offered his hand. "I'm Alex."

"Rebecca," she said. "Nice to meet you."

"Congratulations. Sorry I missed the ceremony."

"We're happy you can be here for the reception. There's still
plenty of food," Rebecca smiled her perfect Instagram smile at
him. She nodded to Logan. "Tessa, I'll take him so the two of you
can catch up."

Before I could respond, Rebecca was lifting Logan out of my
lap and carrying him away.

Alex gathered my hands between his and pulled me up from
my chair. "Your conversation looked pretty civil."

"It was, surprisingly," I said. "But what are you doing here?"

With a gentle hand on my lower back, Alex guided me toward
the edge of the dance floor. I didn't recognize the music, but it was
softer and slower. Much more my speed.

"Apparently your mom somehow worked a miracle with my

mom during their coffee today. Mom called my boss and told him that I had to be allowed to leave early because my girlfriend really needed me tonight."

A laugh bubbled out of me. "That's what happened?"

"I know. I couldn't believe it." Alex fit his hands around my waist. "Your mom shared how hard tonight would be and that none of your friends could come with you. My mom had this lightbulb moment where she not only realized that she's been a little overbearing—" Alex flashed me a grin. "But also that she's fighting a losing battle. All of us are going to leave the nest, she told me with mostly dry eyes, and she wants us to actually want to come back."

"It's her birthday, though."

"We're celebrating tomorrow night instead." Alex pulled me a little closer. "And she'd like for you to come too. Dad's grilling burgers and we're being subjected to a Jane Austen movie."

"That sounds amazing."

Mrs. Simmons and her husband twirled by us like they were competing in a ballroom dance contest while Alex and I swayed like middle schoolers at the edge of the floor.

"Wow." Alex watched them and raised his eyebrows at me. "Life goals."

I arched mine back at him. "If that's a life goal of yours, you'll want to ditch me. I think this is the extent of my skills."

"I don't know. I think you could have it in you." He attempted to twirl me, but all it resulted in was me stomping on his foot and tripping.

I laughed as he helped me regain my balance. "See?"

"Yep, you're right." He took hold of my waist again, exaggerating the act of keeping me steady. "You're completely out of control."

"Not completely, but yeah. Not as in control as I'd like." I grinned up at him. "I'm working on being okay with that."